D0426561

TROUBLE IN MIND

Recent titles by Michael Wiley

A Sam Kelson mystery

TROUBLE IN MIND *

The Detective Daniel Turner mysteries

BLUE AVENUE *
SECOND SKIN *
BLACK HAMMOCK *

A Franky Dast mystery

MONUMENT ROAD *

The Joe Kozmarski series

LAST STRIPTEASE
THE BAD KITTY LOUNGE
A BAD NIGHT'S SLEEP

* available from Severn House

TROUBLE IN MIND

Michael Wiley

severn House

This first world edition published 2019
in Great Britain and 2020 in the USA by
SEVERN HOUSE PUBLISHERS LTD of
Eardley House, 4 Uxbridge Street, London W8 7SY.
Trade paperback edition first published
in Great Britain and the USA 2020 by
SEVERN HOUSE PUBLISHERS LTD.

British Library Cataloguing in Publication Data
A CIP catalogue record for this title is available from the British Library.

ISBN-13: 978-0-7278-8981-2 (cased)
ISBN-13: 978-1-78029-652-4 (trade paper)
ISBN-13: 978-1-4483-0351-9 (e-book)

All Severn House titles are printed on acid-free paper.

Severn House Publishers support the Forest Stewardship Council™ [FSC™],
the leading international forest certification organisation.
All our titles that are printed on FSC certified paper carry the FSC logo.

Typeset by Palimpsest Book Production Ltd.,
Falkirk, Stirlingshire, Scotland.
Printed and bound in Great Britain by
TJ International, Padstow, Cornwall.

For Julie

ACKNOWLEDGMENTS

My deep thanks to Julia, Philip, Lukas, Anne-Lise, Kate, and all the good people at Severn House. My love to Julie, Isaac, Maya, and Elias.

ONE

That January, a month before Sam Kelson took a bullet in the head, word came from a snitch that a kid on the Northwest Side was selling the best dope in Chicago. High grade. Cheap. Lines around the block until a cruiser turned the corner and then a magic disappearing act. Kid looked fifteen, maybe sixteen. They called him *Bicho*. Spanish for *Bug*. *Bicho* because he was little and skinny. *Bicho* because he scurried into a hole whenever a cop showed.

The job went to Kelson, eight years on narcotics, the past five undercover.

Kelson always partnered with Greg Toselli. They went through academy together. Their careers paralleled so closely they could've held hands while riding down the highway on motorcycles.

'Not this time,' said Darrin Malinowski, commander of the narcotics division. 'Toselli's a hothead. Go it alone. Keep it quiet. See what it is.'

'Why the special deal?' Kelson asked.

'This is a kid. You've got a kid, right?'

'A nine-year-old girl.'

'Mine's thirteen. Close enough. You know how it goes. If he looks like someone we can fix, let's take him off the street and put him in a program.'

'You're soft,' Kelson said. 'I like that. What if he can't be fixed?'

'We slam him against a wall and break every bone in his little body.'

'Yeah, you're a marshmallow,' Kelson said. 'A feather pillow. A dish of pudding.'

'You always say what you're thinking?' Malinowski said.

'If I said half of what I was thinking, I'd be divorced, friendless, and, after a day or two on the street, dead.'

Kelson disagreed with Malinowski on Toselli. He wasn't such a hothead. 'I've got principles is all,' Toselli would say.

Principles like *First in on a raid*. And *Safety off*. And *No man left behind*. And *Expect the unexpected from others, and do the kind of unexpected things others don't expect*.

The principles worked for him. They worked for the men and women he partnered with too. On the second undercover job he and Kelson did together, a crackhead dealer got spooked and held a crusty revolver against Kelson's ear. The man's hand trembled, and it seemed likely he would shoot Kelson by accident if not on purpose. In a single fluid move, Toselli slapped the crackhead's gun hand, grabbed his wrist, wrenched the gun around so it pointed at his belly, and pumped a bullet into his kidney. Toselli's signature takedown.

That was the first time he saved Kelson's life.

'No one I'd rather have watching my back,' Kelson told him later when Toselli and a date came to Christmas Eve dinner. Like Kelson, Toselli was thirty-four, but he dated young. He liked white women, black women, Hispanics, a girl from Malaysia. 'Turn out the lights and it's all the same,' he said, 'but I swear I know the difference between eighteen and thirty.'

'Grow up,' Kelson said.

'Don't want to. How old's your daughter?'

'Don't ever.'

'Just messing.'

'Don't.'

Toselli was crossing a hard line they kept between the personal and the professional. When Kelson said *Don't*, he also meant *Don't tell each other about the ones we love. Don't let me feel for you beyond the lockstep coordination we need when taking down an armed dealer high on PCB. Don't make me care, either to love or to hate – though loving's the real danger.*

'Just don't,' Kelson said.

Kelson drove an impounded BMW solo into the Ravenswood neighborhood where Bicho did business. The January sun had softened the snow at the curb, and Kelson crunched the car over ice crystals and cut the engine. He got in line with a bunch of addicts at the head of an alley and bought a teener of coke and two pink OxyContin tablets. When he gave Bicho the twenties, the kid said, '*Gracias, viejo*.' A polite kid, but he had wild, worrisome eyes.

'*Hasta mañana*,' Kelson said.

The next day, he bought an eight ball and four OxyContin tablets. The day after, he bought another eight ball.

'You chug a lot of cola, *viejo*,' Bicho said. *Old man*, the kid called him, though Kelson looked in the mirror and didn't see it.

'You got a name besides Bicho?' Kelson asked.

'Nope.' The kid looked to the strung-out woman next in line. '*Hola, chica*.'

Every time Kelson asked for more coke or pills, the kid obliged. 'Sky's the limit, *viejo*. How high d'you want to fly? I'll take you there.'

But something about the kid got to Kelson. Did he see pain in those wild eyes? Did he hear playful innocence in his insistence on calling him *old man*?

Ten years ago, when Kelson's wife Nancy quit the department and went back to school, in the flipside of his deal with Toselli, Kelson promised never to bring home stories about kids like Bicho.

The stories were too sad.

Too dirty.

And too tempting to Nancy.

She loved working as a cop and she'd done the job better than anyone else. She went through academy with Kelson and Toselli, quietly putting the other cadets to shame – all except their class- mate DeMarcus Rodman, a six-foot-eight, 275-pound giant. She did more pull-ups than even Rodman. In hand-to-hand exercises, she threw down men twice her size. She aced the mental tests. When a sergeant asked why a pretty girl like her wanted to be a cop, she said, 'Because men like you treat me like just a pretty girl, and because my mom and dad want me to be a doctor' – and she left it at that.

In the middle of one of the hand-to-hands, Kelson told her he thought tough women were hot. So she hit him in the nose with an elbow strike. When the bleeding stopped, he asked her out for dinner. She said no. Two weeks later, bleeding from an ear, he asked for a third time, and she said yes. They married a year after their first date.

When she got pregnant with Sue Ellen, she surprised Kelson, her mom and dad, and, if you trusted the look in her eyes, herself by returning to school to pick up the science classes she needed to apply for med school. 'When I finish a shift, I'm so pumped up, I want to hit someone,' she told Kelson. 'Seems like a bad thing in a mom.'

'Sexy,' he said. She gave him a dangerous look, so he added, 'You'll be a good mom. A great one.'

She took her MCATs two weeks after giving birth to Sue Ellen, and her scores were good but not good enough. She could return to the department or pick between veterinary or dental school.

'I don't think you have the temperament to stick your fingers in people's mouths,' Kelson said, 'though I can see you pulling teeth.'

'I hate cats,' she said. 'Can a vet work only with dogs?'

'I don't know. I never heard of it.'

So, along with two partners, she now ran the Healthy Smiles Dental Clinic. She once threatened to knock the incisors out of a seven-year-old who bit her, but mostly the reviews were good and the business thrived.

Now Kelson kept his stories about the street – where Nancy would prefer to spend her days – to himself. Nancy, for her part, promised never to talk about teeth. Or gums. 'Gums gross me out,' Kelson said.

After his eighth purchase from Bicho, though, he broke the promise. He would wake up thinking about the kid's wild eyes. When he watched Sue Ellen playing on the living-room rug or doing homework at the kitchen table, he imagined Bicho beside her.

'I can't get him out of my head,' he told Nancy. 'I think he's older than Malinowski says. Sixteen or seventeen. But he's still a kid.'

'But who *is* he?' she asked. 'Where's he come from? What makes you think you can save him?'

'I don't know,' Kelson said. 'A guy I talked to on the street says his real name's Alejandro Rodriguez. That's more than anyone else knows.'

'Well, he doesn't belong to you,' Nancy said. 'Kick him out of your thoughts. There's only room for Sue Ellen and me and all the good people and good things you like to think about.' She always looked at the world coolly. Her toughness intimidated some men.

He also broke his promise to Malinowski by talking to Toselli. No names or details, just one question. 'If you had a street dealer you didn't know what to make of – someone you wanted to save even though you suspected he was as bad as the worst – would you trust your instincts and help him?'

'Never happen,' Toselli said, 'and I'd bust his ass even if it did.'

'You act hard, but I know you better,' Kelson said.

But some kids are beyond saving, and Bicho looked like one of them. Over the next month, Kelson watched him throw a penniless junkie down on an icy sidewalk. He saw him cheat addicts too broken to argue, sending them to whore themselves before he fed their need. He noticed the bulge in his pocket where he kept a little gun.

'All this dope, Bicho,' Kelson said, 'what'll you do if someone robs you?'

The speed with which the kid got the tiny Beretta out of his pocket and shoved it against Kelson's belly stunned Kelson. Bicho opened his wild eyes super-wide. 'I pop him, *viejo*.' And the gun went back in his pocket so fast you would've thought it was a vanishing coin.

Kelson told the division commander, 'We've got to take him down.'

'Do it,' Malinowski said.

Kelson said, 'Someone trusts the boy with the store. No buffer.'

'Set it up. Let's take whoever wrecked him too. But be careful and keep it quiet. Something feels wrong about this.'

TWO

On one of those viciously cold February days when the sky is clear and the wind seems to hold a knife to your throat, Kelson strapped his KelTec semiautomatic inside his jacket. A couple of rounds would shred Bicho's Beretta if they got down to that. 'What if I want to make a big buy?' Kelson asked him.

Bicho looked at the snaking line behind Kelson. 'Sky's the—'

'Fuck the sky,' Kelson said.

The tone brought the kid's wild eyes back to him. His hand drifted toward his gun pocket. 'All right, *viejo*, what kind of big buy?'

'A kilo of coke and five hundred tabs of Oxy.'

Bicho let his fingers brush against the pocket. 'Hell, what kind of fucked-up friends you got?'

'Friends with friends,' Kelson said. 'Friends that'll pay my friends' friends to be friends. Out in the 'burbs. No competition to you.'

Bicho thought about the proposition for only a second. 'I can do that.'

'You want to ask your supplier?'

'*You* don't want to ask stupid questions, *viejo*.'

'Worry is all.'

'You know that snowstorm in December? It's like that at my coke man's house every day. He needs a plow to get out his front door. Don't worry about what I can get. Worry about if you got the money to buy it.'

'You know that storm?' Kelson said. 'Think if snow was green and paper. That's my house. If this works out, I'll bring you and your coke man over to party.'

Bicho smirked. 'Let's keep it on the street.'

Kelson turned the screw. 'Thing is, if I'm buying that large, I want to deal with your man direct.'

'Ain't going to happen,' the kid said. 'He don't come out of his house, you know.'

'Talk to him. For something like this, maybe he'll put on his snow boots.'

The next time they met, Bicho said, 'He'll meet you. But no bitching about the price.' The number he gave him jumped from low market to high.

'No discount for quantity?' Kelson asked.

'Quantity's expensive too,' the kid said. 'Hard to get. High risk.'

Kelson measured him. 'Fuck it,' he said, and turned away.

Bicho laughed – the only time Kelson ever heard him laugh – and said, 'All right, *viejo*,' and he cut the price by thirty percent.

Kelson reached a hand to shake Bicho's. But Bicho dropped his hand back to his gun pocket.

'Easy boy,' Kelson said. 'We're brothers now.'

THREE

Kelson set up the bust. He told Toselli and four other narcotic cops about Bicho and the Northwest Side operation. When he finished, the division commander took questions. Toselli looked stung by the slight. 'You couldn't've told us?'

'What would you have wanted to do if I did?' Malinowski asked.

'Crush the kid.'

'My point. Now you get your chance.'

They planned a standard six-man action. Kelson at the alley mouth with Bicho and his supplier. Toselli and the four others scattered at a hundred-yard perimeter – Toselli at one end of the alley, the others in a van, in a storefront, and in the shadows of a neighboring house at the opposite end. A separate team would shoot video.

Protocol said Kelson should make the bust unarmed so the supplier could frisk him. But while the others slipped into their vests and strapped on their weapons, the division commander pulled Kelson aside and said, 'Carry a full mag on this one,' and, when Kelson gave him a doubtful look, repeated what he said earlier. 'Something feels wrong.'

The KelTec weighed against Kelson's ribs as he climbed from the BMW and walked to the alley. Bicho usually opened shop at nine in the morning and disappeared around noon or after the last stragglers stumbled up and laid balled dollar bills in his palm. Now it was midnight, and the street was empty except for a van idling at the curb a half block away and a man smoking a cigarette outside a twenty-four-hour laundromat. The kid shivered in the cold.

'Where's the boss?' Kelson asked.

Bicho nodded him into the alley – off video but in the sightline of Toselli at the far end. Kelson followed the kid past a pile of broken wood pallets and an upended trash barrel to where the light dimmed. Another two steps would dissolve him in the dark.

Kelson stopped. 'Where's—'

'You got the money?' Bicho asked.

Kelson pulled a wad of fifties and twenties from inside his jacket. He fanned the bills so the boy could see. 'Your turn.'

But Bicho swept his gun from his pocket. 'You're a cop.'

Kelson's fear felt like a blade on his neck. 'Huh?'

'A narc.'

Undercover cops trained for moments like this – in sessions paid for by taxpayers, in conversations with other undercover cops, in sweaty nightmares. Kelson forced a grin. 'All right, all right, you don't want my money, I know people that do.' He stuck the bills back in his jacket – and his hand came out with the KelTec.

The sound of gunshots slammed against the alley walls. The noises came so fast that one seemed to overtake the other in a single explosion.

Kelson and the boy crashed to the cold pavement.

Last thing Kelson saw, Bicho's pip of a gun flashed in the dark alley.

Last thing he saw, his own hands flung from his body as if his arms detached at his shoulders.

Last thing, he was falling, falling, and the fifties and twenties scattered in the windless air like a blizzard.

Narcotics cops swarmed from their posts, their boots and vinyl glinting in the dark, their guns hot in their hands. One cop radioed for help and swung his pistol left and right in case Bicho had armed friends. Others rounded the wall into the alley and ran to Kelson. He had a neat bloody pock in his forehead. He looked dead. Coming from the far end, Toselli reached the boy first. Bicho had a hole like a melon in his chest. Toselli saw right through to the bloody pavement. He drew a sharp breath and shouldered through the other cops. For a moment, it looked as if he would slug Kelson to bring him to life. Instead, he slapped him with an open palm, the meat of his hand cracking against Kelson's cheekbone, spraying blood.

One of the other cops said, 'What are you—'

Like a diver plunging into a black lake, Toselli sucked a breath and mashed his lips to Kelson's. He gave him life from his own lungs. When he came up – eyes wet with tears, lips oily with blood – he drew another breath. Then he plunged into another kiss of life, another gift of what only God could give if you believed in God and something just as miraculous if you didn't.

For twenty minutes, as an ambulance zigged through city streets toward the alley, Toselli breathed for Kelson. When other cops offered to take a turn, he ignored them. He bucked off the supporting hands they rested on his back. More than a lover, more than a father, Toselli claimed Kelson's body as his own.

Then the ambulance crunched over the ice and garbage into the alley, its siren screaming between the brick walls of the abutting buildings. Toselli stopped and stared down at Kelson. Then Kelson, as if responding to his friend's fierce will, breathed once on his own. That was the second time Toselli saved him.

The paramedics strapped an oxygen mask over Kelson's face and loaded him into the back of the ambulance.

The siren screamed again, and the ambulance backed from the alley. Far, far away, Kelson heard a metallic voice – something singing, something of bells.

FOUR

Two years after that dark, bloody night, the white walls in Sam Kelson's office were bare. His desktop was bare too. A plain light fixture hung from the middle of the ceiling. A gray metal file cabinet stood against the wall behind his desk chair. A gray all-weather carpet covered the floor. A woman sat in the client chair across the empty desk from him.

She was dressed all in pink.

'If I hire you, can you be discreet?' she asked.

'Nope,' Kelson said.

'I can't trust you with a secret?' She said her name was Trina Felbanks, and she'd called Kelson's office at nine that morning and come in at ten.

'Not if you want to keep it a secret,' he said.

'I don't understand.'

So he told her. Even if he didn't want to talk, he couldn't help himself. 'I used to be an undercover cop. Narcotics. For eight years, my survival depended on how well I lied. One night, I didn't lie well enough. A seventeen-year-old street dealer shot me in the head.'

'Oh,' the woman said. She looked about thirty, with short red hair parted at the side.

'Left frontal lobe,' Kelson said. 'In the hospital and later at rehab, I laughed for no reason. I walked into doorframes. I said everything that crossed my mind. The bullet cored the part of my brain that let me keep my thoughts to myself. The doctors call it disinhibition. They say they don't remember ever seeing it as bad as with me. I've also got something called autotopagnosia.'

She looked uncomfortable. 'You don't need to—'

'Actually, I do. I can't help myself. I'm much better now. I make it through doorways ninety-nine times out of a hundred. I watch whole movies without sobbing. I've still got the disinhibition, but I've stopped yelling at people on the sidewalk and screaming out my window when I drive. Mostly. Still, if you ask me a question, I'll answer every time. If you don't ask a question, I might tell you anyway.'

She stood up and backed toward the door. 'Thanks for your honesty,' she said. 'And your . . . openness. But I think I've made a mistake.'

'I'm good at what I do,' he said. 'Very good. That's the truth. The department put me on disability and gave me a payout that covered my mortgage. For eighteen months, I—'

'Stop,' she said.

He didn't even pause. 'I lived with my wife and daughter in my paid-off house. I insulted telemarketers. I swore at the mailman. I propositioned the pizza delivery girl. I was obnoxious in every way you can think of. Then my wife kicked me out.'

'Enough,' said the redhead.

'So I rented an apartment – a studio with a separate kitchenette, but enough for me – and I set up this office, got a private license, and advertised myself to do jobs like the one you're going to pay me to do.'

The woman asked, 'Do you *always* talk so much?'

'Yes.'

'Does it annoy people?'

'My wife divorced me. My eleven-year-old daughter seems to like it, though.'

'Right.' She looked around the office. 'You've had this office for a while? When are you going to—'

'Wall art gives me a headache,' he said. 'Clutter does.'

'At least you could replace the carpet.'

'Outdoor carpet scrubs clean better than indoor. Blood and—'

'That's more than I want to know,' she said.

'Yes,' he said.

She came back and sat. 'Do many of your clients bleed on your carpet?'

'I don't have many clients,' he said. 'But one never knows.'

'And if one did know, one would tell me.'

'Yes.'

'I guess that's reassuring – in a way,' she said. 'Do you have a gun?'

He tapped the desk. 'I keep a laptop and a stapler in the top drawer, a picture of my daughter in the middle, and a Springfield XD-S semiautomatic pistol in the bottom. I've strapped a P3AT KelTec under the desk.'

'You're very forthcoming. Do some people appreciate that?'

'No.'

'Have you ever shot anyone?'

'Sure. The seventeen-year-old who put the hole in my head.'

'Oh,' she said again. 'Did he die?'

'Yes.'

'How do you feel about that?'

'Alive. Which is more than I would be if I hadn't shot him.' He told it all – all except the one point that never came unbidden to his lips, which was strange since that point, that question, haunted his thoughts more than anything else. *Who shot first – Bicho or Kelson?*

'I see,' she said. 'I'll give you a try.'

'Because I shot a seventeen-year-old?'

'Because you seem trustworthy. And because you apparently will do whatever it takes.'

'That's true,' he said.

She pulled an envelope from her purse. 'My brother is selling prescription drugs to his friends. Hydrocodone. Fentanyl. Anything he can get his hands on. I want him to stop.'

'Where does he get them?'

'He's a pharmacist.'

'That's bad.'

'I *know* it's bad. That's why I want you to stop him. Scare him before he gets caught.'

'Is he a user?'

'That's the funny thing. He knows what the drugs do. He barely touches them.'

'He sounds like a jerk. He needs a kick in the ass.'

'I don't want you to hurt him.'

'I only hurt people who hurt other people.'

She gave him the envelope and he looked inside.

A loose-leaf sheet of paper said Christian Felbanks worked at Lakewood Pharmacy on West Fullerton. He had a condo within walking distance, on Ashland. A photo showed a pale thirty-six-year-old with thinning dishwater-blond hair and glasses. An index card gave the name and numbers of the woman who sat across from Kelson – Trina Felbanks, a local phone, an email address.

She reached into her purse and asked, 'Do you mind if I pay you in cash? Unlike you, I value discretion. If Christian ever learns I hired you—'

'I'll tell him if he asks,' Kelson said. 'Can't help it.'

She hesitated. 'I'll deny it. And you'll have nothing to prove it – just a personal knowledge of who I am, which anyone can find out.'

She laid a stack of twenties on the desktop, and a low pain niggled in Kelson's skull above his left ear. 'That works for me,' he said, and swept the bills into a drawer.

She stood up to go, but before she reached the door, Kelson said, 'Wow.'

She stopped. 'Excuse me?'

'Sorry – Just admiring your . . . all of you.'

'You were checking out my ass?'

'I didn't mean to.'

'When I was a kid, I had a dog like you,' she said. 'Is this how it went with the pizza delivery girl?'

'It's how it started.'

She began to leave again, then stopped. 'The thing is, you're not bad yourself, for a man who got shot in the head.'

'That's a lie,' Kelson said. 'My left eye sags. The surgeons did their best.'

'Your face has character,' she said.

'So there's hope for me?' he said.

'You mean, like with you and me? You're really asking that?'

'It crossed my mind.'

'No, Mr Kelson,' she said. 'There's no hope for you. Try again with the pizza girl.'

'The restaurant put me on a list,' he said. 'They won't deliver to me.'

'Good move on their part,' she said, and went out the door.

FIVE

Kelson sat alone in his office. Pleased he had work. Pleased he hadn't embarrassed himself any more than he usually did. Then he took the Springfield from the desk drawer, released the magazine, and rolled it in his palm. 'Some men knock on wood or cross their fingers,' he told the pistol, and he rolled the magazine a second time. 'Some men hold their breath as they pass cemeteries.' He felt the cool metallic weight. 'Some wiggle the doorknob when they leave the office.' He snapped the magazine in again and said, 'Me? I've got you, babe.' He tucked the pistol into his belt holster and put on a jacket.

Outside, the March day was bone-chilling. Worse than the bitter dry days of January. When, at the end of the month, the first promises of spring blew in, they would be, like the rest of the month, cold and wet. Kelson loved March days anyway, as he loved all the seasons in the cold, hard city, and as he loved the millions of people who lived and died there.

'It's a great day to be alive,' he said to the garage attendant before riding the elevator to the third floor. He drove a burnt-orange Dodge Challenger – fast and sleek, though it looked as if he was trying to compensate for something, which he was. He bought it a month after he got out of rehab. 'This car is more than a pretense,' he'd told the bewildered Dodge salesman. 'It's an ambition.'

In the garage elevator, he patted the pistol on his side. His therapist advised against guns. Brain injury victims have trouble with impulse control, he said, and the Percocet Kelson took to control the pain doubled the risk.

Kelson reassured the therapist. 'Even if I want to kill you, which I have the training to do with or without a gun – with a spoon, say, or the pen you're using – I wouldn't do it.'

For his next session, Kelson was assigned a new therapist. Her name was Sheila Prentiss, though she went by Dr P. She had a sense of humor and kept a gun of her own under a seat cushion during all therapy sessions.

The first time they met, she asked, 'You ever hear of a guy named Phineas Gage?'

'I busted his brother for crack on South Jefferson,' Kelson said.

'Must've been a different one. A hundred and fifty years ago, Phineas worked on a railroad gang in Vermont, blasting rocks. One day, a charge went off early and shot a three-foot iron bar through his skull.'

'Ouch,' Kelson said.

'The rod destroyed his left frontal lobe,' Dr P said. 'He survived. He even kept his memory. But he acted like a bastard to his friends. Became foul-mouthed. Started fights. Still, the newspapers wrote him up as a medical miracle – a living, breathing man with a hole in his brain. But compared to you, he was an amateur. It's hard, I know, and it will stay hard, but believe it or not, you're a lucky man. Your injuries are localized, and, of course, you got good, quick care.'

'Of course,' he said.

'It seems your disinhibition mostly affects your verbal functions. That's rare, though not unheard of. See this?' She pointed at a diagram on her desk. 'That's your frontal operculum. It controls your ability to use language. And see this?' She indicated a point to one side of the operculum. 'That's where you took the worst damage. We don't know exactly how this works, but it seems this area regulates how much you say, which also means how much you *don't* say. With your wound, the function is severely diminished.'

'Will it get better?'

'Will your brain figure out how to work around it? Honestly, we don't know. I hope you won't be offended if I say it will be interesting to see.'

'You'll give me cheese and electric prods.'

'I'm sorry?'

'I'll be your lab rat?'

'Except no one will experiment on you,' she said. 'You can walk away and never come back. I admit, though, I would like to administer periodic tests, to see how your cognitive function changes.'

'Cheese and electric prods.'

'We've got something we call the Barratt Impulsiveness Scale,' she said. 'We can measure your behavior with it.'

'What does it look at?'

'Motor control, attention deficit, impulsive behavior.' She folded the diagram, got up from her desk, and put it in a file cabinet.

'Nice ass,' he said.

'Verbal impulsivity. Some of these things we'll measure by talking to your friends and loved ones – to see how your current behavior compares with how you behaved before your injury. They'll be our informants.'

'Don't call them that.'

'I'm sorry?'

'I've worked with informants. CIs. They tend to die when people figure out what they're up to.'

'OK, we'll just call them friends and family. We'll talk to them about interpersonal relations. Sexual behaviors. We'll determine areas of dysfunction so we can work on them.'

'You'll talk to my friends about my sexual behaviors?'

'Your wife.'

'What if I was already dysfunctional before I got shot?'

'We'll cross that bridge,' she said. 'We can also counsel your friends and family about your lack of impulse control and the possibility that not everything you say will accord with reality.'

'You'll tell them I'm a liar?'

'Anything but. You'll almost certainly tell them the truth from your perspective, but they'll want to confirm that your perspective matches reality – at least on the big issues. Otherwise, you might say hurtful things to them. They'll need to make allowances for who you are now.'

'How about when I look in a mirror?'

'What about it?'

'Since I got shot, I don't recognize myself. I don't know who I expect to see, but it's not the man who looks back at me. He's a stranger. It freaks me out.'

Dr P said, 'Shit.'

'Doctors aren't supposed to say that,' Kelson said.

SIX

K elson drove over the gray streets to Lakewood Pharmacy, parked one slot over from the disabled spot, and went inside. An olive-skinned woman with a very round face and a very long black braid came to the prescription drop-off. She wore a white lab coat, and her nametag called her *Raima Minhas*. She smiled and asked, 'May I help you?'

Kelson smiled back. 'I need to talk to Christian Felbanks.'

'Mr Felbanks isn't in today,' she said.

'No? Right, of course not.'

'Anything else?'

'I like the braid.'

Her smile tensed. 'Thanks.'

'What's it . . . mean?'

She frowned at him, turned to the man in line behind him, and asked, 'May I help you?'

'Sorry,' Kelson said, 'I talk when I shouldn't.' He left the drugstore and drove to the Ashland Avenue address where Trina Felbanks had said her brother lived.

Christian Felbanks owned a condo above a bike shop in a four-story redbrick building. When Kelson parked in front and got out, the damp air smelled of the Lebanese restaurant two doors south.

He went into the front alcove and tried Felbanks's buzzer. No one answered it. He tapped the intercom speaker and buzzed again. Still no answer. He tried the lobby door. Open.

When he worked undercover in narcotics, he got used to going into buildings uninvited – hanging out with addicts and dealers in stairwells, popping the locks on security doors so an informant could talk without worrying who was listening, hoisting himself through broken windows to impress suppliers. In those days, if he got into a building as easily as he went into Felbanks's, he would've worried – probably would've left and tried a different deal on a different day. Back then, nothing came easy, and he paid a high price for every mistake. Now he said to the door, 'Shish kebab' – a word that popped from his mouth and also the lunch he would treat himself to two doors south after he scared Felbanks straight.

He went up to the first landing and knocked on the door. Then knocked again.

No answer.

He tried the knob and, when it turned, said to it, 'Two for two. What's the chance of that?' When he worked undercover, such easy access meant an ambush, and even now he said, 'Easy does it,' as he stepped inside.

A blond wood floor stretched to a pair of windows facing the street. On one wall, there was a little fireplace. There was a Naugahyde couch and matching chair, another chair, upholstered in beige, and a glass coffee table with a chip on one edge. On one side, there was a kitchen and dining nook. On the other, a hallway led to a bathroom and a bedroom.

Kelson went into the kitchen. Except for a bunch of bananas by the stove, the counters and cabinets were clean, the stainless-steel sink scrubbed and dry. A ceramic container held matching red spatulas and serving spoons. Two decorative signs – *The Chef Is In* and *Happiness Is Homemade* – hung above the toaster. 'Unlikely,' Kelson said, and opened a cabinet. The bottom shelf was lined with jars of organic protein, fish oil, B-12, N-acetyl cysteine, and a half dozen natural supplements. 'Health nut?' Kelson said. 'Which makes no sense.'

He left the kitchen and crossed to the bathroom. Nothing in the cabinets announced Felbanks's side trade as a dealer of opioids.

Kelson went up the hall to the bedroom. On the far side of the room, sliding glass doors led to a balcony patio with a black metal staircase that went up to the next floor and down to a backyard. One of the sliding doors was open, and the March wind had blown in rain, soaking the carpet. In the middle of the room, there was a queen-size bed, neatly made with a batik cover.

In the middle of the bed, there was a dead man. He was lying

face up, and even with the man's gray skin, Kelson recognized
Felbanks from the picture his sister gave him. Felbanks wore white
jockeys and a pair of black socks, nothing else. Since taking the
picture, he'd shaved his head. And where the bridge of a pair of
glasses would've crossed the top of his nose, he had a bullet hole.

'That sucks,' Kelson said. 'For you.'

Seven or eight prescription bottles littered the bedside table.
Felbanks's shoes, pants, and shirt lay on the carpet.

Kelson touched the man's arm and rested his palm on his naked
belly. Cold.

'Who did you bring home with you?' he asked the body.
'Thought you would get lucky. You almost got there. Maybe you
should've taken off your socks. No romance in socks. Enough
reason to kill a man.' He laughed – the way, in the first months
after Bicho shot him, he laughed even when nothing was funny.

Then he dialed 911.

But as the line rang, the door to the condo burst open, slamming
against the wall. A dozen men and women hit the floor in heavy
boots, charging inside.

Kelson jerked from Felbanks's body, drifted toward the balcony
stairway, and reached for his Springfield.

Three men, in the jumpsuits and vests of a Chicago Police
SWAT team, rushed into the bedroom. They wore black combat
boots and black combat helmets, held black assault rifles with
sniper scopes, and kept black pistols holstered on their legs. Two
pointed their rifles at Kelson's chest, one at his head.

Kelson raised his hands – slowly.

The man pointing a rifle at his head yelled, 'Down.'

Another yelled, 'Now.'

The third tightened his finger on his rifle trigger.

Kelson got face down on the carpet.

A man took his pistol, pulled his arms behind his back, and
snapped cuffs on his wrists.

Another man looked at Felbanks's body and told his companions
or himself or no one at all, 'Dead.'

'You're under arrest,' said the man with the cuffs, and he yanked
Kelson to his feet. Kelson let the man yank him, let him shove
him out of the bedroom and into the hall. For once, he was
speechless.

SEVEN

'You're a monster,' Kelson said when Homicide Detective Dan Peters came into the interview room. Peters towered over Kelson – a six-foot-three, 230-pound man, thick in the belly, thicker in the shoulders. His face was big and bearded. Kelson said, 'Your head needs, what, two hats?'

Another officer uncuffed one of his hands and ratcheted the open cuff through a loop on a steel table.

Peters moved to the back of the table and sat.

Kelson admired him. 'What size shoes do you wear?'

The detective looked cross. 'Sixteen.'

'A wedding ring. Is she as big as you are?'

The detective opened a manila folder and leafed through the papers.

Kelson said, 'Because, a man like you – I mean, how do the two of you—'

Peters stopped him. 'Don't go there.'

'Really? But—'

'Stop,' Peters said.

'Sorry,' Kelson said, 'I can't help—'

Peters gave him a look.

'Right,' Kelson said.

Peters picked up a sheet and read it. 'Huh. Another ex-cop junkie. You know the percentage of guys from the narcotics squad that end up on the stuff?'

'No.'

'Me neither. But in the last eleven years you're my third homicide.'

'It's not like that,' Kelson said.

'Yeah? What's it like?' The detective pulled a paperclip from his shirt pocket. He rubbed it between his big thumb and a big finger.

'First, I'm not an addict. Second—'

Peters cut him off. 'You look agitated. Twitchy. D'you do Oxy?

Maybe a little China Girl?' He pulled the paperclip apart so it looked like rabbit ears.

'Of course I do,' Kelson said. 'Percocet. I got shot in the head.'

'Of course you do. You need a lot?'

'Depends on the day.'

'Sure,' Peters said, and he straightened the clip as if he might use the wire on Kelson's handcuffs. 'A man like Christian Felbanks, he could be a regular pipeline for a needy guy like you. A good friend to have.' He bent the wire in two.

Kelson said, 'Big man with a nervous habit. But I get it.'

Peters stared at Kelson for a moment before realizing Kelson meant *him*. He snapped the paperclip in two and laid the pieces on the table. 'Why did you shoot Felbanks?'

'I found him dead.'

'Yeah? How did that happen?'

'I knocked on his front door. I went in and—'

'He let you in?'

'He was already dead.'

'You broke into his condo? To get the drugs?'

'I didn't need to. The door was open.'

'Like – wide open?'

'Like open enough to go in,' Kelson said. 'Unlocked. I went in.' The pieces of paperclip could be a problem. Clutter. The sight of them needled at his skull behind his left eye.

'You and Felbanks must've been close, right?' Peters was saying. 'For you to go in, familiar like that.'

'I never met him. His sister hired me.' He gestured at the broken paperclip. 'Would you mind taking that off the table?'

'What, this?' Peters left the clip where it was. 'How much Percocet do you need, Mr Kelson? Every day? Two times a day? Three?'

'Some days the pain's worse than others.'

'The craving? I hear it's like rats gnawing on your intestines.'

'Headaches for me. Percocet blunts them. They never really go away.'

'Sounds miserable. Enough to kill for? I mean, if you could blunt them with more pills?' Peters picked up one of the pieces of paperclip and, watching Kelson's eyes, rubbed it between his thumb and finger.

Despite the headache, a little smile came to Kelson's lips. He glanced around the interview room and said, 'I was a cop. I know how this thing works. The cold air pumping from the ceiling vent, the dim lighting, the plain walls. You want to disorient me and make me lose my sense of time. After an hour or two, it could be midnight or noon, winter or summer, here or a thousand miles away. The thing is, though, I like this kind of room. But if you'd throw away the paperclip, I'd appreciate it.'

'You're not going to talk?' Peters asked.

'Just the opposite. I'll talk and talk until you get sick of me. But even with your big fat head and your big fat ears, you won't hear what I'm telling you.'

Peters poked a big finger at Kelson. 'If you don't watch your mouth—' Then he stopped and wagged the finger. 'There was a time in this department when we would break a smartass like you. I kind of miss those days.'

'I only tell you what I'm thinking,' Kelson said. 'I can't help it. I could do it all day.'

So Peters scooped up the other piece of wire and stood. 'You like this place? Well, you can stay until you talk sense. Meantime, make yourself at home. Get cozy. Sorry I can't get you a pillow and hot chocolate. I'll be back in a couple of weeks.'

He left the room.

Two hours later, a uniformed cop came in, unhooked Kelson's cuff from the table, and guided him out of the room. 'You charging me?' Kelson asked.

'What did Detective Peters say?' the cop asked.

'Nothing about charges.'

'All I know is I put you in a holding cell. No hogging the interview room.'

'I want a lawyer.'

'OK,' the cop said, with the same tone he might use if Kelson asked for a Ferrari.

'Now,' Kelson said.

'Tell Detective Peters.'

'Fine. Take me to him.'

'He left for the day.'

'This isn't right,' Kelson said.

'Neither is killing a man.'

'I didn't do it,' Kelson said.

'Tell Detective Peters.'

The cop took him down a stairwell, out into a hall, and down a set of white metal steps into a basement with a drain in the middle of the concrete floor and a line of seven white jail cells. Each cell had a bench bunk and a stainless-steel sink/toilet combo. The first two cells had men in them. The cop took Kelson to the one farthest from them and locked him inside.

'A lawyer,' Kelson said.

'Yeah, right,' the cop said, and turned to go.

'I need my meds,' Kelson said.

'Junkie,' the cop said.

EIGHT

Kelson went to the bunk, lay on his back, and did the breathing exercises Dr P taught him to do to relieve stress and lessen the pain of a headache when Percocet didn't do the trick. He breathed in, long and slow, and breathed out, long and slow. But when he breathed out, words as weightless as the thoughts in his head floated on his breath. 'Percocet – dead man – bottle of – jailhouse bench, ha! Dr P – it ain't working – it ain't.' He breathed in, long, slow. 'Peters is – jackass big-footed big ha! – what he does in bed's his own damn – what he does to me is—' Then the men in the other cells told him to shut up, which made him yell at them, which made them tell him what they'd do to him if they could get out of their cells and into his – which made him laugh so hard his lungs hurt, which relieved the stress and head pain.

Then one of the men said to the other, 'Screw it, he's a nutcase.'

Which made Kelson explain, 'Not a nutcase. Disinhibited.'

Which made the man say, 'Yeah, whatever . . . nutcase.'

At some point, a cop brought lunch. Later, a different cop brought dinner. 'This sucks,' Kelson said out loud more than once, which made the other prisoners laugh at him, but the plain white walls and bars and the plain gray floor suited him well enough, and he announced that fact too – more than once. Lights went out

at ten p.m. and came back on the next morning at six. The cop
who'd put him in the cell the previous day returned at six fifteen
and told Kelson to get out of bed and hold his hands for cuffs.
Kelson stretched his limbs, yawned, and held out his wrists. The
cop sneered at him and said, 'A sociopath, huh? No worries? Slept
like a baby?'

'Babies sleep badly,' Kelson said. 'Up at night – hungry, wet.'

'Go to hell,' the cop said, and took him upstairs to the interview
room.

Kelson's friend and former division commander Darrin
Malinowski was waiting for him.

Kelson raised his cuffed hands to greet him.

Malinowski said, 'Oh, Sam.'

Kelson shrugged.

'You don't look so good,' Malinowski said.

'You've got to help me,' Kelson said.

'Of course. Anything I can do.'

'The cop I talked to yesterday – he thinks I killed Felbanks.
He thinks—'

'It's OK,' Malinowski said. 'We'll straighten it out. Take a seat.
Talk to me.'

So Kelson sat and told him what he'd told Peters. Trina Felbanks
hired him to convince her brother to stop stealing and dealing.
Kelson went to Christian Felbanks's condo and found the body.
The SWAT team raided the condo.

Malinowski sat across from him with his fingers folded on the
steel table. Kelson appreciated the neatness of the gesture and said,
'You're a good man, Darrin. Good haircut too. You've got your
priorities straight.'

'Right,' Malinowski said. 'Look, the story you're telling doesn't
make sense. Not to Peters. Not to me either. You say you went in
and found the body. But if that's all it was, why did you pick up
the pill bottles on the night table?'

'I didn't.'

'The homicide guys did a quick check, made a few calls, did
the preliminary forensics. No one wants an ex-cop in the tank with
a bunch of guys he's busted. Forensics ran the prints from the
bottles through the database – you know, to clear you. But they
got matches on two of them.'

'Bullshit,' Kelson said.

Malinowski gave him a sad smile. 'Saying that is good. But it doesn't change the facts. It doesn't change what's real.'

Kelson shook his head. 'I walked into the bedroom, saw Felbanks, checked he was dead, and called nine-one-one.'

'You called nine-one-one?' Malinowski said.

'I started to,' Kelson said. 'SWAT came in. I moved away from the bed. I didn't touch anything.'

'In the whole apartment, you didn't touch anything?'

'In the kitchen and bathroom, I opened the cabinets.'

'See what I mean?' Malinowski said. 'You aren't making sense.'

'All I can do is tell the truth,' Kelson said.

Malinowski said, 'OK, when you opened the cabinets, what were you looking for?'

'Felbanks's drugs,' Kelson said.

'Good,' Malinowski said. 'The drugs you found in his bedroom?'

'Yes – or no. I don't know. Them or other drugs. His sister said—'

'So you and Felbanks partied and then—'

'I didn't party with anyone. I didn't touch the bottles. I found him dead.'

Malinowski sighed. 'Right.' He leaned back in his chair. 'How's your head now? Your therapist told us you might have memory problems. Any blackouts?'

'Yeah,' Kelson said, 'I woke up this morning in jail and couldn't figure out how I got there.'

Malinowski looked at him, uncertain.

'Irony,' Kelson said. 'I can still do irony – sometimes. My memory's as good as before I got shot. It's in my therapy records.'

'So you didn't touch the bottles. You didn't help yourself to a few pills. You weren't going to run off with the whole stash.'

'I didn't touch them,' Kelson said.

Malinowski sucked his bottom lip. 'OK, we'll let that go. You've got another problem. You say Felbanks's sister hired you to talk sense into him?'

'That's right,' Kelson said. 'Trina Felbanks.'

'Twenty-nine years old?'

'I would've guessed thirty.'

'Short red hair? Carrying a few extra pounds?'

Kelson nodded. 'Carrying them in the right places.'

'Flat face?' Malinowski said. 'Short neck?'

'Not so much.'

Malinowski said, 'Trina Felbanks was born with Down syndrome. A lot of other issues. Trouble with her heart. She's lived her whole life in Sioux City, Iowa. She couldn't get to Chicago unless someone put her on a cart and pushed her.'

Kelson opened his mouth, but no words came out.

Malinowski asked, 'You want to tell me what really happened?'

'I can't,' Kelson said.

'You can't, or you won't?'

Kelson looked at his old commander and said, 'I need a lawyer.'

'Peters didn't arrest you,' Malinowski said.

'He held me here last night.'

'That was him being an asshole. He said you smarted off and needed some quiet time.'

'A lawyer,' Kelson said.

Malinowski gave him a curious smile. 'Peters says you're free to go.'

Kelson held his cuffed hands toward him. 'Then unhook me.'

'Sure.' Malinowski used a key. 'But I'll tell you this as someone that cares about you – the only reason you're walking out of here is you used to be a cop. Another guy, the prosecutor might charge and let you sit in jail or scratch together bail. But Peters has your pistol. If ballistics matches the bullet from Felbanks's head, you'll be right back at this table, and you won't be talking with me. You sure there's nothing else you want to say?'

'Yeah,' Kelson said, 'let me the hell out of here.'

NINE

Back at his apartment, Kelson stood in the shower and spoke to the showerhead as if it was a microphone – about bad luck, bad timing, the woman who arrived in his office calling herself Trina Felbanks, the SWAT team bursting in less than five minutes after he went into the condo, his memory of stepping away from Christian Felbanks's bed, his fingerprints on pill bottles he'd never touched, accidents and coincidences, and his certainty that the woman who called herself Trina Felbanks had set him up.

'Yep,' he told the showerhead, 'she walked in, wiggled her butt, laid money on the desk, and told a story. And I bought it. Then the minute I went into the guy's condo, a SWAT team raided. As if she called in an emergency. As if she held a surprise party.'

The showerhead spat at him.

'But how the hell did she get my prints? Wouldn't be so hard. I throw out pill bottles. Someone could dig them from the trash, strip off the labels, set them on a stranger's night table, and . . . surprise. Wouldn't be so hard. Dozens of ways to do it if she put her mind to it. The question is' – he turned off the faucet and watched the water trickle and stop – 'why?'

He dressed, walked out into the cold March morning, and flagged another taxi. He had the driver take him back to Christian Felbanks's condo, where his car was still parked, with two tickets on the windshield. Then he drove to his office with its plain walls and sat at his plain desk.

He expected that when he dialed the phone number on the contact sheet the woman gave him, he would get a disconnected number or a Chinese restaurant or a bowling alley, but he dialed it.

It rang twice, and the woman answered. He said, 'Trina?'

'I'm supposed to give you a message,' she said.

'Yeah? Who told you to do that?'

'I'm just doing what he's making me do. I'm supposed to tell you, this is from Alejandro Rodriguez. Bicho.'

The name felt like a fist in Kelson's belly. His uncertain memory of the night in the alley cross-wired in his mind.

Bicho shot Kelson, blowing off a corner of his forehead.

Then Kelson fired back, hitting Bicho in the chest.

Or did it happen the other way – Kelson shot first and Bicho shot back?

'Who told you to do this?' Kelson asked the woman.

'A man you should never screw with.'

'Who?'

'You want to know what I call him? Mengele. You know why? He's like a doctor, but instead of fixing your head he wrecks it. You ever hear of Mengele?'

'Everyone's heard of him. The Angel of Death.'

'You know the stories about him giving chocolates to the Auschwitz kids, then torturing them – injecting them with oil, draining their blood, cutting off parts of their bodies? He got off on loving them and then seeing them suffer. The man who's after you is like that.'

'Sounds like a lie. You know, I can trace your phone.'

'You can try,' she said. 'It's not mine. Mengele stole it, or maybe it's a throwaway.'

Kelson said, 'Look, we need to meet and talk.'

'That would get us both killed,' she said. 'Goodbye, Mr Kelson. Good luck.' She hung up.

Kelson dialed the number again. She didn't answer. He knew that no matter how many times he dialed she wouldn't.

'Maybe that's it,' he said into the phone anyway. 'Maybe she's done with me – whoever she is. Or *he* is. *Mengele.* They wanted to scare me. It worked. Maybe it's over.' He stared at one of the bare white walls. Across the city, Detective Dan Peters would be digging into Kelson's records as a narcotics cop. A forensics specialist would be looking through a microscope at the bullet pried from Christian Felbanks's skull, comparing it with bullets test-fired from Kelson's Springfield. The bullets wouldn't – *couldn't* – match, though before this morning Kelson had also thought his fingerprints wouldn't appear on Felbanks's pill bottles. Who knew what the woman – or the man behind her, if he was real – planned for him? They'd scared him and made him feel the powerlessness of a jailed criminal. 'Goddammit,' Kelson said to the wall.

He called a criminal lawyer he'd seen defend dealers back in the day. Edward Davies was a smart, competent man with a nasal voice that somehow wormed into jurors' brains and persuaded them. Davies listened to his story but said he could do little unless the police charged him.

'Then what should I do?' Kelson asked.

'Relax,' the lawyer said. 'This will play out whether you stress about it or not. Do something that makes you happy. No harm in that.'

'Good advice,' Kelson told the wall after he hung up. So he dialed his Nancy and told her he would pick up their daughter Sue Ellen after school.

'That's big of you,' Nancy said, though she'd just done a double root canal, which normally would give her pleasure.

'Typical meanness,' Kelson said.

Three months before he and Nancy split for good, they saw a marriage counselor – a little woman with bristly blonde hair. 'With most men,' the counselor told him, 'the problem is too many lies. With you, it's too much honesty.'

'And your problem,' he said, 'is you look like a toilet brush.'

When they found a new counselor, she asked, 'Can't you just shut up when you have something unpleasant to say? Can't you grit your teeth and keep your lips closed?'

'No,' Kelson said.

'He can't,' Nancy admitted. 'I've seen him try. It's like a mouthful of centipedes.'

'Hmm,' the counselor said. She had a pleasant voice and Kelson told her so.

'I liked him better before his accident,' Nancy said.

'Gunshot wound,' he said. 'Attempted murder. Not an *accident.*'

'Yeah, yeah,' Nancy said.

Kelson told the counselor, 'Nancy's insistence on calling it something it isn't bugs the hell out of me. It's like I'm one of her patients whose tooth she's about to yank out, and she's saying, "This won't hurt . . ." Sometimes I need to leave the room.'

'Be nice,' the counselor said.

'I'm not trying to be unkind.'

'You're being rude,' she said.

'Does it count as rude if I can't help myself?'

'Yes,' the counselor and Nancy said together.

'I'm just being truthful,' he said.

'Try lying a little,' the counselor said.

'Besides,' he said, 'Nancy's always been mean.'

'But you like mean,' Nancy said.

'Hmm,' the counselor said.

Now, on the phone, he asked Nancy, 'Can Sue Ellen sleep over tonight?'

Nancy said, 'I guess she'd like that.'

'So would I.'

'You're good with her,' she said, warming to him as she still sometimes did. 'Maybe good with no one else, but good with her.'

'Thanks,' he said.

'So don't screw it up.'

'I understand,' he said.

When he hung up, he said, 'I do understand. You'd think Sue Ellen would show emotional bruises. But she bounces. Rubber girl. I'd never hurt her. Never.'

TEN

He had four hours before Sue Ellen got out of school, so he drove to Lakewood Pharmacy, where Christian Felbanks used to work.

Raima Minhas, the pharmacist he talked to the last time, stood at the drop-off counter again. She tore into Kelson before he could speak, as if he'd never left the store. 'If you go to grocery store and the checkout girl has blonde hair, do you tell her you like it? If you see a bald white guy, do you tell him you like the shine on his skin?'

Kelson stepped back from the counter. 'Well – maybe—'

As if she hadn't heard him, 'Then why's it OK to ask about my braid? Just because of where I'm from?'

A pasty-faced man who looked as if he might be her manager watched from the oral hygiene aisle.

Kelson told her, 'It looked different – and nice, that's all. *You* looked different.'

'*Different*?' she said. 'I'm a goddamned cliché. What would you think if you came to my counter and I said, "May I help you, you racist, sexist dickhead?" You see, I haven't met a lot of you people – you're *different* – so I don't know how to talk to you nice.'

Kelson laughed and said, 'I like you. You talk too much.'

The pasty-faced man stepped beside him. 'Raima?' he said.

She turned on him and said, 'This guy's a jerk. Two days ago, he—'

'Take a break,' the man said to her. 'A half hour. No, take the rest of the day. I'll talk with Mr—' He looked at Kelson.

'Kelson. Sam Kelson.'

'I'll take care of Mr Kelson,' he said. 'You go get yourself together.'

She opened her mouth to argue.

'*Now*,' the man said. He glowered until she left the counter and disappeared into a back room. Then he said, 'I'm sorry. She normally . . . well, she just heard terrible news. Her fiancé died . . . suddenly.'

'Really?' Kelson said. 'Christian Felbanks?'

The man looked surprised. 'Did you know Christian?'

'Met him only once,' Kelson said. 'Or – he was already dead. I went to his place to talk to him about—'

'I'm sorry,' the man said, 'I'm not sure who you are. Is there something I can help you with?'

'Probably not,' Kelson said. 'But here's the deal. I got tangled up with Felbanks – wrong place, wrong time, you know, except someone wanted me in that place and time – so I'm suspicious—'

'I don't know what you're talking about,' the man said.

'Right,' Kelson said. 'Was Christian Felbanks stealing drugs from the pharmacy?'

The man considered him. 'We're making our records available to the police. I assume you're not with them.'

'I used to be a cop. But ever since I got shot in the head, I'm on my own. Knocked out a chunk of my brain. Can't be a cop when you're missing a chunk of your brain. Didn't even want me for desk duty.'

'I see,' the man said. 'Well, Mr—'

'You're not real bright.'

'I'm afraid if you want information about Christian Felbanks's employment here or our inventory audit, you'll need to get it from the police.'

'Won't happen,' Kelson said. 'They'd rather throw me in jail. But you already told me what I need to know.'

'Did I?'

'You're doing an audit because you don't know if Felbanks was stealing drugs, right? How long did he work here? How long did it go on?'

'Ms Minhas is right,' the man said. 'You're a jerk.'

So Kelson left the store and got in his car.

And waited.

Three minutes later, Raima Minhas came out, wiping her eyes. She wore a plaid jacket and a scarf, against the March chill. She'd tucked her long black braid inside.

Kelson rolled down his window and said, 'Hey . . .'

She stopped short. 'You've got to be joking.' She scurried away.

Kelson got out and followed her. 'You know, *I* found him,' he said.

'No, you didn't,' she said. 'The police did. They—'

'I was there. In Christian's condo when they came in.'

'They didn't say anything about you.'

'They had no reason to. I found him in his bedroom, a bullet in the head right here' – he touched his skin where the nose meets the forehead.

'Don't,' she said.

'Seven or eight pill bottles on the table next to him.'

'He didn't do drugs,' she said. 'He didn't even like aspirin. Only vitamins.'

'Funny thing for a pharmacist,' Kelson said.

'Yeah,' she said, and tears came to her eyes. 'He was funny.'

'A health nut?'

'Yeah, he was a nut,' she said, and more tears came.

'I'm sorry,' he said.

'He didn't steal the drugs,' she said. 'He wouldn't. He *couldn't*.'

'Why not?'

'I would've known,' she said. 'I would've seen it.'

'Did he talk about his sister?'

'Trina? Only a little. She's at a group home in Iowa. Why?'

'A woman calling herself Trina Felbanks paid me to talk to Christian. She said he was supplying his friends.'

'She was lying.'

'I know that – at least about who she was.'

'She lied about all of it.'

'Why would she do that?'

'I don't know,' she said.

'Are drugs missing from the pharmacy?' he asked.

The question made her hesitate for the first time since stepping from the store. 'Who exactly are you?'

'Ex-cop,' he said. 'Spent eight years on the narcotics squad. Five years undercover. The department retired me on disability. Now I run a private firm. Mostly unsuccessful because I talk too much. Recently divorced from a woman who seems to hate me for the same reason, but we have a daughter, Sue Ellen, who's the greatest thing in my world.'

'Got it,' Raima Minhas said.

'I could tell you more, but I would rather you tell *me* if any drugs are missing.'

'But you talk too much. So if I tell you drugs are missing and ask you to keep it confidential because I could get fired or maybe worse, you would tell others?'

'Anyone who asked,' he said. 'If I was standing with strangers and it crossed my mind, I might tell them too.'

She considered him. 'Then, no. No drugs are missing. All right?'

'All right . . .'

'Sorry for calling you a racist, sexist dickhead,' she said.

'You were upset.'

'No, you're a racist, sexist dickhead, but I didn't need to say it.'

'*I* would've,' Kelson said. 'If I thought you were one, which I don't, I would've told you.'

That got a broken smile from her. 'Maybe,' she said. 'Maybe something's missing. Maybe some OxyContin last week. Maybe other stuff before. Maybe a couple of cases were broken into. Nothing I've seen, if you understand what I'm saying – nothing I would swear to. Nothing you can say I told you. But maybe.' Then she hurried away.

ELEVEN

Kelson drove to his office, got his laptop from the top desk drawer, and searched for the name Felbanks in Sioux City, Iowa. There were seven families with the name. But the town had fewer than a hundred thousand residents, and he figured they might know each other – maybe even be related. He typed in the name Christian Felbanks and found a high school photo. He typed in Trina Felbanks and got nothing.

He said to the computer, 'His mom and dad will be here now. Meeting with the police. Asking questions no one will answer. Collecting the body. Taking it home. Should've asked Raima Minhas.'

He made two more searches and found a phone number for one of the Felbanks families. Although he figured no one would answer if he called the right one, he dialed it. On the third ring, a man picked up, and Kelson said, 'I'm looking for Christian Felbanks's family.'

He'd reached Christian's uncle, who confirmed his guess – Christian's parents had driven five hundred miles east from Sioux City to Chicago when they got the message from the police.

'I hate to ask,' Kelson said, 'but what can you tell me about Christian's sister?'

'Oh, she's been at the center since she was fourteen. Too much for my brother and his wife to handle. God knows, they tried.'

Kelson thanked the man, told him he was sorry about Christian's death, and hung up.

He leaned back in his chair. He'd followed the only obvious leads. Now, unless he tracked down Christian's parents wherever they were staying in Chicago, or walked into Dan Peters's office and demanded information the detective would never give him, he was done. His wallet felt a little thicker with the cash from the woman who lied about being Trina Felbanks, his credibility a little thinner, and his overall circumstances about the same as where they'd been since he got out of rehab. He should take the lawyer's advice – stop worrying, relax, and make himself happy. 'No harm in that,' he said as he put on his coat. No harm until the next trouble came. 'It'll come,' he said as he left his office. 'Over my right shoulder. Over my left. Straight on like a truck.'

He drove north through the city to Hayt Elementary where Sue Ellen was in sixth grade. At three fifteen, she came from the building, squealed at the sight of him, and clambered into the Dodge Challenger.

They spent the afternoon at his apartment, playing a game of Stump Dad – which Sue Ellen invented when she realized she could ask Kelson anything and his cross-wired brain would compel him to answer. Today, she started easy. 'If you could be any animal, what would it be?'

'A tiger,' he said.

'Would you worry that you were an endangered species?'

'Yes.'

'If a hunter tried to kill you, would you eat him?'

'Yes.'

'Would you worry that you were a cannibal?'

'Only if *you* were the hunter,' he said.

'Uh-huh,' she said, then turned to body functions. 'Do you fart in the bathtub?'

'I take showers,' he said.

'Do you ever blame someone else when you fart?'

'Not since I got shot in the head.'

'Before?'

'All the time.'

Her laugh sounded like music to Kelson. Then, as she often did, she got personal. 'Do you still love Mom?'

'I have mixed feelings.'

'That's sad.'

'Yeah, it is,' he said. 'She doesn't love me.'

'Yes, she does.'

'How do you know?' he asked.

'She told me. She said she's no longer *in love* with you, but she loves things about you.'

'That's a nice way of saying she doesn't love me.'

She thought about that for a moment. 'Tell me something mean about Mom.'

'Really?'

'Uh-huh.'

'She farts in the bathtub.'

Again Sue Ellen squealed with laughter – as if she needed to laugh the way she needed to breathe.

Kelson said, 'You shouldn't ask me to do that. And anyway, you should play this kind of game with kids your own age.'

'They all lie,' she said.

'Lucky them,' he said.

They went out for dinner at Taquería Uptown, a plain-walled place that made great *carnitas* tacos, and when they returned to his apartment, Sue Ellen did her homework and Kelson spread blankets on the floor to sleep on while she took the bed.

The next morning, eating a bowl of cereal at his kitchen table, Sue Ellen tried to stump him again. 'Will you buy me a kitten?' she asked.

'No.'

'Why not?'

'The building doesn't allow pets.'

'We could keep it at Mom's house.'

'Then yes.'

'Mom hates cats.'

'Then I'll buy you two.'

Sue Ellen squealed with laughter, and Kelson grinned so wide the scar on his forehead hurt. 'Get your book bag.'

She stuck her tongue at him. 'You get it.'

'Don't be a little shit,' he said.

A couple minutes later as they walked down the hall from his apartment, he said, 'Sorry for swearing at you.'

'It's all right, you can't help it,' she said. 'Will you buy me a horse?'

'Won't fit in the elevator,' he said.

He felt so good after dropping her off at school that he skipped his breathing exercises and went straight to his office. He wished good morning to two strangers outside the building, to the man who staffed the downstairs reception desk, and to a crowd outside a conference room used by a computer training company that rented space on his floor.

He put a key into his door lock but didn't need to – it was already unlocked. 'Huh,' he said, and opened the door.

The woman who called herself Trina Felbanks sat in the client chair at his desk. She wore skintight black leather leggings, black leather boots, and a white fluffy jacket. Her purse matched her jacket. She had a half-moon bruise on her cheek.

She arched an eyebrow at him.

He frowned and said, 'Good morning, Hot Pants.'

TWELVE

'First,' Kelson said, 'how did you get into my office?' Once more he sat across the desk from the redhead, his thumb covering the 9 key on his phone so he could call 911 if he disliked anything that came out of her mouth.

'I popped the lock,' she said. 'I learned how as a kid. Sad story. You don't want to hear it.'

'No, I do. Unless you want to tell it to the cops.'

'They wouldn't want to hear it either. I was naughty, so my mom locked me in my room.'

'I can see why she would do that.'

'But my stepdad had a key,' she said. 'He visited me when my mom fell asleep. He was naughtier than I was.'

'Oh,' Kelson said.

'So I figured out how to get past locks – simple ones, like the one on your office. When my mom put on a better lock, I was out of luck. I was thirteen. See? Sad story. It gets sadder if you want to hear it.'

Kelson said, 'It would make me cry.'

'Are you making fun of me?'

'No, I do that – I cry. If you tell me a sad story, I can't help it.'

'I wouldn't want you to make fun of me.'

'I'm not worried about what you want. You set me up at Christian Felbanks's condo.'

'Yes.'

'Why?'

'I do what he tells me to do. Whatever he wants.'

'The guy you call Mengele?'

'That's the way it works. One of us suffers – you or me. Sorry, but that means it's you.'

'And he bruised your face to thank you for a job well done? Or are you one of those people who like to get hit?'

'Don't be a jerk,' she said.

He pressed the 9 on the phone and let his thumb hover over

the *1*. 'Why are you here? I would think you'd stay away from me.'

'I'm sorry about what happened.'

'You don't look it. When I worked undercover, I saw a lot of people like you. Abused girls who turned to ice. It wasn't their fault. I still had to bust them, but I felt rotten about it.'

'Don't be too smart,' she said.

He touched the *1* – once. 'If I was smart, I wouldn't have gone to Christian Felbanks's condo. I would've seen through you.'

'True.'

'So why are you here?'

She looked down at her knees, looked at her arms, ran a finger along the sleeve of her fluffy jacket. 'He set up Christian's death so that if you didn't get blamed, I would. That's the truth. I want you to stop him.'

'How?'

'Any way you need to.'

'He hit your face?'

'My face is the least of it.'

'Take it to the cops.'

She shook her head. 'He has too many friends. High and low. You don't get away with what he does for very long unless you have friends.'

'If that's true, you're taking a big risk here.'

'I'll be taking a bigger risk if you don't stop him.'

'What's your real name? What's his?'

She opened her purse, pulled out a little bundle of cash with a fifty on top, and set it on his desk. If he left it for long, it would give him a headache. He left it anyway.

'Jillian Prindle,' she said. 'I'll tell you his name too if you'll do the job. Too dangerous if you won't.'

'Do you have a working phone?'

She gave him a number.

He ended the 911 call and punched in her number.

'It's not a throwaway,' she said.

Her phone rang inside her purse. She let it ring, and he listened to the voicemail greeting identifying her as Jillian and asking him to leave a message. He hung up.

She said, 'I'm done lying. I'm scared.'

'No,' he said, 'you're ice. What's the man's name?'

'You'll do the job?'

'I don't like men who bruise people. I also don't like getting set up. If he made you do that, I'll nail him.'

'His name is Dominick Stevens,' she said. 'He runs a big real-estate firm on the West Side, out on Division by Humboldt Park. The business lets him move money without anyone asking questions.'

'How long have you known him?'

'Too long.'

'More of your sad story?'

'The saddest part.'

He said, 'I don't trust you.' But he opened his top desk drawer and swept the bundle of cash into it.

When she was gone, she left a scent – a hint of perfume, something of leather and fur, something animal. He breathed it deep into his lungs and said, 'What the hell am I doing?'

Then he took his laptop from the desk. As the first light glowed on the screen, he said to it, 'I know better . . . as if that matters. She'll get me killed. Won't be the first to try. Walked into my office. All but held a gun to my head. And I did what? Rolled on my back. Let her scratch my belly. Kicked my hind leg like a horny dog. Impulse. Blood on the brain.'

The screen finished loading.

'Shut up,' Kelson said to it – or to himself, or to no one and nothing at all – and he typed.

The Stevens Group website included links to office, multi-unit, residential, and industrial properties. Kelson clicked on one for media.

If Dominick Stevens worked with partners or had staff, the photos and news articles on the media page didn't show them. They focused on Dominick himself, a handsome man in his late twenties, with sharp blue eyes. He appeared at industry parties, groundbreakings, and ribbon-cuttings, often in the company of the mayor or a city alderman, sometimes alongside a television or sports celebrity. Kelson looked at a bunch of pictures before realizing that none of the captions named Stevens as the developer or broker of the buildings where he was photographed. He clicked the link for residential buildings and copied three of the listings into an open document.

Then he dialed the Stevens Group office number.

A cheerful woman answered.

'I'm calling about your residential properties,' he said, and gave the first of the listings he'd copied – a fourteen-unit multifamily building on South Ingleside.

Without waiting a beat, she said, 'I'm sorry. It's under contract.'

'Your website doesn't say so.'

'We signed the papers yesterday.'

'I see. How about the four-unit on North Sheffield? New construction?'

'We've experienced delays,' she said. 'I'm afraid it won't be available until June.'

'The West Cortland two-flat with a garage?'

'We lost the listing.'

'Right,' Kelson said. 'Could I set up a meeting with Mr Stevens?'

He knew better than to ask such a question. It begged her to ask why he wished to meet, and if she asked, he would tell her. But she said, 'Mr Stevens has a full schedule right now. Can I refer you to one of the other real-estate firms?'

'Very generous,' Kelson said. 'I see why he gets invited to their groundbreakings and ribbon-cuttings.'

'Mr Stevens is well loved in the community,' she said. 'He believes that what's good for one broker is good for all.'

'You might be the shiniest person I've ever talked with,' Kelson said.

'I'm not quite sure what you mean,' she said.

'You're also a bad liar,' he said, and he hung up. Then, saying, 'We'll see about that,' he took his KelTec pistol from under his desk, checked the magazine, and tucked it into his belt. 'Impulse?' he asked, and then answered, 'No. A *feeling*' – then asked another question, 'The difference?'

THIRTEEN

Before leaving the office, Kelson called Dan Peters at the Harrison Street Police Station. Voicemail picked up, and Kelson left a message. 'The redhead who called herself

Trina Felbanks came to my office this morning,' he said. 'Broke in, but that's another thing. Now she says her name's Jillian Prindle, and she turned me on to the man who paid her to set me up. His name's Dominick Stevens and he's supposed to be a big shot in real estate, though from the little I've seen I don't buy it. Jillian Prindle implies he's a mid-level drug supplier, maybe higher. I'm going to shake him by his ankles. If anything bad falls from his pockets, I'll bring him to you. Or I'll shoot him. You know all the things a man can do to get himself shot.'

He hung up and stared at his phone.

Then he dialed Peters again. When voicemail clicked, he said, 'That sounded bad. Here's all you need to know. I'm going to Dominick Stevens's office. Maybe I'll see you there.'

He hung up again and told the phone, 'Much better.'

A cold mist fell as he left his building, the kind of mist that would get fatter and fatter until the street gutters flowed with gray rivers. He went to the parking garage, where the attendant sat in his booth, reading a beat-up newspaper. Kelson said as he passed, 'Find someone you love, and don't let go.'

He drove to Division Street and out past Ukrainian Village. At the west end of Humboldt Park, a block-long redbrick factory manufactured and warehoused martial arts uniforms and equipment. Next door, a four-story glass-and-steel building housed the Stevens Group. The glass front was mirrored. Kelson pulled to the curb and stayed in his car. He slunk low in his seat, watching the building through the mist.

After ten minutes, he sat up and glanced at himself in the rearview mirror. He felt the shock of having a stranger stare at him, nose to nose. 'You've got a bad case of disinhibition,' he said, 'but not a bad case of stupid.'

Five minutes later, he said, 'Patience.' He made a face at himself in the mirror. 'It's a virtue.'

Two minutes passed. 'But he who hesitates . . .' He reached for the door handle, then heard what he'd hoped to hear – approaching sirens. He waited until two Chicago police cars, white with blue racing stripes, rushed up behind him, crossed into the lanes of oncoming traffic, and stopped, blocking the entrance to the Stevens Group building. Four uniformed cops jumped out of the cars, and while one stood in front of the door, his hand hanging above his holstered gun, the others ran inside.

Kelson waited. 'One way or another,' he said.

More sirens approached. Then the three cops who'd disappeared into the building came back out surrounding Dominick Stevens, who huddled low between the others. The cops guided him into the backseat of one of the squad cars.

'Busted,' Kelson said, and the squad car flipped on its lights, pulled from the curb, and shot toward downtown.

But then another cruiser pulled up, followed by an unmarked police car. Two more uniformed cops got out of the cruiser, and Dan Peters eased his huge body from the unmarked car.

Kelson tucked his KelTec under the front seat and got out too.

He called a greeting across the street, 'Detective Peters.'

Peters and two uniformed cops spun toward him, drew guns from their holsters, and aimed at his chest.

Kelson raised his hands and said, 'Whoa . . .'

Peters yelled, 'Down on the ground.'

Kelson said, 'Not again.'

'Down!'

Kelson looked at the pavement. 'It's wet.'

'Goddammit,' Peters said.

So Kelson got face down on the street, his cheek on the damp grit.

Peters and the others checked him for a weapon, twisted his arms behind his back, and cuffed him. They yanked him to his feet and threw him against his car.

'What the hell,' Peters said, his words coming so fast and angry they tangled. 'What's going on? What was that message? What the hell!'

Kelson said, 'Exactly what I told you. Dominick Stevens killed Christian Felbanks. He's a drug supplier. The real-estate thing is just—'

'No,' Peters said, towering over him. 'You want to know who Stevens is? He's the son of Ernest Stevens, the senator. He's only twenty-nine years old but he's on the Board of Directors at the Chicago Housing Authority. He's on the Board of the Chicago Loop Alliance. He's on the Landmarks Board. He has a voice on the use of about half the property in this city. What the hell are you thinking?'

Kelson said, 'That doesn't mean—' but he stopped, because it *did* mean all he wished it didn't.

'Are you insane?' Peters said. 'Is that what this is about? You being out of your head? Because we lock up people like you – a danger to yourself and others.' He turned to one of the uniformed cops. 'Put him in the back of my car.'

The uniformed cop did as Peters told him, slamming the car door. For ten minutes, Kelson sat listening to a quiet patter on the car roof as the mist turned into rain.

The squad car with Dominick Stevens returned. One of the uniformed cops opened the back door, looking like a moonlighting chauffeur, and Stevens climbed out, ruffled but no longer scared. Peters approached him, shook his hand, and talked with him for several minutes – all of his body language apologetic – until Stevens smiled, glanced at the car where Kelson was sitting, and shook his head. He ran his hands down the front of his suit jacket, shedding the rainwater, as if cleansing himself of the events of the past twenty minutes. Now Kelson understood what had happened. The police had rushed Stevens away from the building, telling him that someone had threatened his life. With the threat gone, Stevens disappeared back through the mirrored glass doors into his life of power and privilege.

Peters talked to the uniformed cops, who looked up at his large head like young kids, and when he finished, they went to their cars and drove away. Peters gazed at the Stevens Group building, as if trying to think of ways to avoid talking to Kelson, then came to the car and climbed in next to him, his knees denting the vinyl on the back of the passenger seat.

Kelson said, 'It's got to be tough going through life that way. Jamming yourself into little spaces. Getting dirty looks from people on airplanes. Bet you get cramps.'

Peters stared at him with disgust. 'The ballistics don't match.'

'What?'

'The bullet we pulled from Christian Felbanks's head,' he said. 'It doesn't match the gun we took from you.'

'I know.'

'Then explain what happened.'

'I told you before.'

'Yeah, a lady came to your office and set you up. And she came back today and set you up again. And you believed her?'

'This time I didn't believe her, but I also didn't not believe her. I called you, hoping I wouldn't have to find out on my own.'

'Yeah, that worked out.'

'No one died,' Kelson said.

Peters looked through the rain-streaked windshield at the Stevens building. 'You know what happens when you make threats like this?'

'I didn't make a threat.'

'You said you would shoot him.'

'Then I corrected myself. My thoughts came out wrong.'

'Sounded clear enough to me.'

Kelson said, 'When Stevens got out of the squad car, he looked freaked out. Why did you talk him down? You could have let him throw me in the fire.'

'I told you,' Peters said. 'The ballistics don't match. Our guys tore apart Felbanks's condo. No other gun. As far as I can tell, you couldn't have killed him.'

'I told you before.'

'Yeah,' he said. 'That's why I don't book you for Dominick Stevens.'

'Really?' Kelson said. 'You going to uncuff me?'

'I kind of like you this way. I can pop you in the jaw anytime I want.'

'Ha.'

'Ha yourself. Just watch me.'

'Anyway, the charges wouldn't stick,' Kelson said. 'I used a metaphor when I said I would shoot him.'

'A metaphor, huh?' the detective said.

'But I tucked my KelTec under my car seat – just in case.'

'Ha,' the detective said again, though he added, 'but you do have self-control issues.'

'Which is why you raced across the city and pulled Stevens into the safety of a squad car, even though you knew I didn't kill Felbanks.'

'If you hurt Stevens and I had a recorded message saying you planned to do it, everyone would stomp on my balls. Not really a metaphor. Tell me about this lady that came to talk to you.'

'About thirty years old,' Kelson said. 'Maybe five-five. Short red hair, combed to the side. Are you going to uncuff me?'

Peters shrugged. 'What's the connection between Christian Felbanks and Dominick Stevens?'

'None that I see,' Kelson said.

'I see one,' Peters said. 'You. You and this lady you say is giving you information.'

'You don't believe me?'

'I have no reason to think either way about it. It's what you've told me – we'll leave it at that.'

'Does Stevens use Felbanks's pharmacy?'

'Different part of town,' Peters said. 'But I'll check. Of course. I'll tell you something that might interest you, though. The preliminary bloodwork on Felbanks came back positive for opioids. Enough to kill him. The gunshot was just frosting. The problem is – and I think you know where I'm taking this – the toxicology keeps you in the mix. Since your prints are on the pill bottles and all.'

'We both know that was part of the setup,' Kelson said.

'I know that's what you tell me.'

'You really think I'm in this?'

'I don't know what to think. And I blame you for that. You've said things that don't make sense. You've told me lies.'

'I've told you the truth, a hundred percent,' Kelson said.

'You embarrass yourself by saying that,' Peters said.

'I'll always tell you the truth,' Kelson said, 'as much as I understand it.'

Peters smiled like a man who's heard it before. 'Will you take a polygraph?'

Kelson laughed at that, though Peters looked as if he might follow through on the pop to his jaw. 'I don't see what's funny,' Peters said. Then he unlocked the cuffs and kicked Kelson out into the cold rain – with a warning. 'I don't want to see you again unless I come looking for you. I don't want to hear your voice unless I ask you a question.'

Kelson said, 'This woman, Jillian Prindle, or whatever her real name is – it isn't over with her. She—'

Peters said, 'Shhh. Did I ask you a question?'

'No,' Kelson said. 'No, you didn't.'

FOURTEEN

Back in his car, Kelson retrieved his pistol from under the seat, released the magazine, fingered it, and snapped it back in place. He tucked the gun in his belt, took out his phone, and called the number the woman gave him.

No one picked up. No voicemail asked him to leave a message. 'What did I expect?' he said.

He turned on the car and watched the wipers smear rain across the windshield. 'As if it was that easy,' he said to them. 'Still, I've got options. None of them good.' He stared at the mirrored building from which Dominick Stevens ran his piece of the city. 'Probably a good man. Probably forgiving. Probably will let this one pass.' If Kelson turned off the wipers, the building would twist and distort in the runnels of rain. He left them on. 'Yep, I have options. She sent me here for a reason. Of all places, here. Of all men, him. Paid me to come.' He looked at the building, which seemed to gaze back like an opaque lens. 'Hell if I know why. Hell if I know how to find out. Her move next. Again. Her move and my countermove. Still, I've got options.' He looked at the wet street. 'Only *one* of them good. Do something that makes me happy.'

He shifted into drive, pulled from the curb, and did a U-turn.

Then he zigzagged across the city until he reached the west branch of the Tree House Humane Society, located in a brown-brick building so small Kelson thought it could shelter no more than a pet mouse. 'Or a gimpy ferret on a leash,' he said. 'Maybe a tank of tropical fish.'

He parked a half block away and ran through the rain, ducking in through a black door.

A man in a black T-shirt stood at the front counter. In the recesses of the building behind him, dogs barked.

'Maybe I'm wrong,' Kelson said to the man. He was dripping from the rain and filthy from lying in the street.

The man looked at him sideways and said, 'Can I help you?'

'I need some kittens,' Kelson said, and smiled. 'To go.'

'I see,' said the man. 'They would be for yourself?'

'My daughter,' Kelson said. 'She'd rather have a horse, but . . . you know . . .'

The man gave him another look.

Kelson caught his breath and said, 'Can I start over?'

'Please do.'

'I would like to adopt two kittens.' He explained that his eleven-year-old would take care of them with his help and the help of his ex-wife, who, he admitted, hated cats.

The man said, 'Your ex-wife is OK with this?'

'No,' Kelson said, 'I thought I would surprise her.'

The man sent him on his way.

Fifteen minutes later, Kelson pulled up outside the downtown Anti-Cruelty Society, a complex big enough to house a circus. 'More like it,' he said. He sat in his car for several minutes, repeating out loud the words *responsible adult*, and then he went inside and adopted a pair of black-and-white kittens, sisters from a litter rescued off a restaurant rooftop. He answered the questionnaire honestly but smiled a lot and managed to keep from tangling himself in the truth or offering worrisome unsolicited information.

He brought the kittens out in a carrier, along with a cat starter kit – food, bowls, a litter box. Then he gave himself a few verbal high-fives and drove straight to Nancy's house.

He was waiting at the street-side with the mewling kittens, which he'd let out of the carrier and were clambering up the seat backs and on to his shoulder with pin-like claws, when Nancy drove her minivan in behind him. Sue Ellen jumped out of the passenger side into the rain, pleased to see his car. Nancy got out, wearing medical scrubs. As had been the case a lot in recent months, she looked annoyed. And mean. 'And sexy,' Kelson said.

He climbed out of his car, holding a kitten in each hand, and said, 'Surprise!'

Sue Ellen squealed happily, then stopped short and looked at her mother.

Nancy didn't laugh. She didn't smile. The rain was making her mascara run.

'Jesus Christ,' she said. 'You're the most irresponsible, the biggest—' She couldn't get the words out. 'You've got to learn to control yourself. You can't just do this to people.'

'To you,' Kelson said.

'That's right. To me. I have a life. I make my own choices. I don't have the patience or energy for this.'

One of the kittens mewled.

Nancy stared at it ferociously. 'Take them back.'

Sue Ellen said, 'I told Mom we talked about kittens this morning. I thought you were joking.'

'So did I,' Kelson said.

She looked at him slyly. 'Where's the horse?'

Kelson said to his ex, 'What makes you think I'm offering them to you?'

She gave him her you've-forgotten-to-floss eyes. 'You didn't plan to leave them here?'

'Well, I thought that made the best sense,' he said, 'since you've got the house – the space.'

She shook her head.

'You don't have to be smug,' he said. 'It's not like you *tricked* me into admitting it. I'll keep them at my apartment.'

'Your building has a no-pets policy,' she said. 'Sue Ellen told me that too.'

Sue Ellen gave Kelson a pretend pout. 'You didn't bring me a horse?'

Kelson winked at her, which made Nancy angrier. He said, 'If the neighbors complain, I'll do what I need to do.'

'That's just cruel,' she said. 'Taking animals into your life and then—'

'You're making assumptions,' he said. 'Maybe I'll find a new place to live.'

'But who will take *you*?' she said. 'I mean, really, if anyone spends more than a minute with you, *who*?' She walked up the sidewalk and went into the house.

Kelson said to Sue Ellen, 'Go with her. But come over tomorrow after school to visit the kittens – if she lets you.'

Sue Ellen started up the sidewalk, then ran back to Kelson and gave each kitten a kiss on the head. She said to him, 'Give the horse a kiss for me too.' She ran up the sidewalk and went in.

'Great kid,' Kelson told the kittens.

Then Nancy stuck her head out the door and said, 'Take them to the pound.'

So Kelson drove home to his apartment. He parked with the hazards on in front of the building, got out, and checked the lobby, then ran inside to the elevator with the cat carrier. He snuck down the hall, hushing the kittens, and fumbled his key into the lock. He stepped inside and yelled, 'Goddamn it.'

Not only was his bed turned down – though he always tucked in the sheets in the morning, smoothing them flat to prevent head-aches – there was a woman in it. The pharmacist Raima Minhas lay with the sheet and blanket pulled to her knees. She wore a black bra and, as far as Kelson could tell, nothing else. She stared wide-eyed at the ceiling.

'Hey,' Kelson said.

She didn't answer. She didn't move.

Something else about her had changed from when he'd seen her before. Her long black braid was gone.

He went to her, and he knew without touching her that she was dead.

He touched her anyway, feeling for a pulse. Her skin had gone a long way toward cold. He wanted to move away from her as he'd moved away from Christian Felbanks in the condo, but he stayed close. She was clutching a prescription bottle, the label showing through her fingers. He leaned over her to read it.

Percocet. Filled at Lakewood Pharmacy. The label made out to Samuel Kelson.

FIFTEEN

Kelson pulled the bottle from the woman's fingers. He just wanted to read the label again, but now it had his prints on it – if they weren't already planted there. He said, 'Stupid. I'm an idiot. A stupid idiot.'

He took the cat carrier back down to his car, moved the car to the parking lot, opened the pet-adoption starter kit, and put food in the carrier for the kittens. 'Be good,' he said, and cracked open a window.

He knew from his time as a cop that if drug evidence *can* be found, it *will* be. So he took the Percocet to the street and emptied it into a storm drain. He peeled the label off the bottle, ripped it, and dropped the pieces into the drain too. In a minute, the rainwater would dissolve the pills. In another minute, the label would disintegrate. No matter if it didn't, it all would wash away with the city dirt into an underworld even the most scrupulous detective would never visit.

Kelson couldn't make the plastic pill bottle vanish, but nothing would tie it to Lakewood Pharmacy. He wiped it clean and tossed it into the dumpster behind the building.

Then he went back up to his apartment and called Dan Peters.

Almost immediately, two patrol cops buzzed Kelson's apartment, rode the elevator to his floor, and stood sentinel outside his door. One of them told him to wait at his kitchen table until the higher-ups arrived. When Kelson asked, 'Are you here to keep me in or others out?' the cop said, 'No one comes or goes – that's all they told me.'

Then Detective Peters arrived with a partner – a dark-skinned, thick-legged woman with straightened hair. They moved around the apartment as if they already knew it, or knew places just like it, ignoring Kelson until he stated the obvious. 'You've done this before.'

The female detective mumbled, 'A thousand times,' and disappeared into the bathroom where she opened the cabinets.

'I could object,' Kelson said.

Peters said, 'Just try.'

'It's all right,' Kelson said. 'After I called you, I checked the cabinets and closets.'

That made Peters stop. 'Did you touch her?'

'Yep,' Kelson said. 'She's been dead a couple hours anyway.'

'What else did you put your hands on?'

'I touched everything,' he said. 'I prepared for that one.'

'Huh?'

'I knew you would ask.'

The female detective returned.

'He touched everything,' Peters said.

'It's my apartment,' he said. 'I always do.' He asked the other detective, 'Who are you?'

She gave him a blank stare. 'Detective Johnson.'

He offered to shake hands.

She ignored him and started opening kitchen cupboards.

'Don't you think I would clean out anything that would get me in trouble?' he asked.

'It's surprising what some jerks overlook,' she said.

Twenty minutes later, two forensics cops came, repeated the steps the detectives had taken, and added more of their own. Peters and Johnson sat down at the kitchen table and asked Kelson to tell them exactly what happened – every detail.

He'd prepared for that too, so he focused on the kittens – how he'd snuck them through the lobby, into the elevator, and down the hall, how he'd stepped inside and seen Raima Minhas lying dead in his bed.

'Kittens?' Johnson said. 'I don't see kittens.'

'They're in my car,' Kelson said.

'How did they get there?' she asked.

'They're too little to ride the elevator by themselves,' he said.

'You left your apartment after finding Raima Minhas?'

'I didn't give them the car key. They're safe.'

In less than a minute, he managed to annoy her as much as he annoyed Nancy in a good half hour or so – enough that Peters stared hard at her. 'Keep cool, Venus.'

'Really?' Kelson said, '*Venus*?'

'What the hell?' she said.

'Do you play tennis?'

She looked at Peters as if to confirm what she was hearing.

Peters told her, 'Stay on track.'

So Kelson jumped back in. 'I took the kittens to my car. I could've put them in the bathroom, but they would contaminate the scene. When I came back upstairs, I called you.' Then, to Venus Johnson, 'No offense. I have a hard time with boundaries and categories. I sometimes forget and think I'm black too. Or Mexican. Then I look in a mirror and say, *What's up, white boy?* or *Hola, guero*, or whatever.'

Before she could react, Peters said, 'Did you check the cabinets and closets *before* or *after* you took the cats to the car?'

'After,' Kelson said helpfully. 'I came upstairs, called you, and then checked. I didn't want anything like the setup at Felbanks's apartment to happen again.'

By the time Raima Minhas's body went out on a gurney, and forensics stripped and bagged the bed sheets, it was almost midnight. After the last cop left, Kelson remade his bed, tucking in the edges and smoothing the top blanket until it looked like a calm sea. He brought up the kittens and told them, 'This is your home now.' He folded a blanket into a neat square and set it in a corner near the radiator.

Then he left the apartment and walked through the rain to the Golden Apple Grill.

He ordered a hamburger and gave the waitress a recap of his kitten-buying experience and the discovery of Raima Minhas in his bed.

'Wow,' she said, 'I didn't want to know all that.' When she brought his food, she avoided eye contact. She never refilled his water. He had to signal her three times to order a slice of cherry pie.

As he ate dessert, the restaurant sound system, which had piped in eighties hits throughout his dinner, started into an instrumental version of Joan Jett's 'I Love Rock 'n' Roll.'

'Dammit,' Kelson said.

On the first night he had sex with Nancy, this song had played. Now, despite all that had happened over the past six hours, he felt . . . stirrings. On the long-ago date, he and Nancy had gone back to his apartment, turned on the radio, and as Joan Jett belted out her love for rock 'n' roll, Nancy did a striptease. The thing was, as they admitted afterward, they'd both always hated the song. It would take more than a bullet in the left frontal lobe for Kelson to forget that striptease.

In a recent session, Dr P had warned him that sounds, smells, and even tastes that had strong associations might trigger disinhibited behavior, especially at moments of stress. Sure enough, as he sat at the Golden Apple Grill, Kelson felt a powerful impulse to do a striptease like Nancy's. 'What the hell?' he said, as he eyed the waitress with new interest. Sweating, he paid his bill and rushed out into the dark.

SIXTEEN

That night, Kelson laid his keys and phone on the kitchen counter and, unwilling to climb into the bed where he had found Raima Minhas, slept on the floor again.

Although he surprised himself every time he looked in a mirror, in his dreams he knew himself well, and the self he knew had the unscarred forehead of an unwounded man. This time, he dreamed that Bicho chased him through a shadowy warehouse. The warehouse had hundreds of rooms, doors that opened into brick walls, and passageways that fell into an abyss. When Bicho trapped him in a last, shadowy room, Kelson ripped open a door that faced a wall. He pounded on the wall until he broke through, and he tumbled through the hole into a space that had no floor. He fell and fell, and Bicho plunged through the hole after him, into the dark, as if to kill or – it was unclear – perhaps save him.

Kelson jolted awake in his dark apartment. His heart beat as hard as if a man had just chased him through a warehouse of a hundred rooms. He sat up on the floor and, in a strange gift from his subconscious, felt a sudden rush of love for Bicho. There was no logic to the sensation, though he felt it as strongly as any love he'd ever felt. But a terrible guilt – for killing a seventeen-year-old – followed hard on the love.

'Ouch,' he said in the dark, and he pulled up a blanket and tried to sleep again.

His phone woke him the next morning. One of the kittens was nestled against his mouth. The other seemed to be sleeping on his ear. He peeled them off, stumbled into the kitchen, and picked up the call.

Greg Toselli was on the other end. 'Hey,' he said, 'just calling to check on you. I heard about the latest. You pinched Peters on the ass. His partner ain't too happy about you either.'

'The tennis player.'

'What? Oh, yeah, right. Look, I'm giving you a heads-up.

Whatever the hell you think you're doing, Peters and Johnson get it. They know about the Percocet you took off Raima Minhas. They—'

'What?' Kelson said. 'How?'

'Jesus Christ, I don't know. I just hear what they're saying. If you were partying with the lady, that's your business, but I sure as hell hope you didn't share your meds. 'Cause if you did, when toxicology comes back on her, you're—'

'For the pain,' Kelson said.

'What?'

'I take Percocet for the pain,' he said.

'Don't tell me that,' Toselli said. 'Don't say anything you don't want others to know.'

'I don't party – not like that.'

'Did you give it to her?'

'No,' Kelson said. 'Of course not.'

'See, that's right. Keep it like that.'

'No, I really didn't.'

'Perfect. No man left behind, right?'

When they hung up, Kelson swore at Toselli. Then he went into the bathroom and swore at the stranger in the mirror. Then he said, 'Deal with it.' He stared at his reflection as if it might tell him how. When it didn't, he showered, dressed, and poured three bowls of cereal – a big one for himself, little ones with extra milk for the kittens. He put the kittens on the table, and they ate together.

Afterward, he carried them into the bathroom where he planned to leave them during the day. The clutter of dishes and kitty litter would usually give him a needling headache, but his head felt fine – better than he could remember since the shooting. The kittens mewled at him. So he snapped a picture of them on his phone.

Overnight, the rain had stopped, and, as Kelson drove to his office, the sky hung gray and low over the city. When he rode up the elevator, his office reassured him by looking exactly as he'd left it, as if not a particle of dust had shifted. Before strapping his KelTec under his desk, he checked the magazine, counting the rounds, rolling their weight in his hand, reloading, and snapping the magazine back into the gun. 'Better than diddling with a paperclip,' he said. 'Better than wiggling a doorknob.' He opened the middle desk drawer and gazed at the picture of Sue Ellen.

'Beautiful,' he said. He settled into his desk chair, then dialed Peters on his phone.

'Whatever you think is true isn't,' he said, 'except when it is – but it still isn't what it seems.'

'What the hell are you talking about?' Peters said.

'Drugs. Beds. The storm drain. The whole thing.'

'Look,' Peters said, 'I'm way too busy for whatever you're ranting about. What do you need?'

'Me?' Kelson hadn't thought about his own needs when he dialed.

'I'm hanging up now,' Peters said.

'I need to know where Christian Felbanks's parents are staying.'

'Why would you need to know that?' Peters said. 'Why are you even calling me? Do yourself a favor and let me forget you.'

'If Christian told anyone about the trouble he was in, it was probably Raima Minhas. But maybe he talked to his mom and dad too.'

'You don't think we're asking them?'

'I'm sure you are. But you guys sometimes get an idea in your heads, and it keeps you from seeing clearly or asking the right questions. You think you know the truth, but it isn't – or it is but it isn't—'

'You're digging a hole.'

'Right. I don't want to point fingers, but when you first grilled me about Felbanks's killing—'

'Maybe you should stop there,' Peters said.

'So are you going to tell me where they are?'

'You're just a little deluded, right?'

'Because I was thinking, they keep their daughter in a special home – and that costs money. And funeral expenses – that's money too. They're from Sioux City. Salt of the earth. The kind of people who put common sense above emotion. So even if their son died in the condo, why wouldn't they stay there to save money? That's what they would think.'

Peters growled into the phone. 'Stay away from them.'

'Thanks,' Kelson said, 'that's what I needed to know.'

Kelson took his laptop from his desk and spent a half hour researching Christian Felbanks and Raima Minhas. Christian had graduated from the College of Pharmacy at the University of Illinois-Chicago twelve years ago and Raima a year after him.

'Probably met there,' Kelson told the computer. Raima seemed to have started working at Lakewood Pharmacy straight out of college, and Christian, who worked at a Walgreens in Sioux Falls for three years, joined her there when he moved back to Chicago. 'Did he move for her?' Kelson asked. 'Or did it start when they began rubbing shoulders in their lab coats?'

Felbanks's Facebook and Instagram accounts had pictures of the couple together – at concerts, on the beach, at the skating rink in Millennium Park – but hers had pictures only of other women in saris or long blouses. 'Trouble in the family?' he asked one of the group photos, taken at a restaurant table. 'Dad and Mom don't like him? Do they even know about him?' He jabbered on for a minute about honor killings and divided cultures and things he had little understanding of and had heard just enough about to be misinformed.

Then he Googled their two names together and got a hit for a wedding-related site with the address www.raimaandchristiansayido. com. It linked to registries at Target, Crate & Barrel, and Macy's, included pictures of the evening they got engaged, and offered information about the wedding itself, which they'd planned for the first weekend in June.

Kelson needed to talk to the parents – Felbanks's first, since they might leave for Sioux City at any moment.

But as he got up to leave, there was a knock on the office door.

He buzzed it open, and two men came in – one in his mid-twenties, the other around sixty – and Kelson guessed from their faces who they were. 'Raima Minhas's relatives, yes?' he said, before either opened his mouth. 'Her father?' he said to the older one, who wore loose blue cotton pants and a zipped-up yellow windbreaker. 'And her brother?' he said to the other, who was thicker and wore blue jeans and a Chicago Bulls hoodie. Kelson smiled at them.

The older one pulled a cheap revolver from under his windbreaker, the younger one a pistol from the front pouch in his hoodie.

The younger one spoke with a British accent. 'And you're the asshole that killed her.'

'That's lovely,' Kelson said, 'though it makes me think you aren't her brother. A cousin? From *auld* England?'

'Shut up,' the older man said.

'Ah, you're definitely the dad,' Kelson said.

The older man was sweating, and although he and his companion held the only guns, his hand shook as he aimed at Kelson.

'Please,' Kelson said, 'have a seat. If you try to shoot me, you'll probably hit each other. Those are lousy guns. Who—'

'Shut up,' the older man said again.

'You make me nervous too,' Kelson said, 'and when I'm nervous, I talk. If you put down the guns, I won't pull my own from under my desk and kill you. I'm thinking you're here because of a misunderstanding, and I would hate to hurt you for it.'

'Rubbish,' the younger man said.

'Ha,' Kelson said, 'I always tell the truth, *chap*. Will you please put down the guns?'

The men shook their heads.

'If you don't, I won't tell you what I know about Raima,' Kelson said, 'and I won't find the person who really killed her.'

The older man said, 'Tell us something we don't know.'

'For example,' Kelson said, 'she planned to marry Christian Felbanks.'

The man stared at him. 'Yeah?'

'You knew?'

'She was growing a wedding braid. My wife reserved the Hilton banquet room. Do you think my own daughter would get married without my blessing?'

'Of course not,' Kelson said.

'You cut off her braid.' The younger man said it as if Kelson had reached down the front of Raima Minhas's pants.

'I didn't touch her,' Kelson said.

The older man said, 'Tell me what you know about her.'

'OK,' Kelson said, 'I know she loved Christian Felbanks. So I know she wouldn't have gone to another man's apartment on her own, which means she didn't go to mine. I know she seemed strong enough to resist one man who tried to force drugs on her, strong enough to resist me. I know – or at least suspect – she knew a secret about the drugs at the pharmacy where she worked. She implied it to me. I know she's dead and I may have less reason than you to want to get whoever did it, but I still have a lot of reason. And, if you want the truth, maybe I'm partly responsible for her death since whoever killed her put her in my bed. If someone killed her to get at me, I'm truly sorry.'

The older man seemed uncertain. His hand shook.

The younger man lowered his gun a notch.

Then the older man said, 'No.' And he pulled the trigger.

Kelson misjudged the time he needed to grab his KelTec. But he was right about the man being a rotten shot.

The bullet ripped past and sank into the wallboard.

Kelson shoved his desk toward the men, knocking them back.

He didn't need to do even that much. At the sound of the gunshot, the older man looked stricken by what he'd done, as if waking from a nightmare to find a bloody screwdriver in his hands. The younger one dropped his gun on the floor.

Kelson was furious. He touched the scar on his forehead. 'Do you see this?' he said. 'This is what happens when someone who knows how to use a gun shoots at me – a kid who probably sucked on a pistol barrel instead of a pacifier. He probably killed a half dozen other men before he shot me. But he couldn't kill me. And *you* – with your pathetic little guns and your pathetic shaking hands—'

'I'm sorry,' the older man said weakly.

Kelson reached under his desk anyway and pulled out the KelTec. He gestured at the revolver still shaking in the man's hand. 'Put that down.'

'Oh, God,' the man said, the fact of what he'd done still blooming in his mind, 'I'm so sorry.' He put the revolver on the floor, and he started to cry.

'Oh, no, you don't,' Kelson said. 'If you do that, you'll get me going too.'

But it was too late. Tears streamed down the man's face, and he spoke disjointedly about his daughter – his child, his pride, his love, the greatest joy he'd ever felt, and now she was gone – which made Kelson think about Sue Ellen and how he'd feel if anything bad happened to her, and so tears streamed down his cheeks too, and the office filled with the sounds of the two men sobbing. Only Raima's cousin remained dry-eyed, and he watched Kelson as if he'd gone crazy. Then Kelson came around his desk and hugged Raima's father, and the father hugged him back.

When they stopped crying, which took a long time since each could set off the other again, Kelson straightened his desk and once again asked the men to sit.

This time they did.

'Now, where were we?' Kelson asked, dabbing an eye with a knuckle.

The old man looked sheepish. 'I was shooting a hole in your wall.'

'Right. Let's try again. My name's Sam Kelson. And you are . . .?'

'Jaipal Minhas,' the older one said.

'Amit Minhas,' the younger one said.

'He's my brother's son,' the older one said.

'Very good,' Kelson said. 'And why did you try to kill me?'

'You killed Raima in your bed,' the older one said. 'The police detective said they also put you in jail for Christian.'

'Dan Peters,' Kelson said. 'I didn't kill your daughter, and I didn't kill Christian.'

'This is what you say,' the man said. 'Raima was a good daughter. How did this happen?'

He looked as if he might cry again, so Kelson made a show of strapping his gun back under his desktop and asked, 'Did she have problems with drugs? I worked in narcotics for eight years, and sometimes kids from good families—'

The man interrupted him. 'Not Raima, no. You must believe me – she was a good girl. Very clean.'

'I believe that you believe that,' Kelson said. 'Did she talk to you about the pharmacy? Missing inventory? Shipments being tampered with? Thefts?'

'No, no, nothing like that. She wouldn't steal drugs.'

'I mean someone else,' Kelson said. 'Did she ever think someone—'

'No, she was happy at work. She did nothing wrong.'

'No one says she did, Mr Minhas.'

'She died in your bed,' he said. 'The police say—'

'In my bed, or somewhere else and then she was put there. But I get your point. Don't worry too much about what the police think about her. They're trained to think that way about everyone.'

'What about you?' he asked. 'Do you think that way too?'

'I don't know what to think.'

'Raima was a good child,' the man said. 'A good woman.' Tears pooled in his eyes.

The nephew said, 'She told me the manager harassed her. He said things to her. He tried to touch her.'

His uncle said, 'That was nothing.'

'She laughed it off,' the younger man said. 'She liked the job and didn't want trouble.'

'What did Christian think about that?' Kelson asked.

'It was nothing,' the older man said again.

'Christian wanted them to quit,' said the nephew. 'But Raima convinced him they wouldn't find another shop where they could work together. She convinced him she could handle it.'

'Did it ever get out of hand?' Kelson asked.

'Not that I know of.'

'No,' the older man said, 'everything was OK. Raima was happy.'

They talked like that, around and around, and then Jaipal and Amit Minhas picked up their guns and shuffled out of the office.

Thirty seconds after they got on an elevator to the lobby, the building security guard accompanied a cop to Kelson's door.

'We got a call,' said the security guard, a fat guy everyone knew only as Steve. 'Sounded like a gunshot.'

'A lot of things sound like gunshots,' Kelson said.

'Including gunshots,' Steve said. He looked into the office over Kelson's shoulder. 'You didn't shoot a gun in here?'

'Me? Never.'

'Are you here alone?' the cop asked.

'Yep.'

'You mind if I take a look?'

Kelson let him take a look.

The cop saw the desk, the chairs, the file cabinet. He didn't look at the bullet hole. 'No one's hurt, then?' the cop asked.

'Not here.'

SEVENTEEN

A man wheeled a bicycle from the shop under Christian Felbanks's condo. The smell of garlic wafted from the Lebanese restaurant two doors away. On the sidewalk, pigeons pecked at a gray discarded piece of French bread. They looked as cold and bleak as the harshest winter. 'Me too,' Kelson said.

He tried the handle on the street door to the condo. Locked. 'Closing the barn door,' he said, and he hit the button for Felbanks's address.

A man's crackling voice answered through the intercom.

Kelson introduced himself, and, after a moment, the man let him in.

Jerry and Ann Felbanks were staying in their son's place. But as if nervous about putting down more than feeler roots, they'd unpacked their suitcases only on to the living-room couch, making neat stacks of underwear and socks. They wore jeans and flannel shirts, and looked tired and uneasy, maybe scared. When Kelson said how sorry he was about their son, though, Jerry gave him a big handshake and Ann a small one, and when Kelson asked if Christian had told them of trouble at the pharmacy or elsewhere, Jerry answered with a firm but quiet voice that suggested he was used to talking in silent, wide-open spaces and being listened to.

'Christian had a way with people,' he said. 'You'd call it charm. It could be hail and hell outside, and he'd see the good in it. The benefit. He never said a mean word. Never complained.'

'So he never said anything about someone stealing?'

'He wouldn't. He liked to be your friend. Saw the good in people.'

'Sounds like words in an obituary.'

'We've been writing his,' Ann Felbanks said.

Her husband said, 'The police say you found Christian.'

'Yes.'

'Will you show us where?'

Kelson didn't want to return to the bedroom. 'If it will help.'

They went in. Curtains were pulled over the sliding door to the balcony, and the woman turned on the bedside light. Kelson showed them how their son was lying on the bed and, because she asked, where the pill bottles were on the night table and where Christian's pants and shoes were on the floor.

She touched the bed. 'Too many losses.'

Kelson asked the husband again, 'Do you know of any problems he had?'

'We wanted him to stay near us,' he said, 'but he was head over heels for Raima.'

'Head over heels,' his wife said.

'Don't get me wrong,' the man said. 'Raima was a sweet girl. She made him happy. No, he had no problems we knew of. He left any problems behind when he moved back to Chicago.'

'Do you mind telling me what those problems were?' Kelson asked.

The man screwed up his mouth and glanced at his wife. 'Our family has had its share of difficulties.'

'Like any family,' his wife said.

'There's his sister Trina,' the man said. 'She has needs. And—'

'Christian was good with Trina,' his wife said.

'But he also wanted a life of his own,' the man said.

'It was understandable,' she said. 'Raima was here. With *her* family.'

'It's hard,' the man said.

Then, in the other room, the door buzzer buzzed.

'I should warn you,' the man said, 'the homicide detective asked us to call if you came. I did, as you were coming up. I'm sure you don't mind.'

But Kelson said, 'Is it OK if I go out through the balcony?'

'Why would you do that?' the man asked.

'The detective will want to talk, but I need to get home to my daughter.'

The man stared at him, uncertain.

'New kittens,' Kelson said.

The couple exchanged a look. Then the woman went to the curtains, pulled them back, and opened the balcony door.

Kelson went out into the cold and dropped down the staircase two steps at a time.

EIGHTEEN

That afternoon, Sue Ellen played with the kittens until they fell asleep in little balls of fur and bone. Then she said, 'Now, let's Stump Dad.'

'No, thanks,' Kelson said.

She grinned. 'What's it like—'

'No, really.'

'—to be you?'

Kelson fought it but there was no fighting it. 'Dr P told me there's something called autotopagnosia,' he said. 'People who've got it can't recognize their own body parts. Like, they'll look at their legs and freak out. They'll think someone else's legs are sticking out of their bodies. Then there's something else, just plain agnosia, which is when you can't recognize other people's faces. With me, it's like you put those things together. I forget what I look like, or I think I look like someone else. I stare in a mirror and the face that stares back surprises me.'

'Weird,' Sue Ellen said.

'Yep.'

'Do you ever think you look like an animal?'

'Nope.'

'Well, you look like a monkey.'

'Ha.'

'But you don't know for sure, right? Unless you look at a mirror?'

He touched his face with his hands. 'The ears are wrong.'

'Do you ever think you look like a girl?'

'Nope.'

'How about . . . someone who's Chinese?'

'It happened once.'

'Did you think you could *talk* Chinese?'

'Of course not.'

'Must be confusing.'

'That's a good description. Now it's time for you to do your homework.'

'I want to play with the kittens some more.'

'You've exhausted them. Let them sleep.'

'Let's name them.'

'Fine. Anything you like.'

So Sue Ellen said, 'Payday and Painter's Lane.'

Kelson raised his eyebrows. 'Those sound like names for—'

'Horses,' Sue Ellen said. 'I work with what I've got.'

'Smart girl,' Kelson said. 'Don't let me catch you trying to ride them.'

*   *   *

An hour later, as Sue Ellen did her math at the kitchen table and Kelson started cooking dinner, the phone rang.

When Kelson answered, the caller hung up.

Five minutes later, the phone rang again.

This time a woman at the other end said only one word. 'Run.'

One word was enough. Kelson recognized the voice of the woman who'd set him up to find Christian Felbanks's body and lied about Dominick Stephens. 'Did you also kill Raima Minhas?' he asked, and Sue Ellen looked up from her homework.

'Run,' the woman said. 'While you can.'

'You got me twice. You won't get me a third time.'

'I never hurt anyone in my life,' the woman said.

Kelson said, 'I'm going to ask you nicely to leave me alone.'

'I'm telling you – get out of your apartment now. He's coming.'

'"Mengele"? If he wanted to get me, he could've done it any—'

'At least get Sue Ellen somewhere safe,' she said, and her words felt like ice. 'Don't let her get hurt because of you.'

'How do you know—'

The woman hung up.

Kelson yelled, 'Shit.'

'You shouldn't swear,' Sue Ellen said. 'You'll scare Payday and Painter's Lane.'

'Fuck Payday and Painter's Lane,' Kelson said – and now real alarm fell over his daughter's face. 'Get your books,' he said. 'I'm taking you home.'

She tried once more, weakly. 'This *is* my home. My kittens are—'

'Your mother's home,' he said. 'Yours too.'

Sue Ellen's eyes dampened, and only his fear kept him from tearing up too.

She put each book, each pencil, each sheet of paper in her bag separately, as if lagging would break the spell that seemed to have rushed into him from the phone. When she raised her eyes to his, he swore again and told her to hurry. If she'd asked about the call, he would've told her, and so he bullied her out the door, downstairs, and into his car.

She leaned sullenly against the passenger door as he drove to Nancy's house. Then she got out, slammed the door, and disappeared up the path and into the house. As the front door closed, he said, 'I love you.'

On his way back to his apartment, he called Dan Peters but got voicemail, and so he hung up. He dialed Greg Toselli, who picked up on the second ring.

When Kelson told him what happened, Toselli said, 'She's trying to scare you.'

'Yeah, and it's working,' Kelson said. 'She threatened Sue Ellen. How does she even know—'

'Calm down,' Toselli said. 'You'll blow a fuse. Seems to me like you've got two choices. Go home and take it easy or do like she says and get out of the way of whatever's coming. If you go home, what're the chances anyone's really coming for you? She's been messing with your head is all—'

'No,' Kelson said, 'she's killed two people. Or whoever she's working with has.'

'*Mengele*?' His tone said enough. 'Then run. Go into hiding. If someone comes after you, don't let them find you.'

Kelson thought about that, mostly out loud, then asked, 'Can I come over and hang out with you tonight?'

For the first time, Toselli hesitated, as if Kelson's story scared him more than he let on. 'I don't know that's such a good idea,' he said. 'I've got a date – and sometimes you say things you shouldn't.'

'I don't mean to.'

'Maybe you should just hole up tonight. Read. Watch a movie. I'll call every couple of hours to make sure you're OK. If you want, I'll stop by later and have a beer with you.'

'Yeah, the calls would be good,' Kelson said. 'Don't worry about the beer.'

'Another time?' Toselli said with false cheer.

'I hear pity,' Kelson said. 'I don't do pity.'

'Well, what do you expect?' Toselli said. 'You call, scared shitless, because a woman's making prank phone calls in the middle of the afternoon—'

'A woman connected to two killings,' Kelson said.

'OK, understood,' Toselli said. 'But you call, scared, and that makes me sorry. Once was a time when nothing scared you. You went as deep as anyone ever went in the department, and I admired that. And when a seventeen-year-old thug shot you in the head, what did you do? You killed him. That's the stuff of heroes. So when I hear you scared, it makes me sorry.'

'None of the guys I dealt with on the street threatened Sue Ellen. Not even Bicho. But I'll tell you what, don't bother checking in tonight. I wouldn't want to lower myself in your eyes.'

'That's not what I was saying,' Toselli said. 'You're—'

But Kelson hung up on him. 'Asshole,' he said. 'Love him, but he doesn't have a fucking clue.'

That evening, Toselli telephoned anyway, once every two hours, and Kelson thanked him for the calls.

Between the calls, Kelson cooked dinner, then stared from the window as if whatever attack the woman warned him about would come rolling down the street. He stretched out on the carpet and then on the bed where Raima Minhas lay dead twenty-four hours earlier, and then he got up and stared out of the window again. The kittens practiced their claws on the carpet, played a game of hide-and-seek under the bed, and scaled the bed cover as if it was a rock face, before falling asleep on his pillow. 'So damn cute,' Kelson said, and he watched a utility truck cruise down the street.

After Toselli's midnight call, Kelson said to himself, 'No sleep tonight.' After the call at two a.m., he kicked the kittens off the bed and climbed in again. The sheets were new, the blanket fresh, but he thought he smelled Raima Minhas. Maybe something physical but beyond the range of the human senses remained of her in the room, like an odorless gas. 'Or some sixth-sensory thing,' he said. 'Don't think about it. The world is full of the dead. The dirt under our fingernails is composted bodies. The air we breathe has already passed through the lungs of dead men. Get used to it. She died here. Just the most recent of many. No reason for nightmares. No reason to let her into my dreams at all.' He lay awake talking like that for a half hour and then swore at himself. He ripped the sheets and blanket from the bed, spread them on the carpet, and lay down again. 'No reason to worry,' he said, and he closed his eyes. 'Only a fool worries about what he can't see.'

NINETEEN

The next morning shined dully through his window, and he woke with the same shock he felt when he looked in a mirror and saw a stranger. 'Good morning,' he said to one of the kittens – he was pretty sure it was Painter's Lane, though he hadn't paid close attention when Sue Ellen told him which was which. He felt a weird joy at seeing the gray sky and hearing the stale heat hiss from the radiator. When he cooked breakfast, his eggs and toast tasted better than usual, and he told them so. Dr P had said some brain injury victims experienced sudden manias as they recovered. He'd never had that happen but wondered if he was feeling one now. He explained to the eggs that, *no*, happiness was perfectly reasonable after making it through the night.

The ringing of his phone startled him, but when Nancy's irate voice spoke to him from the other end, he laughed. Sue Ellen was refusing to go to school. He'd upset her yesterday afternoon and now—

'Put her on, put her on,' he said. 'Shut that luscious mouth of yours and give her the phone.'

'Dad?' Sue Ellen said when she picked up. 'Are you all right?'

'Couldn't be better,' he said. 'I'm sorry I acted like a bastard yesterday.'

'You shouldn't use words like that,' she said. 'They upset Mom.'

'Then I'm sorry for being a dickhead.'

'That's better?' she said.

'And I need to know, which one is Payday and which is Painter's Lane?'

When she told him, he swore again because he'd gotten it wrong. They hung up a minute later, having agreed that she would go to school and he would pick her up afterward. He consented to another game of Stump Dad when she warned him that once she hit puberty, she wouldn't want to play games with him – at all.

*   *   *

As he put on his jacket, he looked out at the street again, and something bothered him about how the cars were parked at the curb – the dirty van in the tow-away zone, the two cars across the street idling with exhaust pumping into the cool morning air – and about the absence of pedestrians. 'Slipping?' he asked himself and kept staring at the street. 'Imagining monsters?' he said. 'Nothing and nothing. Peek under the bed and find . . . kittens.'

He rode downstairs, went outside, and started up the sidewalk.

Then the side panel of the dirty van slid open and three men in green coveralls and black vests poured out, carrying rifles, running toward Kelson. Plainclothes cops with bulletproof vests over their jackets and service pistols in their hands got out of the idling cars and jogged toward him. He'd participated in similar maneuvers dozens of times himself on the narcotics squad.

So he put up his hands and leaned against the cold wall of his building.

One of the cops patted him down and caressed the inside and outside of his legs for guns, then yanked his hands behind him and snapped cuffs on his wrists.

Peters got out of a car Kelson hadn't noticed from his window. The cop who cuffed Kelson spun him around to face the detective.

The big man peered down at him and said, 'You're under arrest for the murders of Christian Felbanks and Raima Minhas.'

Kelson said, 'But—'

Peters shook his head. 'Shut the hell up. Is that enough of a caution, or do you want the rest?'

TWENTY

In the police lineup, Kelson felt he had an advantage. He didn't know what he looked like, and he sensed his own confusion would make it harder for anyone to identify him. He knew the problem with that logic. 'Like a baby hiding behind his hands and thinking no one can see him,' he said as he and four other men filed into the room. The man in front of him glanced back as if Kelson was crazy, and the cop directing the lineup told him to keep his mouth closed. Nerves made Kelson talk, though, so when the cop told the men to face the mirror, then turn left, then turn right, and then stand still, Kelson said, 'And shake your booty.'

Rather than single him out, the cop said, 'Quiet, please, gentlemen.'

'Good protocol,' Kelson said.

'Shut your goddamned mouth,' the cop said.

Twenty minutes later, as Kelson sat again in the interview room, Peters came in and said, 'Well, you're screwed.'

'Do you mind telling me what the witness saw me doing?' Kelson asked.

'Entering your apartment building with Raima Minhas. Ms Minhas was stumbling – incapacitated. The witness said she looked drunk, though she could've been high. You mostly carried her.'

Kelson thought of the possibilities. 'Let me guess. The witness is about thirty. Short red hair.' When Peters stared at him blankly, he added, 'Nice ass.'

'You seem sort of fixated,' Peters said. 'Nope, the witness is nothing like that.'

'Then I'm screwed.'

'As I said.'

'You know I didn't do it.'

'How would I know that?' Peters asked.

'Check the witness. See who this person is. Whoever it is, there's going to be dirt.'

'I'll tell you something I shouldn't,' Peters said. 'You're right. We've got credibility concerns. We wouldn't take this one in front of a judge unless we had good evidence.'

'Addict?'

'Not quite. But who knows, this one might not even show up for the trial. Maybe there isn't even enough to arrest you.'

'But you just did.'

'Sure, because you've got bigger problems. I hear that a street cop and a security guard visited you in your office yesterday morning. Something about gunfire.'

'That's right.'

'And when they came, you said no one shot a gun.'

'No, I said—'

'I've got it in the report.'

'They only asked about *me*. And they didn't notice the bullet hole.'

'You're wrong,' Peters said. 'They noticed. The cop called it in and ran your name. So the report got passed to me, and I'm guessing you know the rest.'

'You got a warrant and checked my office,' Kelson said.

'Hell, I brought a team with me. We pried out the bullet and bagged it. We looked inside your desk. Cute picture of your little girl – you should hang it up like a normal person. Clever under-the-desk rig for your KelTec. We bagged it too.'

'So why did you arrest me?'

'We tested the bullet from the wall. I'm guessing you know the rest again.'

'No, but I'm starting to worry.'

'Fireworks. A match with the bullet that killed Christian Felbanks.'

'Fuck.'

'That's what I would say too if I was sitting where you are.'

'Raima Minhas's father shot it.'

Peters laughed at him. 'You sure it wasn't the redhead?'

'Raima's father and a cousin came to my office and blamed me for her death. I convinced them I didn't kill her.'

'But the father shot the wall anyway.'

'Yes.'

'You must've done a lousy job of convincing. Why'd he shoot?'

'He was aiming at me.'

'And he missed you by what – eight feet?'

'He was jumpy.'

'You know what?' Peters said. 'You should stick with the redhead. She's at least got a nice ass.'

'I want my lawyer.'

Peters shook his head. He reached into his pocket and pulled out a paperclip. He bent it in half, as if it was Kelson. 'Why don't you first tell me what really happened?'

'My lawyer.'

'Where's the murder weapon?'

'Talk to Raima Minhas's father.'

'Go to hell. Where is it?'

'My lawyer.'

'There's no one I hate more than a dirty ex-cop. You shit on your whole life and my life too.'

'My lawyer.'

TWENTY-ONE

Edward Davies arrived before noon. With his fingers laced as if he was praying, he listened as Kelson told him his story. Then he asked for details about the phone call in which the redhead implied that someone set him up at Christian Felbanks's condo to avenge Bicho Rodriguez's death. He didn't roll his eyes, but he asked Kelson to repeat the part about a man the redhead called Mengele. He directed Kelson back to his legal concerns when he sidetracked to the story of Sue Ellen and the kittens.

'Got it,' he said, when Kelson finished. 'Each of the killings is a life sentence. With two together, courts like to go exponential.'

'You've got rotten bedside manner.'

'You want me to hold your hand, or you want me to do my job?'

'I want you to get me out of here.'

'Would this afternoon be too early? I mean, if everything you say checks out?'

'You're not *that* good.'

'Even a bad lawyer could do it,' Davies said. 'If what you're saying is true, it's a sloppy arrest. Plenty of drama. A lot of flash. A big effort to shake you up. But easily undone if Jaipal Minhas has the gun.'

'The guy seemed too nervous to kill Christian Felbanks.'

'That's what I'm guessing. And it would make no sense for him to kill his daughter and then show up at your office like that. So let's work with the idea he didn't kill Felbanks and he might not even know that his gun is the one that did it.'

'How about the cousin?' Kelson said. 'I didn't get much of a read on him.'

'He's worth looking at,' Davies said. 'I'll talk to the father first.'

'What can I do from here?' Kelson asked.

The lawyer shrugged. 'Get some rest. Think happy thoughts.'

Kelson said, 'So, you *can* do bedside manner after all.'

Kelson spent the afternoon in the same holding cell where he'd slept after Felbanks's death. It smelled like a dank basement until a cop brought a disheveled man down the steps and put him in the cell next to his. Then it smelled like sweat and urine. 'Monkey house,' Kelson said.

He lay down on his bunk and tried to think happy thoughts, though all he could think of was Sue Ellen waiting for him to pick her up at the end of the school day as he'd promised and then Nancy rushing from the Healthy Smiles Dental Clinic to get their sad daughter. 'Bad dad,' he said. 'I'm a bad, bad dad.'

He was still lying on the bunk when a cop slid a dinner tray into his cell.

At eight that evening, the cop came back and opened his cell. He led him up the steps and along a corridor to the Homicide Room. In Dan Peters's office, the detective and Edward Davies sat at a desk looking as if they'd just finished a heated argument. Davies smiled as Kelson came in. Peters didn't.

'Detective Peters owes you an apology,' Davies said. 'It seems your arrest this morning was based on a . . . what did you call it, Detective? A misunderstanding? A miscommunication?' When Peters gave no answer, he said, 'Let's call it both. A misunderstanding and a miscommunication. Seeing that this is the second time the detective has locked you up for a crime you didn't commit, less charitable people might call it harassment. People might suspect the motives of the detective. Lawsuits have been filed for less. But I've assured him you're in no way vindictive. I hope I haven't overstepped. But I've also told him you would like an apology and an assurance that he'll avoid this kind of action in the future – a complaint or lawsuit remaining an alternative.'

'I don't need an apology,' Kelson said.

'Do you see that?' Davies said to Peters. 'He'll save you the embarrassment.'

Peters stared at Kelson. 'Stay out of the way. I've got two killings. If you step out, I'll run you over.'

'I'm already flattened,' Kelson said.

'And I'll flatten you again.'

Davies said to Peters, 'From a criminal defense standpoint, that's a bad tactic.'

Peters kept his eyes on Kelson. 'Leave. Now.'

Davies smiled at Kelson. 'From all standpoints, that seems like a good idea.'

Davies took Kelson out for a second dinner – this one at Benny's Chop House. 'Jail food lowers the spirits,' he said. 'Just walking into the station lowers mine. I'll bill you for this dinner by the way. Get the filet or the rib eye.'

'Tell me what happened,' Kelson said.

But Davies insisted on ordering first – a ten-ounce filet for himself, a ten-ounce filet for Kelson, and a bottle of Bordeaux because, he said, 'You don't walk out of jail so easy every day.'

After he wiped salad dressing from the corner of his mouth, he said, 'Jaipal Minhas admits he shot the gun. He bought it and the cousin's pistol two days ago from a woman who looked a lot like the one who identified you in the lineup – dirty blonde, skinny. She went to the father's house to offer condolences for Raima's death. She said she was a college friend.'

'And what?' Kelson said. 'She brought guns instead of flowers?'

Davies shrugged. 'I guess she brought flowers too. Jaipal's angry about his daughter's death. The woman encouraged the anger. She could help him do something about it.'

'The guns were lousy,' Kelson said. 'The kind I used to take from kids on the street. Nothing professional.'

'I don't know about that,' Davies said. 'I found out a little about the woman. She's a twenty-six-year-old named Barbara Lisle – goes by the name Raba. The witness report – which I wasn't supposed to see but did because I'm smart and persuasive and also good-looking – lists her occupation as "adult entertainment." No porn – I Googled her. She used to dance at a club up by the Wisconsin border. Now she's an escort who, the reviews say, will do anything and then some, at a price.'

'Including identifying me in a lineup.'

'It looks like it. The police will put out a warrant for her, but it'll be low priority. I'm sure she's already disappeared – to LA or somewhere else nice if she's got a good ticket, Cleveland or

Detroit if she doesn't. You don't pull a stunt like this and sit tight.'

An hour later, Davies dropped Kelson at his apartment. As Kelson got out, Davies said, 'Hold on, I've got a present for you,' and he popped the trunk. In a cardboard box, he had Kelson's KelTec. 'They couldn't reasonably keep it once forensics cleared you,' Davies said.

'How about my Springfield XD-S? They took it off me at Christian Felbanks's condo.'

'See? That's what I mean,' Davies said. 'The assholes never told me they had it.'

Kelson released the KelTec magazine, thumbed it, and slid it in again. 'This'll do the trick for now.'

Davies said, 'Do me a favor. Don't shoot anyone tonight. I've got other clients to deal with.'

Kelson went up to his apartment and called Nancy's house.

The call woke her – and he knew he'd made another mistake. He asked anyway, 'Can I talk with Sue Ellen?'

'It's almost midnight.'

'It is?'

'She's been asleep for two hours. Use your so-called head.'

'Tell her I love her – in the morning.'

'You were supposed to get her from school. Where were you?'

'In jail.'

'Again?' She was wide awake now.

'Funny, huh?'

'No, not funny at all.' The line went dead.

'I still love her,' he said to Payday.

TWENTY-TWO

The next morning, Kelson woke up without a headache but popped a Percocet with breakfast just in case. He went to his office early, strapped the KelTec under the desk, and took his laptop from the drawer. 'The problem is,' he said to it as it booted up, 'you can't stop people who go after you like this. Unless you kill them.' He considered the idea. 'But you can't do that.' He connected to the internet and brought up Google. 'Can you?' He looked up news articles about Bicho Rodriguez – the boy's shooting of him, his own killing of the boy. Again, he felt the haunting, sickening question – *Who shot first?* He could live with the knowledge that he returned fire if Bicho meant to kill him, but if Bicho only meant to scare him with his tiny Beretta and then Kelson panicked and killed the kid, that knowledge would rip him apart. During his months in the hospital and rehab, he hadn't wanted to see the details. If they clarified that one blot in his memory, they might destroy him. But after he got out, Dr P encouraged him to do all he could to understand what happened because knowing could help him heal.

'It would be like peeling back my skin and looking inside,' he told her.

The metaphor didn't put her off. 'How else are you going to clean out the wounds?'

But now others were peeling back his skin anyway, and so he read every word he could find. He expected the stories to give him pain – maybe pain he couldn't bear, if they revealed him as a trigger-fingered coward – but they sounded cold and dead. The articles painted the shooting scene as Kelson wished he remembered it. They said that, struck in the head by a bullet, he managed to take a gun from inside his jacket and plug the boy once in the chest. He skipped the profile articles about his history in the department and his family life and the day the mayor, the police superintendent, and his district captain came to his hospital room with a service medal and news cameras. He lingered on the *Tribune* profile of Bicho's hard-luck childhood. When he finished it, he wrote notes.

> Alejandro Rodriguez – Bicho
> Father OD'd/DOA when B was 8
> Mother died when B was 9
> Raised by grandmother and uncle – Names? Other family?
>   Neighborhood?
> Amundsen High Sch – Damen Ave. – dropped out 9th
>   grade – Friends? Teachers?

Drug charges at 16 – Juv Detention 7 months – Friends?
   Guards?
   Girlfriend – Francisca Cabon

Then he searched social media sites. If Bicho had accounts, they were deleted after his death. Francisca Cabon had posted a picture from the funeral, though – Bicho stretched in a casket, wearing a white suit coat with a white carnation boutonniere, his dark hair slicked back, his thin lips stretched in a smile.

Kelson searched for more on Francisca and found an address on West Lawrence three blocks from where he and Bicho shot each other.

Then he put away the computer and left a voicemail message for his friend Greg Toselli at the police department. 'I need to see the Alejandro Rodriguez file,' he said. 'I want to know about his relatives and friends. I want to know who supplied him with the coke.'

When he hung up, he looked at his window. Drizzle was spitting on the glass. 'Might as well,' he said. He holstered the KelTec and left his office.

TWENTY-THREE

Francisca Cabon lived in an apartment above a storefront west of Seely Avenue. Kelson pulled to the curb and cut the engine. The business that had once occupied the storefront was long gone, and the sign-mount hanging over the door was empty and rusting. Kelson jogged through the drizzle to the street entrance. When he read the display of tenant names, he froze. At the top, a little plaque said *Stevens Group Rental Properties*.

'What're *you* doing here?' Kelson asked, before deciding it didn't necessarily mean anything since Dominick Stevens owned properties throughout the city. But he said, 'What are the odds?' before pushing the button for Francisca Cabon.

A woman answered through the intercom, and Kelson said, 'I need to ask you some questions about Bicho Rodriguez.'

'You one of his friends?' she asked.

'I'm the guy who killed him.'

'Oh.' She buzzed him in.

The woman at the third-floor landing looked about eighteen. She wore jeans, flip-flops, and a blouse she'd knotted above her belly. She'd bleached a blonde streak in her brown hair. She held a diapered baby against her shoulder. As Kelson came up the last step, she held a free hand to shake his. 'Elena,' she said. 'Francisca's roommate. You're the guy that did Bicho?' She invited him into the apartment and said, 'Francisca's in the shower – worked late. You want orange juice?'

The front room was fitted out with a mix of furniture, the kind you buy used or scavenge when one of your neighbors gets evicted. When Kelson turned down the drink, Elena sat on a brown couch with the baby.

Kelson took a chair that once might've been part of a set, and Elena said, 'Don't believe what Francisca tells you. She'll say she wasn't with Bicho anymore, but that *pendejo* got her pregnant. You want the truth, ask me.'

'Is this their baby?'

'*Si*, this is Miguel. He's the only good thing that ever came out of Bicho.' She turned the child so he faced Kelson. He had the brightest blue eyes Kelson had ever seen.

'Wow,' Kelson said.

'*Muy hermoso*, yes?'

'How old is he?'

'He was born the day before you killed his daddy,' she said. 'If Bicho had been at the hospital with Francisca instead of selling drugs, he would be here with his little boy, and I would—'

A voice spoke from a doorway behind Kelson. 'Bicho was making money for Miguel and me.'

'Yeah, yeah, yeah,' said Elena.

Like Elena, the woman in the doorway was about eighteen. She'd wrapped herself in a white bath towel. Otherwise, she was golden and naked, but with eyes as dark as the baby's were blue.

Kelson asked, 'Francisca?'

She took the baby from Elena. 'Yeah, and who are you?'

Elena smiled and said, 'He killed Bicho.'

Francisca seemed to pale. She held the child close. 'You're the cop?'

'Ex-cop,' Kelson said. 'But he shot me, and I shot him.'

'Why are you in my apartment?'

'It seems some of Bicho's friends want to finish what he started. I don't know what it's about, but they're coming at me hard.'

'Good,' she said.

'Pretty bad,' he said. 'They killed two others. Innocent.'

'How do you know I'm not one of these people coming after you?'

'I don't,' he said. 'So I'm carrying a gun.' He showed it to her. 'I hope I'm good enough to shoot you without nicking Miguel. I used to be, though when I first came out of rehab, I couldn't hit the body silhouette at the gun range, much less the concentrics on the head and chest.'

She hugged her child.

He said, 'If you've got friends hiding in the back and you call them out, I'm screwed.'

Elena said, 'You don't sound like a killer.'

'What does a killer sound like?' he asked.

Elena and Francisca looked at each other and said, 'Bicho.'

'I'm sorry I shot him,' Kelson said, 'I'm sorry he isn't here with you and the baby.'

Something eased inside Francisca – not enough to lessen her anger at Kelson but enough for her to say, 'Some people think Bicho had it coming. But you just got lucky.'

'I never saw the luck in it,' he said. 'He took off part of my forehead. I lost my wife and my job.'

'He shot people before you,' she said.

'I figured as much.'

'You're the only one who ever shot *him*.'

'Lucky me.'

'What do you want?'

'Do you know a woman who's around thirty and has short red hair, parted on the side?' he asked. 'She calls herself Trina Felbanks . . . or Jillian Prindle . . . or something else.'

'No, no one like that.'

'How about someone around that same age? Blonde. Skinny. Barbara Lisle. Raba. Works as an escort.'

'No.'

'Really no? Or no because you don't want to talk to me?'

'I don't want to talk to you, but really no. I don't know a Barbara Lisle.'

'How about Bicho's friends? Have any of them talked about getting even for his death?'

'If they did, I wouldn't tell you.'

'Do you know what it's like to have a man point a gun at your face?'

The baby struggled in her arms. She hushed him. 'Bicho wasn't a man. He was a boy.'

'He shot like a man.'

'You killed a boy,' she said.

'I wish I hadn't,' Kelson said.

'Easy to wish that now.'

'Which of his friends would want to get even?' he asked again.

'Maybe all of them.'

'Two people are dead. They planned to get married.'

'I'm not telling you the names of his friends.'

Elena said, 'Hugo. Esteban. A guy they call *Chango*. He hung with them.'

Francisca said, 'You bitch.' The baby started crying.

'Talk to Hugo,' Elena said. 'They call him *Chilito – little dick*. He's like four feet tall.'

'*Puta*,' Francisca said.

'Shut up,' Elena said. 'They'd mess you up if they could.'

'You have last names for them?' Kelson asked.

'Hugo Nuñez,' Elena said. 'Esteban Herrera. I don't know Chango's last name.'

'You talk that way, you get hurt,' Francisca said.

Kelson asked, 'Who was Bicho dealing coke for?'

Elena shrugged.

He looked at Francisca.

'Yeah, like I would tell you.'

Elena said, 'She don't know. Bicho didn't talk about that.'

'If I knew, I wouldn't tell.' Francisca glared at Elena. 'Girls who talk get hurt.'

Kelson said, 'Girls who hook up with guys like Bicho get hurt.'

That seemed to sting her. 'I do OK,' she said. 'No one messes with me.'

'We all get messed with sooner or later.'

'Not me. Get out of my apartment. I got nothing more to say. Elena either.'

But he had one more question. 'How's your landlord here? Dominick Stevens.'

She glanced at Elena.

'He's OK,' Elena said. 'Nice. And *muy generoso*.'

'Yeah?' Kelson said.

Francisca glared, but Elena said, 'When Bicho died, he heard about Francisca. She had a new baby, and he had an empty apartment here. He let her stay in it. No one lives upstairs, and the store downstairs is empty. We watch the building for him.'

'No rent? What a guy.'

'*Guapo* too,' she said.

'Everyone in Chicago loves Mr Stevens,' Francisca said.

'I've heard that before.'

TWENTY-FOUR

K elson sat in his car outside Francisca Cabon's apartment and added to his notes.

Elena – roommate
Hugo Nuñez – 'Chilito'
Esteban Herrera
Chango
Dominick Stevens – Apt./gift/why?

Then he drove through a steady rain to the Stevens Group building. He parked on the street and ran up the slick sidewalk. The wild, wet face staring at him from the mirrored door startled him, but he went inside and crossed a black marble floor to the reception desk. A wide-shouldered man with a soft voice said, 'May I help you?'

'You got a towel?'

'No, sir.' He looked about twenty but had one of those faces that you can't tell.

'Then would you call up to Mr Stevens and say Sam Kelson is here to see him?'

The man stared at him, as if assessing his state of mind.

'Please?' Kelson said.

'You're the one the cops chased off two days ago?'

'Please call Mr Stevens and let him make up his own mind.'

The man did. When he hung up, he said, 'Mr Stevens is busy right now.'

Kelson said, 'Call back and tell him—'

'Busy means he don't want me bothering him with pointless calls.' He straightened himself in his chair. He was a big man.

'Tell him it's about Francisca Cabon.'

Something fierce appeared on the man's face. 'How do you know Francisca?'

'I just came from her apartment. How do *you* know her?'

'I've always known her,' he said.

'Yeah? What's your name?'

'Esteban.' He offered it as if it was a challenge.

'Herrera?'

'Now, how do you know that?'

'Francisca told me about you.'

The man started to say something but instead picked up the phone again and dialed it. 'He's asking about Francisca,' he said to the mouthpiece. When he put down the phone, he said, 'You can go up – fourth floor.'

'You're a happy family here, aren't you?' Kelson said. 'But I don't understand, what's Dominick Stevens's interest in you?'

'I've worked here since I was fifteen,' he said. 'He kicked me and my mom out of our apartment and gave me a job.'

'You took a job from a man who evicted you?'

'My mom was a bum and didn't pay rent.'

When the elevator doors opened at the fourth floor, Dominick Stevens, dressed in a closely tailored charcoal-gray suit, was waiting for Kelson. He led him to an office with a large steel-and-glass desk and big windows that looked out at Division Street. He closed the door and said, 'Why shouldn't I call the police?'

'Because they might ask the same questions I have,' Kelson said.

'And what are those?'

'Why do you have the friend of a gangbanger drug dealer like Alejandro Rodriguez manning your front desk?'

'I knew Esteban a long time before I heard of Alejandro Rodriguez.'

'I'll bet he can get all the party drugs you and your rich pals want on the weekends.'

'I'll bet you have no idea what you're talking about.' Stevens walked to the other side of the desk. 'Esteban's mother was an addict and a prostitute. She was also one of my tenants in the first building I owned. I tried to work with her. When I kicked them out, that damn kid helped carry the mattresses to the curb. You want to know what guilt feels like? I talked to Esteban, and he impressed me. So I gave him an after-school job, and when he finished high school, I hired him full-time. The kid has problems – a possession arrest, a breaking and entering – but he's always done right by me. When you got shot, I could help his friend's girlfriend, Francisca, and so I did.'

'No wonder everyone in the city loves you. You steal from your own pocket and give to the poor.'

'Did you see where she lives? It's crumbling. That apartment was no gift. She watches the building, and if anyone breaks in, she lets me know. Saves on a security service.'

'So you aren't Robin Hood – you're self-serving?'

'If you keep that up, you can explain yourself to Detective Peters. I'm practical, but I do good when I can. Agreeing to talk to you instead of kicking you down the stairs is another example – if you can handle the truth.'

'I can always handle the truth,' Kelson said. 'Why didn't you tell Peters about Francisca when he came two days ago?'

'I did tell him. Apparently, he didn't let *you* know. I thought my connection to her might give you a reason to come after me.'

'That would be a dumb reason to want to hurt someone.'

'I understand you suffered . . . some impairment.'

'Sure, a hole in the head. But nothing that makes me stupid or violent.'

'But I wouldn't know that, would I?'

'I have the sense that for a young guy you know a lot. But, look, I got set up for two killings—'

'That's what Detective Peters says you say. It's also what I saw in the news.'

'The people who did it left big holes in the setup. If they were smart enough to set me up the way they did, they should've been smart enough to cover the holes. They wanted to knock me off balance, but they also wanted me out of jail – making trouble. The thing is, when they sent me after you, they didn't leave any holes. They couldn't know I would call Peters and tell him I was coming here, and so they must've thought I would get to you.'

'But as you say, you aren't violent.'

'Almost everyone who knows who I am thinks of me as the guy who killed a seventeen-year-old in a gunfight. *You* thought I'd come to hurt you when you scurried out two days ago. Peters is half convinced I killed a couple of pharmacists because I'm out of my mind. Whoever sent me after you probably thought they could make me flip out. I flip, but I don't flip that way – yet.'

'They wanted you to hurt me?'

'I don't know what they wanted. But at least they wanted me to get to you. That means they see us the same way. They're screwing with me. They sent me to screw with you.'

Stevens gave him a tolerant smile. 'Why?'

'Because of Alejandro Rodriguez. Bicho. He's the only link between us. I know what I did to piss them off about him, but I don't know what you did.'

'I never met the boy. I've helped his girlfriend and the baby. That shouldn't make me a target.'

'Whatever you did, you can expect them to come at you again.'

The smile. 'Just as long as they don't send you to do the job.'

'Since I got booted from the department, I pick my own jobs.'

'Next time one of them points you toward my office, take a detour, all right? We don't want to bump into each other too much. I think we'll both be happier if we don't.'

So Kelson rode down in the elevator but, before going back out into the rain, stopped at the front desk. Esteban Herrera said, 'You get what you came for?'

'Stevens seems like a good man.'

'The best.'

'Do you know how I can get in touch with Hugo Nuñez and someone called Chango?'

Herrera gave him a hard look but said, 'Chango's at Marion. Eight to ten for selling *bombita*.'

'Heroin? How long's he been there?'

'Three months. He was in Cook County for ten before that.'

'How about Nuñez?'

'You don't want to talk to Hugo. You might think you do, but you don't.'

'I hear there's not much to him. You call him *Chilito*.'

'*I* don't call him that. No one does to his face if they want to stay alive. You know how people worry about big dogs but it's the little ones that get nasty? That's Hugo.'

'I thought you, Bicho, Chango, and Hugo were all friends.'

'I don't know where you heard that. I don't talk about *my* friends. Hugo was more like Bicho's guy. I do my own thing. I stay clean.'

'Except when you're getting busted.'

Herrera's grin was unapologetic. 'Yeah, except for that.'

'Where can I find Hugo?'

'If you really want to – and I'm telling you that you don't – try Bomboleo on Huron. He's there most nights, drinking and eating and dancing.'

'Look for the short guy?'

'Look for the meanest *hijo de puta* in the place.'

TWENTY-FIVE

That afternoon, Kelson drove to Sue Ellen's school and parked outside of the pick-up lane. It was Nancy's day with her, but Kelson wanted to see her, if only from a distance, as she bounded out with her friends. 'No harm in that,' he said to the man in the mirror. He waited until the last of the kids left the building, but Sue Ellen never came, and he didn't see Nancy's car. Maybe Nancy picked her up early for an appointment – the kind of thing they once would've discussed at the breakfast table but now left unmentioned in their separate lives. 'Bummer,' he said, and he drove to his apartment.

As the kittens played with one of his socks, he dialed Nancy's cell number.

'Did you take Sue Ellen from school early today?' he asked.

'I've started her with a therapist,' she said.

'Why?'

'Are you really asking that?'

'I think we're handling this well,' he said. 'I think she is.'

'Pull your head out of your butt. She cries herself to sleep every night.'

'Not when she stays at my place,' he said.

'Don't do that.'

'What?'

'Don't say she prefers to be with you.'

'I didn't,' he said.

'How did you even know I took her out early?'

'I swung by her school to watch her coming out.'

Nancy barely contained her anger. 'See what I mean?'

'What?' he said, and after she hung up on him, 'What?' again.

For a long time, he watched the rain falling outside his window, graying the city. Then he took a nap but jerked awake after he dreamed he crept behind Bicho in an alley, held a gun to his ribs, and pulled the trigger.

The sky outside was dark, and so he made dinner for himself, Payday, and Painter's Lane. Then he pulled a chair to his window, turned off the lights, and listened to the rain whisper against the glass. The lives of strangers in strange apartments shined from windows in the building across the street – TVs flickering, shapes of bodies moving – but the rain smeared and blurred the details of their lives. 'Probably for the best,' Kelson said.

He sat until ten o'clock, when the lights in the apartments started to go out, and then he got up, took a shower, and dressed again. He strapped his KelTec into an ankle holster, popped a Percocet, and went back down to the street.

Bomboleo occupied the bottom of an old eight-story redbrick factory building. The club served white-tablecloth dinners from a Latin menu before converting the dining room to a dance floor where a DJ blasted music until early morning.

The valet looked at Kelson's Dodge Challenger with hungry eyes.

Kelson said, 'Don't even think it,' and handed him the key.

Inside, the women wore skintight dresses, and the men's hair was stiff with gel. In the main room, the party was just getting started. The DJ switched between English and Spanish as he called the crowd to dance. As Kelson crossed to the bar, the room went dark, and then a mambo tune blasted from the ceiling speakers and a strobe light made the people jerk toward the dance floor.

Behind the bar, two blonde women and a bleach-blond man in a black silk shirt mixed purple and green cocktails, topping them with sliced fruit.

When the man saw Kelson waiting, he shouted over the music, 'What'll it be?'

'Grape Kool-Aid and a cookie,' Kelson said.

The bartender said, 'Huh?'

'Hugo Nuñez?'

As if used to people asking, the bartender pointed his thumb at a corridor leading from the side of the room and said, 'VIP.'

So Kelson crossed the dance floor and went into a hallway lit only by dim, ankle-level bulbs. It took him to a door that he expected to be locked or guarded but wasn't.

He stepped inside.

A very short man sat at the head of a table with twelve other men and women. The short one wore a white suit that he could have stripped from Bicho's body in the coffin. Despite what Esteban Herrera said about him, he had a pleasant smile. The women at the table were young and pretty and looked extremely stoned. The men were tightly wound and kept their sharp eyes on the stoned women, as if they would keep flicking pills at them, like peanuts at pet monkeys, until they kicked them out of bed the next morning. A waiter stood near a wall, ready to answer any needs.

Dishes – mostly empty – covered the table from a feast the group had just finished – glass bowls with the remnants of octopus and crab ceviche, a platter with stray pieces of a blood sausage, a dozen stripped skewers with fat clinging to them, the head and feet of a suckling pig. 'So much for the zoo,' Kelson said.

None of them paid attention. Maybe they thought he'd come to clear the table or offer another roast pig.

So he went to the short man and said, 'I hear I shouldn't call you *Chilito*.'

Nuñez blinked at him. 'Whoever told you that gave you good advice.' The white in his left eye was bloodshot solid. 'Yes, that's advice you can live by.' He spoke in clear, accentless English.

The bloody eye transfixed Kelson. 'Are you touching yourself with dirty fingers?' he said.

Nuñez gave him a stony stare. The others at the table quieted.

Kelson said, 'My dad got that sometimes in the corner of one of his eyes. He said tension did it – a bad day at work, a fight with my mom. He died of a heart attack. I don't know if it was related – blood pressure or something.'

'What the hell do you want?' Nuñez said.

That snapped Kelson out of it. 'My name's—'

'I know who you are. You're the one that killed Bicho. And you were on television yesterday.' Now he had an accent.

'That's because of your friend Bicho again.'

'Bicho was too big for his pants.'

'His britches.'

'His what?'

'Britches,' Kelson said. 'It's "too big for—"'

'Do I look like I care what it is?'

'No, you look like a little guy who's acting tough by dressing in a shiny jacket and lowering his voice an octave below where it would naturally fall.'

One of the women took in a sharp breath. The waiter moved toward the door to the corridor.

Nuñez said, 'I could shoot you in the head.'

'It's been done before,' Kelson said. 'No glory in it. Like the second man up Everest.'

Nuñez narrowed his eyes, which made the bloodshot one look all black. 'I hear Bicho took out a piece of your brain. Like a doctor. He gave you a lobotomy.'

Two of the men laughed.

Nuñez liked the laughter. 'I also hear they used to do lobotomies with icepicks. A bullet's quicker. We could try the old-fashioned way since you disrespect me in front of my friends.' He nodded at the waiter. 'You got an icepick in the kitchen, Juan?'

'No, Señor Nuñez,' the waiter said.

But Nuñez didn't care about icepicks either. He said to Kelson, 'You think you're smarter than me?'

'I think most people are smarter than you,' Kelson said, 'but you're meaner and littler than the rest of us, and that counts for something.'

'You say stupid things,' Nuñez said.

'You ask stupid questions.'

That made Nuñez break into a wide-mouthed smile full of mean little teeth. 'Bring me some knives,' he said to the waiter. 'A bucket of them.' Then, to Kelson, 'What does a smart question sound like?'

Kelson said, 'Here's one. Are you setting me up to get back at me for Bicho?'

Nuñez gave a rapid shake of the head. 'No, that's stupid. Why would I do this? I'm grateful to you for taking care of Bicho.'

'How's that? I thought you were friends.'

'He was a pest. I didn't trust him.'

'Because he was as tough as you?'

Nuñez said to the waiter, 'Do you think I am joking about the knives?'

'I don't know, Señor.'

'Yes,' he said. 'It's a joke. But when I ask for something, get it. To be on the safe side.' Then, to Kelson, 'No, I didn't trust him because he didn't answer to me. I trust only men who do what I tell them – like Juan here, who will get me knives next time I ask, even if I am joking.'

'Who did he answer to?' Kelson asked.

Nuñez showed his mean little teeth again. 'No, no, I don't do that. There are men who are tougher than I am – not many, but there are men. They know who they are, and I know who I am. That's enough. Maybe one of these men is going after you. I don't know. All I know is I was eating a nice dinner with my friends, and you came in and interrupted us. You don't want me for an enemy.'

'You've always been my enemy,' Kelson said. 'I used to work in narcotics. Any man like you—'

'Enough,' Nuñez said. He didn't raise his voice, and his accent seemed to melt away again. 'You can leave now. You can walk out the door and straight to the exit. Do not look back. Do not *think* of looking back. Or I can have my friends remove you. I advise you to leave on your own. That's more advice you can live by.'

Kelson opened his mouth to reply – he thought he *should* say something – but no words came to his lips. So he just said, 'Have a good night, *Chilito*.'

But instead of crossing the dance floor to the exit as Nuñez advised, he went back to the bar and signaled the bleach-blond bartender. He handed him a twenty and said, 'I forgot to thank you.'

'A pleasure,' the bartender said and pocketed the bill.

'Can you help me with one more thing? What time does Señor Nuñez leave?'

The bartender gave him a wary look. 'You couldn't ask him yourself?'

Kelson took another twenty from his wallet and laid it on the bar top. 'I left in a hurry.'

Without glancing at the bill, the bartender folded it into his fingers. 'I wouldn't be surprised if he stayed until closing. Tonight, that's two a.m.'

Then Kelson headed for the exit.

He almost made it.

Two men by the hostess station grabbed his arms and guided him back into the club. They were no bigger than many other guys who work out at the gym for a few hours each day, but there were two of them.

While couples did the rumba to a tune heavy with guitars and clave rhythm, the men pushed him into a narrow hallway covered with graffiti.

One of them shoved him through a restroom door, while the other stood guard outside. The first threw him against a stall. As Kelson bounced back, the man planted a fist in his jaw. All the Percocet in the world couldn't take away the pain of a punch like that. The man seemed to grunt his words – 'Don't' – he threw a punch into Kelson's ribs – 'ever' – Kelson slid toward the tile floor, but the man hoisted him up by his jacket – 'call' – the man punched him in the jaw again – 'Señor Nuñez' – Kelson felt himself falling and falling – '*Chilito*.'

The man kicked Kelson and kicked him again. In the head, in the ribs, in the head, in the ribs. Kelson pasted himself on the dirty bathroom tile as if the cool and wet could open an escape hatch. The man grunted with each kick. Kelson groaned, lips to the tile. The man kicked him exactly ten times, as if doling out lashes written in law. Sometime after the last kick, Kelson fingered his ankle holster, tugged out his gun, and aimed at the man. But the man was gone.

Kelson pried himself from the floor and looked at the mirror. He felt exactly like the man who stared back – wincing from pain in his ribs, his face bruised, his top lip cracked. He set his pistol on the sink and splashed water on his face. He mumbled something as incoherent as his thoughts. He straightened his pants, his shirt, his jacket. He ran water over his hands, splashed it on his face again, and slicked back his hair. He didn't like the man in the mirror.

He tucked his pistol in his belt and stumbled out into the club. The DJ was playing a song with a hard, thumping beat. If Kelson didn't get out soon, he felt his head would explode. But he stumbled past dancing couples toward the VIP room. No one seemed to care about a bruised man lurching through the strobe light.

In the dim corridor, Juan the waiter brushed past with platters from the table.

'Ghost,' Kelson said – and he meant himself.

Outside the room, he pulled his pistol from his belt. He took out the magazine, checked it, and slapped it back in place. He shoved open the door.

The room was empty. Nuñez and his guests – gone. Only a food-stained tablecloth showed the damage they'd done.

Kelson stood, bewildered. He raised his pistol and aimed at the chair where Nuñez had sat. He tightened his finger on the trigger, then eased it. 'Probably for the best,' he said.

He went back out and crossed to the bar. He signaled the bleach-blond bartender. The bartender – mixing a highball the color of blood in water, topping it with an orange wedge – ignored him. Kelson waited. 'No rush,' he said.

The bartender filled another customer's order – green with jalapeño slices – before coming to Kelson. 'What can I do for you?'

Kelson fumbled with his wallet, taking out another twenty and putting it on the bar top. 'Where'd Nuñez go?'

The bartender ignored the bill. He stared at Kelson as if he'd never seen him before and asked, 'Who?'

TWENTY-SIX

The next morning, Kelson had an appointment with Dr P. Overnight, the rain had stopped, and the sky was clear and cold. As Kelson walked from the parking lot to the Rehabilitation Institute building, he tried to whistle from his swollen jaw. 'Nothing doing,' he mumbled.

After he told Dr P about the past few days, finishing with a blow-by-blow account of the Bomboleo men's room, she shined a penlight at his pupils, had him perform a coordination exercise, and asked questions from a cognitive acuity test.

She sighed when he touched his finger to his nose and again when he nailed the answers. She said, 'You can't let people kick you in the head.'

'I didn't *let* him—'

'Repeat injuries could be catastrophic,' she said. 'Even a minor concussion might—'

'I thought you would be sympathetic.'

'Because you saw a roaring fire and jumped into it?'

'I didn't light the fire. Someone set me up.'

'What would be your best response to that?' She had the tone of a parent who was more disappointed than angry. 'I mean, would it be better to jump in or run away?'

'Is this a brain test?' he said.

'It's a test of whether you have any common sense.'

'What lobe is that in?'

'Would you have shot that man if he'd been sitting in the chair?'

'I don't know,' he said. 'At the time, I thought I would. But it didn't happen.'

'I think you should give up your weapon until we understand your impulse control more fully.'

'I got sent to a condo to find a dead man. I came home and found a dead woman in my bed. A killer is targeting me. And you want me to give up my gun?'

'I think it would be best.'

'I like a fighting chance,' he said.

'It worked out well for you last night.'

'The gun gave me a chance.'

'It did you no good, and it put others at risk. At least lock it up. Put it in a gun safe.'

'I'll think about it.'

She wrote notes on a clipboard. 'The kittens are good.'

'Sure,' he said. 'Fluffy. Sue Ellen likes them.'

'They help with the headaches?'

'They seem to. It's nice to have company.'

She wrote another note. 'Just don't shoot them.'

TWENTY-SEVEN

When Kelson pulled from the parking lot, he glanced at the mirror and asked, 'Who does she think I am?' A half block away, he glanced again. 'Kittens, for God's sake.' He turned the corner toward Lake Shore Drive and looked a third time – now to check the green Audi behind him. As he'd come out of the parking lot, the car had pulled from the curb across the street, and now it turned with him. No big deal if he hadn't gone through what he'd gone through lately, but the side windows on the Audi were tinted, and glare from the sun kept him from making out the driver.

So instead of continuing on to Lake Shore Drive, he turned again.

The Audi turned behind him.

He turned again. The Audi turned.

'As if I didn't already have enough,' he said. He slowed as he approached the stop light at Michigan Avenue, then punched the gas as the light turned yellow. It flipped red as he entered the intersection, but the other driver gunned it and followed him across to the music of car horns and screeching brakes. 'Must be important,' Kelson said, and he turned, drove to Lake Shore Drive, and headed to his office. When he pulled into the parking garage, the other car went past, slowing at the curb. When he walked out to the sidewalk, the driver's door on the Audi opened. The redhead got out. She wore black leggings and a red angora sweater. She'd gelled her hair into spikes.

Kelson stopped. 'Not again.'

'Fancy driving,' she said. 'You'll get us both killed.'

'That'll save you the work,' he said. 'How did you find me at the Rehab Institute?'

'I followed you since you left your apartment this morning.'

'Damn,' he said, and he looked up and down the street to see who else she had brought. He pulled out his phone. 'I'm calling nine-one-one.'

'Hang up or I'll drive away,' she said.

'Really? Do you promise not to come back?'

'You'll be glad if I stay. Come on.' She walked toward his building.

He stood still. 'You've gotten me twice. There was a time when you wouldn't have gotten me at all.'

She came back, close enough that he felt her breath. 'The thing is, standing out here, we're both taking a risk,' she said. 'The cops think you're making me up – or else you're involved with me in ways you haven't admitted. And the guy who's setting you up thinks I'll do anything he tells me to do because he has me on a string too. If he found out I came to see you—'

'Hugo Nuñez.'

'What?'

'Hugo Nuñez. *Chilito*. Is he Mengele?'

'I don't know anyone named Hugo Nuñez.'

'The damned thing is, I don't know if you're lying.'

'Let's go inside,' she said, and either she was scared or she did a good job of pretending.

Kelson said, 'I think whatever game this guy is playing has just started. I think he's out to wreck me.'

She said, 'You want to hear what I have to say.'

'Tell it to me.'

'Take me inside.'

He just stared at her.

'Fine,' she said, and she walked toward her car.

'You follow me back and forth across the city and then drive away?'

She got in the car.

He shouted, 'You've got great legs.'

She started the engine, rolled down the window, and flipped him off. Then she hit the gas, and the Audi jumped from the curb. As it turned the corner and disappeared, he said, 'Impulse control.'

He went up to his office and took his computer from his desk. Then he pulled out the picture of Sue Ellen and walked around the office holding it against the walls. Maybe Peters was right – he should hang it. Maybe Sue Ellen's gaze wouldn't give him a headache. Maybe he should hang a photo of Payday and Painter's Lane next to hers.

The phone on the desk rang.

When he picked up, the redhead said, 'The funny thing is, I could help you.'

'Why don't you leave me alone? Tell whoever's behind this I got the message. Tell him I'm sorry about Bicho. Tell him I wish the kid never shot me and I never shot him. I wish I never met him and he was selling coke to some other undercover cop and I was far away.'

'Did anyone ever tell you you're intriguing?'

'Yeah, a word that gets used for me a lot, mostly as an insult,' he said. 'Why don't you harass someone else?'

'When I drove away, you were supposed to yell at me to come back. That's what I thought you would do, based on your behavior.'

'Sorry to disappoint you.'

'I learned how to read people when I was little,' she said. 'Survival instinct.'

'With the stepdad who used to come to you in your bedroom?'

'Exactly.'

'If he's even real.'

'All too real,' she said.

'What would've happened if I'd brought you up to my office? What would you have told me?'

'I would've told you about Bicho's girlfriend Francisca and her baby. Bicho wasn't the father.'

'If that's true, I'm sure Bicho would care – if he could. But why should *I*?'

'Because the father owns most of the apartment buildings in

Bicho's old neighborhood, including the one where Francisca lived
with her mom until her mom kicked her out.'

'Dominick Stevens?'

'Uh-huh.'

The thought sent a shiver through him.

She said, 'With a good-looking man like him – young, lots of
money, lots of power – who could blame her? But if Mengele
wants to get people who hurt Bicho, what happens to Stevens?'

'I see your point,' he said. 'But I've also seen it before. What
do you want me to do? Rush over to his office and get myself in
trouble again?'

'Not his office, no. His townhouse in Lincoln Park.'

'I'll bet you'll even give me the address.'

'Would you believe me if I told you I don't know it?'

'No.'

'Yeah,' she said, 'you're intriguing. Cute too.' And she hung up.

'I know what you're doing,' he said to the phone anyway. 'And
it won't work.'

To clear his mind and dull the urge, he looked out the window
at the mid-morning traffic. He half expected to see the Audi
parked at the corner, the redhead staring at him through the windshield. He thought about what the redhead said about Francisca
Cabon. 'Must've been, like, sixteen when Stevens got her pregnant,'
he said. 'If he really did.' He thought about Miguel, Francisca's
baby, with his intense blue eyes. 'You don't get eyes like that
except from pain or joy,' he said.

He went back to his desk and called the Stevens Group office.

The receptionist said Stevens was out and asked who was calling.

Kelson told her and asked, 'Has he come in today?'

'I'm afraid his schedule is private,' she said.

'If he's supposed to be there and hasn't arrived, call the police,'
he told her. 'Have them check him at home.'

When he hung up, he Googled Stevens's name along with the
word 'townhouse.' He got hundreds of real-estate listings. So, he
Googled the phrase 'Dominick Stevens's home.' He got a link
to a *Chicago Magazine* feature titled 'Chicago's Designing
Entrepreneurs' that profiled five men and women who dug deep
into their bank accounts as they rehabbed old houses. The profile
showed Stevens standing outside a two-flat on North Burling that

he'd converted into what the magazine called 'the ultimate retro bachelor pad.'

He went back to the window and tried to fight the urge for another twenty minutes. He fogged the window glass as he told it all the reasons he should ignore the redhead's call. Then he grabbed his coat and went down to his car.

Kelson drove down Halsted and cut over to North Burling. 'Jackpot,' he said. A block and a half away, a half dozen squad cars, their lights flashing, filled the street.

Kelson pulled to the side and turned off the engine. 'Not such an idiot after all,' he said.

He watched as cops went to the front steps of Stevens's house and returned to their cars, then went back to the house. They looked overexcited. Although every impulse said *Go close and see*, Kelson stayed put. 'Not *so much* of an idiot,' he said.

He sat for ten minutes. An ambulance approached the squad cars from the other direction, and two paramedics got out and talked with a uniformed cop. They stayed outside. Five more minutes passed. Another cop came from the house, and then the paramedics got back into the ambulance and left. Kelson said, 'That's either very good or very bad.' More cops came out, got in their cars, and drove away too, leaving three squads.

'Dammit,' Kelson said. He started the car.

But before he could pull from the curb, a grimy blue Ford Interceptor rushed down the street behind him, braking hard and blocking him in.

Peters climbed out.

If Kelson opened his door, Peters might shoot him, so he rolled down his window and said, 'Good morning, Detective.'

Peters said, 'You're a real asshole.'

Kelson said, 'Some people think I'm intriguing.'

Peters yanked the car door open as if he would drag him out. 'Why did you make the call?'

'What?'

'It's like you're making bomb threats.'

'I figured, better safe than—'

'But why? What made you think?'

Kelson couldn't help but answer. 'The redhead with the great ass.'

'Goddammit.'

'Is Stevens all right?'

'No, he's not all right – he's pissed off. With good reason.'

'He was supposed to be at his office. If his people called, they must've been worried.'

'He was at home – with a companion.'

'A *companion*?'

'Yeah, a goddamned companion.'

'Stevens had a kid with Bicho's girlfriend. At least the redhead says he did.'

'We know that. We've known for a long time.'

'You have?'

'Who do you think the companion is?'

'Oh,' Kelson said. Then, 'She was sixteen when he got her pregnant. There're laws against that.'

'There are also laws against calling in false threats.'

'You're letting him slide on the girl?'

'It's complicated.'

'Because he's connected to power.'

'Because the girl won't testify. And she won't allow blood tests on the baby. And yes, because Stevens has power. What the hell did you think? I've never known a guy who was a cop for fourteen years but was so naïve.'

'I was a cop for fourteen years and I have an eleven-year-old daughter who'll be sixteen in a few years.'

'Oh, Christ, don't be sentimental. That's as bad as naïve.'

'The redhead said—'

'Shut up. OK? I don't want to hear it. If this woman's more than a fucked-up figment of your fucked-up imagination, next time she tells you to do something, do the opposite, OK?'

Kelson could've argued.

He could've explained.

He said, 'OK.'

TWENTY-EIGHT

'What made me do it?' Kelson said as he drove back to his office. 'Judgment. I always trusted my judgment.' Next time he saw Dr P, he would ask if his brain injury could change his judgment the way it initially changed his ability to walk through doorways, skewing him by ten or fifteen degrees, smacking him into doorframes any normal man would thread without bumping shoulders. But he already knew Dr P's answer. *Sure, why not?* She'd told him a dozen ways already. *With the brain, we're always in new territory. You're one of a kind, Mr Kelson. Sometimes a brain injury even leads to new characteristics and abilities – a fondness for piano music, a facility with foreign languages.*

'*Tak jest,*' he'd said when she told him that last bit – Polish for *Yes, sir*, a phrase an informant used with him when he worked an undercover job in the Noble Square neighborhood.

Dr P gave him a don't-screw-with-me look.

Now, he thought about each step he'd taken with the redhead, testing his judgment. The redhead paid him to talk sense into Christian Felbanks, who, she said, was her drug-stealing brother. He reasonably took the job. Then she sent him after Stevens at the office building on Division Street. That time, he should've known better. When she called him at his apartment and told him to *run*, warning him to get Sue Ellen out of harm's way, he reacted fast and sensibly – taking Sue Ellen to Nancy's house, then holing up alone. The fact that Dan Peters brought a tactical team to arrest him the next day in no way undermined the soundness of his decision to stay. If he'd run, as the woman told him to, he would've looked guilty and his circumstances might've been worse. As for today, what choice did he have? What if Dominick Stevens had died? Kelson had a responsibility and he fulfilled it. Could he have done it without getting Stevens's office staff to call the cops? Maybe. He would count this morning as a partial failure – though even a partial failure went down in the bad-judgment column. That made him two for four.

'Batting five hundred,' he said. 'Pretty good for a player just off the disabled list.'

Still, when he parked his car, went up to his office, and found the redhead sitting in one of the client chairs again, he fumbled his phone out of his pocket and called Peters.

When Peters answered, Kelson yelled, 'She's here right now.'

'What?' Peters said. 'Who?'

'The redhead.'

'Yeah? Go to hell. Get some help, OK?' Peters hung up.

Kelson scrambled to redial but dropped the phone.

The redhead watched, arching an eyebrow.

Kelson grabbed the phone, dialed, and, when Peters answered, said, 'Goddammit—'

'Goddammit yourself.' The line went dead again.

Kelson shoved the phone in his pocket and told the woman, 'I'll take you in myself.'

'Don't get all weirded out. It makes you less attractive.'

Kelson went to his desk and reached for the KelTec in the hidden rig. It was gone. He opened the bottom drawer. It wasn't there either.

The woman pulled it from her purse and aimed it at him. She said, 'Having a good ass doesn't make me stupid.'

'Clearly.'

'Now sit down and listen.'

'Why are you doing this? You could just shoot me.'

'Sit down.'

He did.

'We all pay for our mistakes,' she said. 'Mine are the only reason I'm here.'

'*Mine* was shooting Bicho Rodriguez when he pulled a gun on me?'

'Seems almost unfair, doesn't it?' She held the KelTec lightly. 'But he was a kid, and you know how that goes. From Mengele's perspective, you have to understand the anger. I mean, you have a daughter. You know—'

'Don't bring her into it. Don't ever,' he said. 'And what about Christian Felbanks and Raima Minhas? What mistakes did they pay for? He was corn-fed and wholesome. Straight from farm to table. And her? An immigrant girl makes good.'

The redhead ran a free finger down the length of the pistol barrel. She tried to sound coy, but her face showed pain. 'We all have secrets.'

'Not me,' he said. 'Not anymore. I can't keep them, no matter how hard I try.'

'That could become a problem. Mengele has a job for you – one you won't want to talk about. No money in this one. He wants you to kill Dominick Stevens.'

Kelson laughed at her. 'Not happening.'

She looked pained, ill. 'Stevens hurt Bicho by sleeping with Francisca Cabon. Mengele uses me to get you, and he'll use you to get Stevens. He says you can't pretend you aren't already involved. He says that's what you tried to do with Bicho.'

'You're an excellent spokesman for him. What's he got on you?'

'You don't want to know.'

'But I do. I couldn't be more interested.'

'He says you're delusional. You think you're better than others.'

'I won't kill Dominick Stevens,' he said. 'No one will.'

'At this point, I'm supposed to ask about your ex-wife and daughter.'

He rose from his desk chair, furious – unthinking.

But the redhead raised the pistol with him and aimed it at that spot on his forehead where Bicho had shot away a part of the man he'd been.

And he flinched.

Sweat breaking from his neck, he sat in his chair. 'If you ever – if Nancy and Sue Ellen ever even *think* someone might hurt them, I'll – *why* are you doing this?'

'I don't want to be here. Just like you didn't want to shoot Bicho. But it's you or me. You angered the wrong man, and he wants to destroy *you*. He doesn't want you dead. He wants you to carry the guilt.'

'Who is he?'

She shook her head.

'What will he do to you?' he asked.

'If I didn't do this, he would destroy me too. I've been destroyed enough times in my life. I can't take it again.'

'What's he got on you?'

She ignored the question and said, 'Do you think three days is enough? You know where Stevens works, and now you know where he lives. Since you've harassed him so much lately, he'll probably be on guard, but you can get close enough to do it.'

'Uh-uh. We go to the police.'

She stood and set the KelTec on the desk. 'They won't believe a word that comes out of your mouth.'

Then she walked out of the office.

He sat for a full minute, speechless, staring at . . . nothing. Then he popped the magazine from the pistol, rolled it in his palm, and snapped it back in.

He knew better than to call Peters. So he called Greg Toselli. Toselli had spent the previous night raiding a building that supposedly housed a child-trafficking operation but had found only a single mattress and a bunch of empty rooms. He was tired and cranky and seemed to have a hard time listening as Kelson told him his troubles.

'But why would anyone do this?' he said.

'Exactly what I asked,' said Kelson. 'She made it sound like revenge for Bicho.'

'But the kid shot *you*.'

'I'm aware of that.'

'Unless they think you shot him first.'

'That question never went public.'

'Either that or someone loved the kid a lot – the kind of love that makes a person violent. What does the redhead get out of this?'

'She makes it sound like the man's setting her up too. If she doesn't do what he says, he'll spring the trap.'

'Do you believe her?'

'Well, this is about more than Bicho – at least enough to get Christian Felbanks and Raima Minhas killed. So maybe there's something in what she says. But it's mostly about Bicho. Did you get the records I asked for on him?'

Toselli hesitated. 'First rule – no man left behind. That includes me too. I'll do anything for you, but you won't let this blow back on anyone, right? You've got Peters coming at you on one side and these people on the other. Anyone who's in the middle with you or helping . . . I mean, if I can get the files for you, will you keep it quiet?'

'I don't know if I can. You know, things come out.'

'That's what I'm saying. Don't ask me to do something that hurts you – or me.'

'So what would *you* do?' Kelson said. 'If you were where I am. You've always played the game smart. You get things done.'

Toselli sounded frustrated. 'You shouldn't have been in that alley with that kid. You shouldn't have had a gun. But you were there – and you did – and so how do you get out now? Seems like you've got two choices, and you won't like them. One, you can do something to show you're listening to this woman. Something that shows you're taking the threat seriously. Delay the game and give yourself time to figure it out.'

'Unless it pisses this guy off and he goes after Sue Ellen and Nancy.'

'I don't think so. He's playing you – running you over the psychological ropes, seeing what you'll take. Sue Ellen and Nancy are his last move – game over.'

'What's the other choice?'

'Take the redhead out of it. Completely out. Whoever's hiding behind her – if there's even such a person – either gives up or comes out in the open.'

'Or finds someone new to front for him.'

'Hard to find someone like her, from what you say. Of the two choices, that's the better one. It's what I'd do. Take care of yourself and take care of your own. Self-defense. She's holding a gun to your head, right? Same as Bicho. And with Sue Ellen and Nancy, she's got hostages.'

'More or less,' Kelson said.

'Then do what you've got to do.'

'Maybe so.'

'But whatever you decide, do it all the way.'

'Sure.'

'You've got to live by it,' Toselli said. 'Make it an absolute principle.'

And they hung up.

Toselli was right – Kelson disliked both choices. Part of him admired his friend's ability to act decisively in bad situations. He *lived* by his principles – and other cops owed him their lives. But he also seemed unconcerned about the damage he caused to people outside of his circle.

'Rough justice,' Kelson said. 'Stay on the right side of a man like that. Still, you've got to admire him.' Then he added, 'Admire but not emulate.'

So instead of gunning for Stevens or the redhead, Kelson went looking for a man he hadn't seen in two years, since before Bicho shot him in the head.

TWENTY-NINE

DeMarcus Rodman could've been a great cop, the kind newspaper articles get written about when they retire and who become legends in the bars where cops hang out. Kelson and Rodman started police academy together, at the same time as Greg Toselli and Nancy, and while Nancy scored in the top three percent and Kelson and Toselli scored in the top ten in both the intellectual and physical testing, Rodman blew through the charts. He was tall – taller than even Dan Peters – and as wide at the shoulders as two men. His eyes were set a little too close together, he wore a goatee, and his brown skin was soft. When he did the bench press, the academy instructors called the other cadets to watch. When a classroom instructor handed back an exam, he said, 'You've got to be kidding, Rodman' – in a good way. Instead of trying to break him the way they did most of the others, the instructors treated him like one of their own.

Then, a month before graduation, his little brother stepped into the middle of a street bust. Something on him flashed. Maybe his belt buckle. The cops said he had a knife, but none of the bystanders saw him pull it. It didn't matter, though. When the cops saw the glare, they fired fourteen bullets into him. The mayor and the police superintendent promised a full investigation, but ten days later a review board ruled the killing justifiable. And Rodman quit.

'The review board *lived* by it too,' Kelson said now as he drove downtown toward Rodman's apartment.

In the years since Rodman quit, rumors about him floated back to the department. He'd joined the army. He'd left the city to live with relatives in Maryland. He'd gone rogue and was climbing the ladder in the El Rukn street gang. But three years ago Kelson learned the truth.

Kelson was working on a drug operation in Bronzeville, on the city's South Side, pretending, as usual, to be a south suburban businessman with a coke habit and plenty of friends whose habits he wanted to supply. Twice a week he drove along Forty-Fifth Street in a black Corvette the narcotics squad had confiscated from a meth lab operator, and a kid would run from the alley by the Ebenezer Baptist Church, take Kelson's money, and give him a baggie. Once the dealer recognized him as a regular, the process relaxed, and soon Kelson was standing outside his car explaining his needs to a man who sold coke to most of the neighborhood users.

One morning as they chatted, a police cruiser – sent by a narcotics liaison – drove past, and the dealer and Kelson slipped into the alley and deep into the dealer's world. After some friendly prodding, the dealer sent a lookout to the end of the alley and then showed Kelson the wares he had on hand – more than enough, he promised, to keep Kelson and his buddies screaming high for a month. That was all Kelson needed to see. He told the dealer he would bring cash the next morning, though he planned to arrive instead with Greg Toselli and a raid team.

But before he could go back to the Corvette, DeMarcus Rodman came out of the back door of a third-floor apartment that reared to the alley, and jogged down the wooden stairs. He was enormous, and before he put a foot on the asphalt, the dealer pulled a small pistol out of his belt and pointed it at his wide chest. Rodman winked at Kelson and raised his hands.

'You come closer, I'll cap you,' the dealer said.

Rodman answered with the softest, gentlest voice. 'You've got to wonder with a man like me, how deep a bullet from a little gun'll go. If it kills me, you win. More likely, it stops in the muscle layer. Then you've got to wonder what it'll feel like to have me cram that pistol through your teeth and down your puny throat. If I was a man like you, that's what I'd wonder about with a man like me.'

The dealer lowered the pistol, and Rodman lowered his hands. Rodman ignored Kelson, though Kelson sensed he was performing for him when he told the dealer, 'See that apartment up there? Me and my girlfriend just moved in. A nice place, and you know what? We don't even need an alarm clock. Old Ebenezer Baptist tells us the time with his bells. If you like, you can come up for coffee.'

The dealer stared at him with contempt. 'I don't drink the shit.'

'Or tea,' Rodman said. 'Cindi likes the tea. But she don't like this business you got going down here.'

The dealer smirked. 'She don't like it, she can—'

Rodman held a single huge finger to silence him – nothing especially threatening but enough. 'She don't like it because this is our home now, and all that pretty church-bell music sounds cracked if a man like you is making junkies out of the neighbors.'

The dealer tried again. 'It's a free—'

'No,' Rodman said, as soft as before, 'it ain't, and it never was. If you think it's free, you're confused. I could tell you stories – over a cup of coffee, or tea – that would make you reconsider that falsehood. It ain't free, and you ain't free.'

'I'm working this block for five years,' the dealer said. 'No one tells me where I do business. A man that tries gets some of this.' He raised the gun again.

'I'm sorry to hear that,' Rodman said, 'because I thought we could be pals. I thought you liked your teeth in your mouth and liked your throat without blood running into your lungs.' His gentle voice scared the hell out of Kelson and the words weren't even meant for him.

The dealer's hand wavered. He stuck the pistol inside his belt.

Rodman moved close to him and looked down as if he would pat the top of his head. He took the gun from the man's belt and held it in his palm, and the man looked relieved he didn't take more of him than that. Then Rodman pulled a trash bin away from the church wall, reached into a hole in the bricks, and took the dealer's stash.

'You can't do that,' the man said.

'Wrong again,' Rodman said. Then he winked at Kelson again and climbed the stairs to his apartment.

That afternoon, Kelson reported to his squad captain that the Forty-Fifth Street operation had imploded. These things sometimes happened, and when the captain asked, Kelson said only, 'The dealer cut and ran. He spooked.'

And the next afternoon, Kelson went back to Rodman's Bronzeville building. The lock on the street door was broken, and after going up to the apartment, he knocked. Rodman, wearing a pair of huge boxer shorts and nothing else, pulled the door open. He grinned and enveloped Kelson in a hug. 'Goddamn, it's good to see you,' he said, and his gentle laugh made Kelson think of a volcano. 'You know how surprised I was when I looked out yesterday and saw you?'

He made Kelson wait as he started a pot of coffee, and then they went into the living room.

'I've never seen anything like that,' Kelson said.

'When you move into a new place, you've got to sweep the trash out of the gutters.'

On the wall behind a sofa, there were three portraits that looked as if they were painted by the same hand – Marty Luther King, Jr., Malcolm X, and, between them, a woman with beaded hair who looked about twenty-five. 'That your girlfriend?' Kelson asked.

'Cindi,' Rodman said. 'Working right now. She's a nurse at Rush Medical.'

'How're *you* getting by?'

'I do what I need to do,' Rodman said. 'Hustle some. Take jobs when I find them.'

'Everyone wondered what happened to you.'

'I got hit by a truck that's called America. It's a good truck but it hurts like hell to get hit by it.'

So Kelson asked what he'd come to find out. 'What'll you do with the coke?'

Rodman said, 'A guy my size, that stash lasted an hour. Had to go looking for another guy to rip off last night.' He watched for Kelson's smile and, when he got it, said, 'Nah, there's a bunch of happy Lake Michigan fish right now. I flushed it. What I always do.'

'We were about to bust him.'

'What good would that do? If the judge put him away at all, he'd be out in a year and set up right here again or down the block.'

'What good is stealing his stash going to do? He'll set that up again too, if his supplier doesn't kill him.'

'And I'll take it too. I'll take it again and again until he loses the heart to try anymore. Then maybe he'll come up and have a cup of coffee. It's happened before.'

'More likely, he'll get a bunch of friends and kill you.'

'More likely he'll *try*.'

THIRTY

N ow, three years later, Kelson drove back into Bronzeville and found Rodman's apartment building looking exactly as he'd last seen it. A woman wearing an enormous man's shirt opened the door and called into the apartment, 'DeMarcus, you've got a friend to see you.'

Rodman came out and enveloped him in another hug. 'I saw you in the news when you got shot,' he said. 'I thought you were dead or dying.'

'I don't go down so easy,' Kelson said.

'That kid hit you hard.' He told Cindi, 'This guy's got steel for brains.'

Cindi said, 'I've seen you in the news. Maybe you don't have brains at all.'

Rodman said, 'So, what's up?'

For the next hour, Kelson told him.

Rodman said, 'At least you got kittens out of the deal.'

'I need help,' Kelson said.

'What kind d'you think I can give you?'

'You're maybe the smartest and strongest guy I've ever known.'

'First, you don't *know* me. Second, see where it's gotten me?'

'That doesn't mean a thing.'

'So, what do you want from me?'

'From what I can tell, you handle people when they try to screw with you. If they see you as a challenge and try, they quickly realize they aren't up to it.'

'Mostly true.'

'That's what I want.'

'I don't do hired muscle.'

'I want to partner with you. It's paid work – though I don't have a lot of income right now.'

'Partner, huh? Who bosses who?'

'You do what you want, and I do what I want, and we get the job done.'

'The job being saving your ass.'

'Yep, that's the first job.'

'So there's a future to this relationship?'

'Depends on if we get through this one. If we don't, there's no partner in me for a partnership.'

Rodman considered it. 'Maybe I could give it a try.'

'Good,' Kelson said. 'You got any ideas?'

'Sure, we'll go beat the hell out of Dan Peters.' When he saw Kelson's eyes, he said, 'Kidding. Jesus Christ, who do you think I am?'

'You got any *real* ideas?'

'Yeah, same as yours. You need Alejandro Rodriguez's sheet.'

THIRTY-ONE

B ut first they drove to Christian Felbanks's condo. When Christian's parents let them in, they looked awed by the big man. 'In the last couple of days,' Kelson told them, 'I've gotten the sense that whoever went after Christian and Raima wanted something the police don't know about. The police think this is about prescription drugs. Maybe drugs are in it too, but there's something else.'

The Felbankses exchanged a glance.

'Can you think of anyone Christian hurt? Anyone who—'

'No,' the man said. 'No one.'

Rodman spoke with his low, gentle voice. 'A pretty, red-haired girl.'

The woman made a sound, as if something stung her.

Her husband said, 'Like all boys, Christian . . . tested boundaries. But he never hurt anyone, never would.'

'What do you mean, tested boundaries?' Kelson asked.

'The same as every boy,' the woman said.

'He smoked a little pot? Snuck a drink from your bottle of gin?'

'We don't drink,' she said.

'What did he do?'

'Nothing the other boys didn't,' the father said.

Rodman asked softly, gently, 'Whose daughter did he fuck?'

Again, the mother made a sound.

'I need to ask you to leave,' the man said.

'You don't like how I talk?' Rodman said.

'I don't like what you insinuate.'

'It was an innocent question if the answer's innocent,' Rodman said.

Kelson said to the woman, 'When I worked on the narcotics squad, I met parents who tried to protect their kids by denying their addictions, as if the denials kept them from something even worse – jail, humiliation, maybe breaking the last trust between them. Some of those kids died – OD or a bullet or a knife – and, even then, a lot of the parents kept up the act. At first that surprised me. I thought they would want to take down the dealers who killed their kids. But then I figured it out. All they had left was illusions. They could talk to me or they could keep imagining their kids before the drugs. It hurt too much to talk. You see what I'm saying? They pretended they were honoring their kids by keeping their secrets. But really, by allowing the people who sold the drugs to keep selling, they were just killing again.'

'Get out,' the woman said.

'Please,' her husband said.

Kelson said, 'You need to take responsibility for Christian.'

The husband had tears in his eyes. '*Please.*'

Kelson and Rodman went down to Kelson's car.

'They're scared shitless,' Rodman said.

'Yeah.'

'Whoever got their boy is bringing it to them too. You see that man's eyes? I'm guessing whoever's threatening you is threatening them twice. How much did you look into that family?'

'I talked to one of their cousins in Sioux City,' Kelson said. 'Heard about the daughter they keep in a home. And I checked Christian's record. Clean.'

'How about his fiancée – Raima?'

'Good people even when they're waving guns at me, I think. Scared too.'

'You'd better get back on the phone,' Rodman said.

'I'll ask Greg Toselli if he'll call the Sioux City PD and see if they ever heard of Christian. Maybe he'll do that much.'

'Leave Toselli out. He's a hothead and a player.'

'He saved my life. Twice.'

'Yeah, well, there's that,' Rodman said, 'but when things go bad, he's always there. He's no one's surprise ending.'

'What did he do to deserve that?'

'When my brother got killed, he told me the cops had it right. A few more dead boys like my brother, and the bangers would scare back to the holes they crawled from.'

'He's a true believer,' Kelson said. 'A purist.'

'In my neighborhood, we call that a heartless motherfucker – when we're being polite. I'll make the call.'

'Who's going to talk to *you*?'

'Seems like everyone does.'

So they both pulled out their phones. Rodman dialed Sioux City and talked in his low, gentle voice – a voice that might coax a wild horse into a corral or a psychopath out of a hostage situation. Kelson dialed Harrison Street Police Station and asked to talk to Venus Johnson.

He told her, 'I've burned through Peters's patience. Big man, thin skin. If I call him again, I think he'll take out a restraining order.'

'So now you're calling to burn through *my* patience? Here's some news – you burned through it the first time we met.'

'You're much hotter than Peters, though,' he said.

Rodman gave him a sidelong.

She said, 'I'm hanging up now.'

'I need help,' Kelson said.

'I don't practice that kind of medicine,' she said.

'You talk this way to everyone?'

'Just guys who don't see past my skin – and other people I find despicable.'

'The tennis thing, huh? Maybe I earned that.'

'Maybe so.'

'All right, forget it.'

But before he could hang up, she said, 'Tell it to me. What do you want?'

'Peters doesn't believe what I tell him, and I'm not asking you to. But I'm in trouble.'

'Not much I can do,' she said.

'When will the department release Christian Felbanks's body to his parents?'

'You planning to go to the funeral?'

'I want to know how much longer the parents will be in town.'

'Peters told me he warned you away from them.'

'He warned me about a lot of things. He also threw me in jail twice.'

'Maybe the third time will stick,' she said.

'That's my worry. When will you release the body?'

'You know I can't tell you that.'

'Then do something that'll really help. Get me a copy of Alejandro Rodriguez's case file.'

'I don't think so.'

'He's dead,' he said. 'The case is dead. I can sue to see it.'

'Then you should do that. Look, I don't think you mean to be a jerk – you're just what you are. You tried to do your job and got hurt, and that sucks for you. I'll take a look at the file, OK? And if there's anything important, I'll let you know.'

'Thank you,' he said.

'No promises.'

'Can you answer one more question?'

She hesitated. 'Yeah, I've got a wicked forehand.'

'Barbara Lisle. The woman who picked me out of the lineup when Peters brought me in the second time. What else have you found on her?'

'You shouldn't even know her name,' she said. 'Even if I could tell you, I wouldn't.'

'Just tell me if you've found out anything important – not what it is, just if.'

'Conversation's over.'

'Right,' he said.

'You should stop while you're ahead.'

'I'm no good at that. Sorry again, about the tennis thing.'

She laughed, and for the first time it was a nice laugh. 'You want to know something? I really do play. But I'm lousy at it. So the comments irritate the hell out of me.'

When he hung up, he listened to the soft, soothing cadence of Rodman's voice and watched the sunlight in the leafless black branches of a curbside tree. Rodman hung up a couple of minutes later and said, 'Sioux City's a small town, and the Felbankses are a big family. The lady I talked to is married to someone's nephew or a friend of the nephew – distant relations but close enough to hear the gossip. About twelve years ago, she thinks, Christian got caught with a girl who turned out to be a cousin. They were teenagers – thirteen or fourteen – and they said they were in love. The Department of Children and Family Services went out and made a report. There was a lot of screaming and yelling and threats in the family. I don't know if the girl was pregnant or what. The lady didn't want to talk about it even when I whispered in her ear.'

'Did she say if the girl had red hair?'

'She said, "Honey, if she wanted red hair, she could buy a bottle of it."'

'So the girl wasn't a redhead?'

'The lady didn't say.'

'Did she have a name for her?'

'She said everyone called her "Red."'

Kelson gave him a look.

'OK, OK. The name's Doreen.'

'You're good. Weird eyes – set too close together – but a big brain behind them.'

Rodman gave him a long stare.

'Sorry,' Kelson said. 'You got any more ideas?'

'A couple, if you don't mind zigzagging to get where you're going.'

'I don't even know what a straight line feels like anymore.'

'Is Venus Johnson going to get you Bicho's file?'

'She'll look at it and tell me if it matters – maybe.'

'You say his dad and mom died when he was a kid, and then he got put in juvie?'

'That's all I know.'

'Maybe it's enough.'

THIRTY-TWO

R odman had Kelson drive to a cold white concrete building on the Southwest Side. The building housed the juvenile court and a temporary detention center. Blue wooden barricades blocked the street by the front doors.

'No matter where they sent Bicho, they processed him through here,' Rodman said.

When they went inside, the guard, a thin black man with a starched white shirt, came around from the metal detector and bumped fists with Rodman. 'You come for Tyrice?' the guard asked.

'Nah, judge sent him out to Adams County.'

'Sorry to hear that. You'll check on DeShaun?'

'Not today. This is my friend Sam Kelson. We're here to see the big man.'

Kelson held a fist to bump the man's too, but the man just narrowed his eyes as if Kelson was trying too hard. 'Say hi to DeShaun if you got time,' the man said to Rodman. 'He could use it. And we got a couple new kids from that thing last night in Woodlawn.'

Then the man let them in, and Kelson said, 'Who're DeShaun and the "new kids"?'

'I come to see the boys sometimes,' Rodman said. 'Talk to them. Scare them and give them hope.'

'Huh. It do any good?'

'I'll tell you in about ten years.'

They went down a gray hall to the detention center director's office. Charlie Jenkins, the man who worked in it, stood about five eight with glasses perched on top of his bald head. He bumped fists with Rodman too.

Rodman explained Kelson's situation and said, 'He needs a favor.'

Instead of pulling up Bicho's record on his computer, the director looked Kelson in the eyes and said, 'The boys here are animals, most of them. They've got all the problems of grown men, plus a kind of kid insanity. We put them here to keep them safe from

adults, though, and, except for the worst of them, we let them
out at eighteen or twenty-one because maybe they've grown out
of it. A lot of them are every bit as vicious as the worst of the
men. But like all animals, they do what they do because it's what
they are – you can't really blame them for ripping up their prey.
So I protect my boys. Maybe that makes no sense to you?'

'Makes plenty,' Kelson said. 'I do what I do because I am what
I am too.'

Rodman said, 'Charlie and I disagree on the animal part.'

'Yeah,' the director said, 'wild cats are gentler than some of
these boys.' Then to Kelson, 'This Alejandro Rodriguez is dead?
That doesn't change my legal obligation to him. I want you to
understand what you're asking me to do.' He looked from Kelson
to Rodman and back. Then he went to his computer and sat. He
said, 'When DeMarcus first came and wanted to visit the boys, I
told him the same thing, isn't that right?'

'Word for word,' Rodman said.

'How many times you come before I let you in?'

'Four?' Rodman said.

'Something like.' And then to Kelson, 'So you understand,
DeMarcus has saved more than a couple of boys from themselves.
I'm doing this for them and for him – because he asked for it.
You understand? Because if this comes back on me and hurts me,
that hurts the boys, and, vicious as they are, that would be as bad
as hurting an innocent animal.'

'I can't make any promises,' Kelson said.

The man took his fingers off the keyboard.

Rodman laughed. 'Just the way he talks.'

The man said to Kelson, 'Are you fucking around?'

'No, sir,' Kelson said.

'Because *I'm* not fucking around,' the man said.

Five minutes later, the printer kicked out sixteen pages. It was
a small portion of what Venus Johnson could give Kelson, but
when the assistant director handed it to him, he felt as if the man
might be saving his life – and he told him so.

'Just don't let it come back on me or my boys,' the man said.

Kelson and Rodman sat in the car and read the file. Mostly it gave
dates and numbers – the January day when a judge remanded

Bicho to temporary detention, the August day when Bicho left
for the Kewanee Youth Center, the schedule and quantities of
Zoloft the nurse dispensed to him, and a meal schedule for a
period of time when he was isolated from the other boys. A page
of infractions listed three incidents over a period of two months
– all for fights in the cafeteria, the third of which led to the isola-
tion. A visitor list mentioned an 'uncle' – nameless – who came
once a week. Toselli's words returned to Kelson – *Someone loved
the kid a lot – the kind of love that makes a person violent.* 'Got
to find the uncle,' Kelson said.

'Uh-huh,' Rodman said.

A separate page gave an intake evaluation completed by a social
worker three days after Bicho entered the facility.

> Physical Health – good
> Intelligence – high
> Sociability/Social Characteristics – manipulative
> Emotional/Psychological Status – paranoia? Depression
>   (refer for further evaluation)
> Suicide Risk – moderate
> Family – uncle, grandmother. Mother and father deceased.
>   0 siblings
> Support Range – low
> Education – completed 9th
> Acquaintances Currently at Detention Center – 0

Another page listed the charges that landed Bicho in detention.
There were four, all involving drugs – one for marijuana posses-
sion, one for possession of Ecstasy, and two for selling cocaine.
Kelson recognized none of the arresting cops' names.

The final page contained contact information for Bicho's lawyer,
a man named Rob Chalmers, surprising only because he came
from a private firm instead of the Public Defender's Office.

'See anything?' Kelson asked Rodman.

'Just the uncle and the jump the boy made from kid-stuff dealing
to serious business by the time he shot you.'

Kelson said, 'Want to go talk to his lawyer?'

'You do that. I'm going to go back in and see DeShaun and
the new kids.'

'I'm fighting a clock,' Kelson said.

'What did you say about me doing this my way and you doing it yours?'

'I'm scared.'

'Yeah,' Rodman said. 'You should be.'

'Thanks for the boost.'

'You do it your way, and I do it mine.'

THIRTY-THREE

Rob Chalmers worked from an office on West Devon Avenue, just inside the northern city limit. The beige-brick building was set back from the street three doors from Novelty Golf & Games, where replica elephants, circus seals, a statue of liberty, and a helmeted conquistador adorned the mini-golf greens. No one played on the cold March afternoon, and the Astroturf looked beaten down. 'Like the rest of us at funnyland,' Kelson said as he pulled past.

In the law firm office, a receptionist in a tight wool dress and thick-framed glasses took Kelson's name and asked him to wait. The classical music piping into the room reminded him of doctor offices he'd visited since getting shot, and he said, 'I don't like needles.'

As if he'd spoken perfectly sensibly, the receptionist said, 'Me either.'

Ten minutes later, a short-haired man in a navy-blue suit came from a door behind the reception desk, smiled like an old friend, and said, 'Mr Kelson?'

They went back to a windowless interior room, lighted by a row of fluorescent bulbs. When Kelson was still a cop, he sometimes put suspects in a room like this and left them until they became jittery, but the lawyer seemed at ease and interested in making Kelson feel at ease too. He offered him a chair and, when Kelson took it, sat across from him and folded his fingers over his belly. 'What can I do for you?' he asked.

'I killed one of your former clients,' Kelson said.

'Yes, I know.'

'Yeah?'

'Sure. You're Sam Kelson. Ex-narcotics cop. Recently in the news again for a variety of incidents. You met Alejandro Rodriguez in tragic circumstances.'

'That's me. Tragic.'

'For Alejandro at least.'

'I'm hoping you can give me some information about him.'

'I thought perhaps you wished to hire me to handle your recent troubles. If so, I would need to turn you down. Conflict of interest.'

'Because of Bicho?'

'Alejandro, yes. And an ongoing relationship with family members.'

'That's what I'd like to hear about. His family. Especially any funny uncles.'

The lawyer didn't quite laugh at Kelson. 'I work for them. I can't divulge anything.'

'Not even who they are?'

'I would consider that a breach, as would they.'

'I understand his mother's dead.'

'That's true.'

'And his father too?'

'OD'd a year before the mother died,' Chalmers said.

'So it's just the uncle and a grandmother.'

He smiled instead of answering. 'May I ask why Alejandro's relatives interest you? Are you considering legal action against them?'

'No, I'm worried they're trying to rip me apart.'

'I doubt that.'

'They're part of a small circle who might do it. Them and a midget named Hugo Nuñez and a pretty redhead.'

'I can't pretend to understand what you're talking about,' Chalmers said. 'But I assure you that Alejandro's relatives are upstanding members of the community. I believe you would respect them.'

'I would feel better if I could check them out myself. I'll trade you.'

'Pardon me?'

Kelson said, 'I'll give you information about Bicho's death if you'll tell me the relatives' names.'

'I don't work that way.'

Kelson said it anyhow. 'I might have shot Bicho first. Before he shot me. That part of my memory is gone.'

The lawyer nodded. 'I've heard the rumors.'

'You shouldn't have. It's whisper-whisper – and only around people involved in the investigation.'

'Whenever there's a police-involved shooting, there're rumors,' the lawyer said. 'People wonder, did the cop really sense immediate, life-threatening danger? Did the victim really own the gun found on his body? Or, in your case, did the boy really shoot first? But may I ask another question – perhaps a sensitive one? Are you getting help? Therapy?'

'Once a week,' Kelson said. 'Twice if I need it.'

The lawyer kept his fingers laced over his belly. 'You should consider taking advantage of everything they make available to you.'

On his way out, Kelson stopped at the receptionist's desk. 'Can you tell me his hourly rate?' he asked. When she told him, he said, 'That's a lot for this neighborhood. Does he do *pro bono*?'

'You know how you feel about needles?' she said. 'That's how he feels about giving work away for free.'

THIRTY-FOUR

'The guy's a creep,' Kelson told his rearview mirror when he got back in his car. 'A cartoon lawyer. Stick him on a platform between a plastic elephant and a conquistador and putt golf balls under his scrotum.' The man in the mirror looked back and said, 'He's just doing his job.' Kelson laughed at the man – 'Said the executioner.'

So he drove back to his office and spent the rest of the afternoon at his computer, searching for a Sioux City girl named Doreen who would be about the same age as Christian Felbanks. The combination of 'Sioux City' and 'Doreen' got him more than six thousand hits on Google. He figured she might have Felbanks as a last name, though, and so he tried 'Doreen Felbanks.' He got nothing – which didn't mean she had a different last name, just that there was no trace of this one. 'If the thing with Christian went public,' he told the computer, 'she would've switched schools and done a presto chango.' Which gave Kelson another idea. He went to Classmates.com, which archived yearbooks, and he searched Sioux City high schools for the name Doreen in the years he calculated Christian Felbanks would've been there. There were four public high schools and a handful of private ones. The four public schools were named after the directions on the map – North High School, East High School, and so on – and he worked his way around the compass. At North High School, he found one Doreen – skinny and curly-haired. 'Sorry,' he told her. At East High School, there were two Doreens – one a couple of years older than Christian, the other a year younger – and neither looked like the redhead. The listing for South High School had one Doreen, and Kelson grinned when he saw her last name. Felbanks. He clicked on the file, a picture popped up, and he said, 'Ha!'

The Sophomore-year picture was black and white. At fifteen, a year or so after she climbed into bed with Christian, she had blonde, shoulder-length hair and a minor acne problem that her lipstick only accentuated. She smiled at the camera with the face of a girl who liked cameras – none of the self-consciousness and irony that Kelson saw in pictures of Sue Ellen lately. 'Beautiful in your own way,' Kelson told the picture. A strand of loose hair lay across her forehead, and he felt the impulse to touch the screen to move it from her eyes. 'When did you become a killer?' he asked, and clicked on a second link. It brought up a picture of the girls' volleyball team. There was Doreen Felbanks again, in a middle row, her arms draped over the shoulders of girls on either side. Beaming at the camera. 'Happy,' Kelson said. 'A hundred percent, corn-fed happy. When did you turn to ice?'

He closed the yearbook site and searched for variations on the name Doreen Felbanks – on social media sites, credit history sites, sites offering access to criminal records. He found nothing.

He put away the computer and called Peters. 'Doreen Felbanks,' he said to voicemail. 'That's the redhead's name.' He hung up and said to his phone, 'He'll delete it,' and so he called DeMarcus Rodman. He told him too, adding, 'She almost definitely goes by a different name now. From Sioux City. Blonde when she was a teenager. Something bad must've happened to turn her.'

'Nice job,' Rodman said.

'She played high school volleyball.'

'A fact I don't know what to do with.'

'*You* get anything?'

'Nah,' Rodman said. 'I just finished talking to a couple of boys who beat up an old lady in a liquor store.'

'In the meantime, I'm dying.'

'We've all got problems.'

'I'm just saying, I have less than three days.'

'Don't be dramatic,' Rodman said. 'It'll slow you down. I'm going to go back to Mr and Mrs Felbanks and drop Doreen's name – see what happens when it hits bottom.'

'I'll meet you there,' Kelson said.

'Let me go solo on this one,' he said. 'I'll whisper at them, and I'll bet they'll talk.'

'And if they don't?'

'Why wouldn't they with a cuddly guy like me?'

So Kelson went back to his apartment and, as the kittens wrestled on the kitchen floor, boiled a pot of spaghetti. Again, he set dishes of food on the table for them, then served himself.

When his phone rang, he grabbed it. 'DeMarcus?'

Sue Ellen said, 'Can I come over and play with Payday and Painter's Lane?'

Kelson wanted nothing more. 'Too risky,' he said.

'What do you mean?'

'Daddy's gotten himself in trouble.'

'Again?'

'Still.'

'Oh,' she said. 'Mom says you'll never change.'

'She's smart.'

'My therapist says the same thing.'

'Your therapist is stupid.'

'I think so too. Can we play Stump Dad?'

'Not this evening, honey, OK?'

'How's a bowl of baked beans like a swimming pool?'

'Next time, OK?'

'If you fart in it, you make bubbles.' She squealed with laughter.

'That makes no sense,' Kelson said.

'Maybe my therapist is right,' she said, and hung up.

A moment later, the phone rang again, and he snatched it. 'Hey, honey, I'm sorry—'

But another voice spoke. 'Dominick Stevens was on the five o'clock news – at a groundbreaking for new public housing.' It was the redhead.

'All publicity is good publicity,' Kelson said.

'Not good for you,' she said.

'Not good for you either, Doreen.'

'True.' She didn't deny the name – didn't seem surprised. 'Mengele hoped he'd see you in the crowd at the groundbreaking. Maybe taking care of business right there on camera. At least looking for a good way to get to Stevens.'

'I won't touch him,' Kelson said. 'I'm coming after you.'

'Don't be ridiculous,' she said. 'I'll tell you something about myself. I've been gone for a long time. The girl I once was? I haven't been her since I was seventeen. You're looking for the wrong person.'

'What happened to you?' he asked.

'Don't worry about me,' she said. 'Worry about what'll happen to you and your family.'

'Isn't it the same thing? Whatever happened to you, that's why this is happening to me – at least partly?'

'Don't be a fool,' she said, her voice shaking, and, like Sue Ellen, hung up.

'Gotcha,' Kelson said.

He waited through the evening for Rodman to call and, when his phone stayed silent, tried calling him. Rodman's phone rang and rang and didn't go to voicemail or a machine. After the eleventh ring, Kelson hung up. 'Huh,' he said.

That night, he talked to the moon. It was yellow and so full it looked swollen. He stood at his window, the lights off in his apartment, and told the moon his problems. The moon didn't seem to give a damn.

THIRTY-FIVE

In his dreams that night, Kelson was whole – never shot by Bicho, living with Nancy and Sue Ellen in a single house, feeling at one with his split personality as an undercover cop. Whole and content. He woke in the early-morning light with Payday purring on his chest and Painter's Lane draped over an ankle. 'Whole and content,' he said.

He got up and checked his phone. Rodman hadn't texted him overnight. There was no sign that Kelson was anything but alone in the universe. 'Except for the kittens,' he said. He took a picture of Payday on his phone, then one of Painter's Lane. 'So damn cute,' he said. He took another picture of Payday. He made breakfast for the three of them, showered, and then followed the kittens around his apartment, taking more pictures. At nine fifteen, as he took his hundredth shot of them, someone buzzed from the lobby.

He ran to the intercom and said, 'DeMarcus?'

A girl's voice answered. 'Me.' Sue Ellen.

He buzzed her up.

'You should be in school,' he said when she was standing inside his door, her tie-dyed knapsack hanging over one shoulder.

'Yup.' She scooped Painter's Lane into her little hands.

'You're playing hooky?'

'Yup. What happened to your face?'

'Someone kicked it. Does your mom know where you are?'

'Nope.'

'You can't do this.'

'Why not? You do.'

'I don't play hooky,' he said. 'I'm always here, always doing my job – always.'

'Always here for your eleven-year-old daughter who loves you very much?'

'Don't make those eyes at me. When the kittens do it, it's bad enough.'

'Let's go to the zoo.'

'No.'

'We'll take Painter's Lane and Payday. Introduce them to their relatives.'

'No.'

'Let's buy a horse.'

'I'm taking you to school. *Now*.'

'I'd rather play with you.'

'I have work to do.'

'What were you doing before I came?'

'We're not playing Stump Dad.'

'What were you doing?'

'Taking pictures of the cats.'

'Let's see.'

He handed her his phone, and she scrolled through the pictures.

'Jesus, Dad, this is weird.'

'Don't swear,' he said.

'Why did you take so many?'

'They're so damn cute.'

'Don't swear,' she said.

'That's it, you're late for school.' But before they left, he gave her a key to the apartment. 'In case you play hooky again,' he said. '*Don't*. But in case you do and I'm not here.'

In the car, she stared at his bruised face and asked, 'Is someone trying to hurt you again?'

It came out. 'Yes.'

She had tears in her eyes.

'Don't do that,' he said. 'I'll be all right.'

'Really?'

'I don't know.'

After dropping her off, he drove to his office. Rodman was sitting in the desk chair, eyes closed, feet kicked up on the desk, head tipped back, a gentle snore rumbling from his enormous chest.

But when Kelson closed the door, the big man's feet slid from the desk, and, as he opened his eyes, he reached for the gun on his hip. Then he saw Kelson. 'Ah,' he said, with his mild smile.

'I don't know why I bother to lock the door,' Kelson said.

'I don't know why you use such a lousy lock. You know how easy it is to pop?'

'Yeah, I heard. Doreen Felbanks came through it a few days ago.'

'For a guy who values his life, you could do more to protect it.'

'Why didn't you call last night?'

'The Felbankses are gone,' Rodman said. 'When I went to the condo, I got no answer. So I let myself in there too. There was blood in the bathroom sink – not like nicked-myself-shaving, more like slit-my-wrists or took-a-knife-in-my-ribs. I went looking for them. The hospitals have no records, no surprise. A car parked up the street from the condo is registered to them.'

'Which means someone took them.'

'Seems like it,' Rodman said.

'So why are you here?'

'I didn't want to interrupt while you took your girl to school.'

'You were outside my apartment?'

'Since four this morning. If someone went after the Felbankses, maybe you'd get it next.'

'I didn't see you.'

'You seemed distracted,' Rodman said. 'An army could've surrounded your building and you wouldn't've seen it. You had something on your mind.'

'Kittens.'

'What?'

'Any idea what happened to the Felbankses?'

Rodman gave him a sideways look. 'None. But I got another lead. D'you know how many strip-club buffets it takes to fill a man my size?'

'I don't follow.'

'The answer is five. Five strip-club buffets. Cocktail weenies. Burnt slivers of pizza. Chicken nuggets. But a man's got to eat. So, after leaving the condo and checking a couple hospitals, I decided to ask around about the escort lady who picked you out of the lineup. I started at the Pink Monkey on Clinton. They had calamari and wings – not bad – and a bunch of skinny blonde girls strutting their monkeys on the stage. I asked the bartender if he knew any skinny blonde dancers who part-time as escorts. He gave me this look like, *You're in over your head, black man.* So I told him the name Barbara Lisle, but I'd already lost him. Next, I tried Renegade's Gentlemen's Club – pepperoni pizza. Same thing as at the Pink Monkey, more or less. Repeat that twice more. Finally, I went to the Lucky Horseshoe on North Halsted. That one's a gay club and I figured the odds were low, but I was still hungry. Good-looking bartender with pierced nipples said he'd never heard of Barbara Lisle, so I gave him the name I should've tried at the other clubs – Raba. The boy lit up. Oh, yeah, everyone knows Raba. She mostly does the escort thing now, he said, which I already knew, but she sometimes dances for the truck drivers at a place by the Wisconsin border, which I also knew, and – get this – she also dances at the Pink Monkey. Long story short, I went back to the Pink Monkey, and they said they hadn't seen Raba in a week.'

'That's a lead?'

'That's dinner *and* a lead. One of the other Pink Monkey dancers told me Raba's got a boyfriend just over the Wisconsin border, which is why she dances up that way, even though the truck drivers are shit tippers, and when Raba disappears for a week, that's where she goes.'

'Huh,' Kelson said.

'I should say so. I also know about a place in Kenosha that makes a hell of a chili and cheese omelet, and it's already past breakfast time, so unless you've got a better idea?'

THIRTY-SIX

Kelson and Rodman drove up I-94, crossed the state line, and rode into downtown Kenosha. The cold air smelled like fish and iron as they neared Lake Michigan. The restaurant was a half block from the harbor, a place with soda-fountain stools, vintage signs for coffee and milkshakes, and gray-haired diners. 'A chili and cheese omelet and coffee for me,' Rodman told their waitress. 'And one of those milkshakes for my friend.'

'No one here will know Raba Lisle,' Kelson said when she left.

'Let's talk about it after we eat,' Rodman said.

Kelson tried his best to be patient. But before Rodman could swallow the last of the omelet, Kelson stood and stepped on to his chair.

He took two twenties and a ten from his wallet and held them in the air for all to see. 'I beg your pardon,' he said, 'but my friend and I have fifty bucks for anyone who can point us to a stripper named Raba Lisle. She's hooking up with one of your local boys.'

The diners held their forks in the air and stopped chewing. The waitresses exchanged glances.

Kelson looked from face to face. 'No?' He put the money back in his wallet. 'Then we'll pay our bill, leaving a generous tip, and be on our way.'

As they walked outside, Rodman said, 'Nice one. You'll get us busted in a town like this.'

'How else're you going to find out if you don't ask?'

'Right – that lady with the walker, *she* looked like she was hiding something. Her husband? Even if he sneaks across the border to a strip club, you think he's going to stand up with his neighbors around and grab the fifty?'

'You never know.'

They got into Kelson's car and pulled across the lot to the street.

Then a long-haired kid in a stained dishwasher's apron scurried out of the restaurant and flagged them down. Kelson stopped, and the kid went to Rodman's window.

'Fifty bucks?' he said.

'Depends on what you tell us,' Rodman said.

'Let's see the fifty.'

'Let's hear it first.'

The kid looked hesitant. 'I don't know Raba's boyfriend, but I know someone that does.'

'Sounds like a stretch. What's the name?'

The kid shook his head. 'The fifty.'

Rodman said to Kelson, 'Let's go.'

'Benny,' the kid said. 'His name's Benny. He works at the Save-A-Lot. Behind the butcher counter.'

Kelson and Rodman had passed the store on their way into town. 'Get in back,' Rodman said. 'You can introduce us.'

The kid's eyes got wide. 'No way.'

'Do I scare you?'

'Hell, yeah. Plus, I've got a job here. They'll fire me if I walk off.'

'He's got a point,' Kelson said.

'Do I get the money?'

'Sure, kid,' Rodman said. Kelson fished out the money, and Rodman gave it to him. 'Go to college or something.'

'Yeah, right. I'm going to go watch Raba.'

THIRTY-SEVEN

Five minutes later, in the low-slung building that housed the Save-A-Lot, Kelson and Rodman walked past the checkout counters, down the cereal aisle, to the meat case. A stock boy was unloading shrink-wrapped pork chops into a refrigerated display.

'Benny around?' Kelson asked.

Without looking up, the stock boy said, 'Smoke break.'

'Yeah? Where's that?'

'Um . . . behind the store.' As if he'd heard no stupider question all week.

Kelson and Rodman went back out to the front. Kelson turned left and Rodman right, cutting around the sides of the building so they would meet in the middle. Rodman rounded the rear corner, and a short-haired version of the restaurant dishwasher dropped a cigarette and took off the other way.

Kelson came around the other corner and almost caught him in his arms. 'Where're you going, Benny?'

The kid did a shoulder check to see Rodman, who closed the gap to about ten feet before stopping.

'No escape,' Kelson said.

'Who are you?' the kid said.

'Sam Kelson, ex-narcotics cop, current private investigator, father of one, owner of two kittens. Why are you running?'

He gave Kelson a long, bewildered stare, then gestured at Rodman. 'You see a guy like that coming after you, what would you do?'

'I'd give him a hug, but I get what you're saying. I'll tell you a secret, though. He'd rather talk to you than pound you into the ground.'

'What do you want?'

'We hear you know the boyfriend of a woman named Raba Lisle.'

The kid looked as if he wanted to run again. 'I don't know who would tell you that, but I don't talk about no one.'

'No one wants to hurt you,' Kelson said.

'Ha,' said Rodman.

The kid glanced at an empty lot behind the store, then back at Kelson, trying to decide between fight and flight. He stepped toward Kelson. '*You* don't look like much to worry about,' he said.

'That's what another kid your age thought.'

'I'll bet he was right.'

Rodman said, 'They cremated him because he was too wrecked to bury him.'

'That's not true,' Kelson said. 'It was a nice burial. They patched him up and put him in a white suit.'

'Yeah, and you're fucking with me,' Benny said.

'We need to find Raba Lisle,' Kelson said.

'Why? What did she do?'

'It's more like what her friends did,' Kelson said, 'and what they're going to do.'

'Who's the boyfriend?' Rodman asked, and moved close.

'All right, all right' – as if Rodman had already put his hands on his neck – 'his name's Jeremy. He's my brother's friend, not mine.'

'His last name?' Kelson asked.

He looked at Rodman. 'Boyd. All right?'

'Where can we find him?' Kelson asked.

'I don't know. He's my brother's friend.'

'Come on, Benny,' Rodman said. Gently.

'My brother will beat the hell out of me.'

'If he touches you, tell him about me,' Rodman said. 'Tell him I'm your friend now.'

'And you'll be waiting outside our house when he goes after me?'

'You never know.'

He tried to walk away. 'I've told you all I'm—'

Rodman stepped in front of him but spoke to Kelson. 'I don't think I'll need to put a finger on him, what do you think?' Then he rested a big hand on the kid's shoulder. 'I think he'll tell us all we need to know.'

'If I tell you where he lives, you'll let me go?'

'Sure,' Rodman said.

The kid double-checked with Kelson.

'Sure,' Kelson said.

'He's at Oakwood Housing,' Benny said. 'It's about five miles from here.'

'The address?' Kelson asked.

'I don't know.'

Rodman squeezed his shoulder.

'Poplar Lane. A little red house. Basketball net in front. That's all – I swear.'

Rodman took his hand off him. 'That'll do it.'

'Don't tell Jeremy who told you,' Benny said.

Rodman gave him the mildest smile. 'I promise.'

Kelson felt bad about it. 'I don't.'

THIRTY-EIGHT

The Oakwood Housing Community was a drab neighborhood just south of a bar called the Rat Race Lounge, which sported a sign of a cartoon rat holding a pink cocktail. The houses were mostly mobile homes, single- or double-wides, the nice ones with a carport, a concrete birdbath, or a skinny garden. Jeremy Boyd lived in the best house on the block – maroon, wood-sided, older than the places surrounding it. On one side, it even had a little tree.

The metal plating on the front door rang under Kelson's knuckles. Rodman waited on the dead grass beside the porch.

After a minute, the door opened. A barefoot man in dirty blue jeans and a white T-shirt squinted into the sunlight. He had greasy brown hair that needed combing. 'What?'

'Dirtbag,' Kelson said.

'Huh?'

'Sorry, that came out wrong. Jeremy Boyd?'

'Who the hell are *you*?'

Rodman smiled from the lawn. 'You're the kind of guy who answers questions with questions?'

The man looked down at him. 'Get the hell off my property, n—'

He didn't get the word out of his mouth. He never had a chance. Rodman seemed to float up the steps, rising to the porch. The man jerked back into the house, recoiling the way he might if he stepped into a street and saw a truck coming. Rodman went in after him and said, 'Don't mind if I do.' The man's hand reached under his T-shirt for something shiny, but Rodman said, 'Leave it,' and gripped him hard enough to rake his face with pain.

'What d'you want?' the man asked, as Kelson came in and closed the door. The front room smelled of marijuana and damp wood.

'*Still* asking questions?' Rodman said. 'Answer one. Are you Jeremy Boyd?'

The man tried to shake free of Rodman's grip. 'Yeah, yeah, I'm Jeremy Boyd.'

Rodman eased his hold. 'Where's Raba Lisle?'

Boyd glanced from Rodman to Kelson, searching for an angle. He looked as if he'd always be searching for one. 'She isn't here.'

But just then a woman's voice – sleepy and slurring – called from the back of the house. 'Who's that, Jeremy?'

He yelled back, 'Shut the hell up.'

Rodman gripped him again. 'Don't talk like that.'

Boyd's voice got a pleading. 'For her own good.'

'Let's see about that.' Rodman marched him through a dim hallway into a dim kitchen.

Raba Lisle sat at a brown table, her skinny legs pulled up under her. She was smoking a joint and looked as if she'd emptied the medicine cabinet down her throat. She wore a white camisole, which clung to her ribs, and pink underwear – nothing else. When Kelson's lawyer described her, he hadn't mentioned her tattoos – a swirling, colorful mass covering her arms and shoulders, coating her legs from her underwear to her ankles.

'Christ, you're like a cartoon snake,' Kelson said to her.

Rodman shot him a concerned glance.

'These guys are asking about you,' Boyd told the woman.

She gave him a stoned smile that she might have meant to be sexy. 'I'm very popular. With the boys.'

Kelson got a grip. 'We're looking for Doreen Felbanks,' he said.

'Oh, don't do that,' she said. 'You'll wreck my – wait, I know you. You killed that Paki girl. I picked you out.' For unclear reasons, the thought made her giggle.

'I didn't kill her,' he said.

'They said you did. Doreen and . . . that man.'

'What man?'

She wagged her finger as if he was being naughty. Then she looked at Rodman. 'You're not so special,' she said. 'I see guys like you every day.'

'Where's Doreen Felbanks?' he said.

'Guys just like you,' she said to him, 'sitting in front, their legs wide open like they're pieces of meat. Like I'm . . . so hungry. *But* . . .' She offered the joint to Boyd, who took it and inhaled. She watched as he held the smoke in his lungs and giggled again. Then she looked at Rodman as if she hadn't interrupted herself. 'But I'm a vegetarian.'

'Good for you,' he said.

'Good for the planet,' she said.

Rodman said, 'D'you know what Doreen and this man have done? Two people are dead – the woman you accused my friend here of killing and Doreen's cousin.'

'Christian?'

'That's right.'

She reached for the joint and drew in a lungful. It made her cough. When she stopped, she said, 'That fucked with Doreen. She couldn't stop crying.'

'Christian's death?' Kelson asked. 'What did she say about him?'

She wagged her finger again. 'You're not . . . *not* special. You kill girls.'

'I told you, I didn't kill her.'

'I know who you are, and you know what? Even the cops hate you. They liked it when I picked you out.'

'It meant nothing. They couldn't use your testimony even if you told the truth. Juries like their witnesses to wear clothes.'

She looked at Rodman again. 'What would you do if I took off my shirt? Would you give me twenty bucks?'

'*I'll* give you thirty if you keep it on,' Kelson said.

'Shut up, man,' Rodman said, then to her, 'I'll give you a hundred if you tell us how to find Doreen Felbanks.'

'Doreen's special,' she said. 'Special to me.'

Her boyfriend said, 'You talk too much.'

She gave him a look and said, 'But no one listens. See this one?' She meant Kelson. 'I told the cops he killed a woman. Now he's standing in your kitchen.'

'*I* talk too much,' Kelson said. 'But I'll listen to everything you tell me.'

So she peeled herself from the chair and stumbled to him. She ran a finger down his chest and said, 'You're one of them that like to listen. Fifty bucks?'

'You work it too hard,' he said. 'That makes me think you're scared.'

She giggled. 'When I'm scared, I don't work anything. I hide. Not that it does any good. Men knock on the door when I'm getting a morning buzz on.'

'How about Doreen? What's she do when she gets scared?'

'Nothing scares Doreen. She'll do anything.' The way she said it, it sounded like love.

Kelson said to Boyd, 'I wouldn't count on your girlfriend sticking around.'

'Jeremy gets what he pays for,' she said, 'just like everyone else.' She turned to her boyfriend for support. 'Isn't that right?'

'I'm good with it,' Boyd said.

Kelson said, 'He keeps you high, and you keep him happy?'

'We're both happy, honey,' she said.

Rodman said to Boyd, 'If you know where Doreen is, you should give her up. You don't, and you'll find yourself on the wrong side of her, especially if you talk to Raba the way you did when we came in. You won't like the wrong side of her.'

'Doreen's cool with it,' Boyd said. 'Like I said, I'm good.'

Then, out front, a car door slammed. Kelson and Rodman exchanged looks. They glanced at Boyd, who shrugged.

Kelson spoke to Raba. 'People are getting hurt. If you know where Doreen is, you can stop it from happening. I know you're hurting too—'

She started to argue.

But the front door opened.

And Boyd darted across the kitchen and into the hall.

Kelson and Rodman went after him. When they stepped into

the front room, Boyd was rushing a woman back out the door. It was Doreen Felbanks – in a short black skirt, a hot-pink vinyl jacket, and matching pink shoes.

She'd driven up in a yellow VW Beetle, the kind of car Kelson's Challenger could do donuts around on an open highway. Before getting in, she reached into a little purse that matched her jacket and her shoes and pulled out a little handgun. She stopped by the front of the Challenger and, as Kelson and Rodman came down the porch steps, popped a single bullet into the driver's side tire.

She smoothed her skirt and was in her car with the doors locked by the time Kelson and Rodman reached her. Rodman slammed a fist on the VW roof, denting it. But she turned a key in the ignition and, waving at Kelson with a little finger, drove off.

A noise came from Rodman's chest, and he went after Boyd, charging as if he would flatten him. Boyd reached into his belt and pulled out the shiny thing – a knife. Rodman took it from him and chucked it into a neighbor's yard. He picked Boyd up and slammed him against the Challenger. Raba Lisle made a high sound, like an animal whining. Rodman gave her a fierce look and she shut up. He picked up Boyd again as if he would break him.

After watching Rodman cruise through police academy and sweet-talk everyone he met, Kelson thought the man never lost control. Now Kelson said, 'Everyone's a monster' – at which point, Rodman winked at him, then spoke to Boyd in a voice that seemed capable of blowing down forests. 'Never wreck a man's car. Where I come from, a car is a man's life. For some men, it's like their child.'

Boyd pled with him. 'I didn't. *She* shot—'

'You're accessory,' Rodman said.

Boyd said, 'You're insane.'

So Rodman slammed him against the Challenger again.

Then he made him take the spare tire from the trunk and replace the punctured one.

Afterward, he marched him and Raba back into the kitchen and sat them at the table. 'Tell us everything. Every goddamned word. If I think you're holding back, I'll tear you apart, and then I'll tear your house apart, and then I'll burn it down with you in it.'

They talked. Raba seemed as sober as a nun. Boyd's voice shook.

As far as Kelson could tell, they told the truth and told all they knew.

But they knew little.

Raba said she met Doreen at a party at the Sofitel Hotel in Chicago, where they were hired to entertain three visiting Japanese businessmen. The girl-girl act worked out so well they put it on their menus of services they would perform for individuals, couples, or groups. Raba got her dates from a business called Second City Escorts, and Doreen got hers through a boutique operation run by the man she called Mengele. Raba didn't know the man's real name – she swore she didn't – and Boyd knew less than she did. Raba had seen him twice when he picked up Doreen, though, and she gave a rough description – white, thin, thirty or thirty-five years old, dark-haired.

'Short?' Kelson asked.

'He was sitting in a car,' she said.

'A screwed-up left eye? Bloodshot solid red?'

'He had on sunglasses one time. I don't know.'

'Could he have been Mexican?' Kelson asked.

'He could've been anything,' she said.

'Could his name have been Hugo Nuñez?'

She smiled nervously, trying to help. 'It *could've* been.'

Kelson looked at Rodman. Rodman shook his head and said, 'Could it have been Kanye West?'

'I mean, I don't know,' she said.

'Tattoos?' Kelson asked. 'Scars?'

'I don't know,' she said, and she looked at Rodman as if afraid her answer would cause him to hurt her.

Kelson asked, 'What's his relationship with Doreen? She sleeping with him?'

'Do you mean, does he fuck her? That's her job. Does she want him to? You'll have to ask her that yourself.'

Rodman asked, 'What does he drive?'

She seemed relieved to be able to answer with specifics. 'A silver Mercedes when he picked her up from the Japanese party. A Lexus the other time.'

'How does he treat Doreen?' Kelson asked.

A bitter smile formed on her lips. 'The way Doreen describes him, he makes her do things, and everything's got to be done his way. You wouldn't want to do those things. He hurts her if she messes up.'

'I've seen the marks.'

She asked, 'Did she tell you she likes it?'

'No.'

'Sometimes she says she does, but she's lying. Even people who *need it* don't really like it. Something's broken that makes them think they do, that's all.'

'You seem to know her real well,' Kelson said. 'She walked right into your boyfriend's house. Has she been hiding here?'

'I told you, she doesn't hide,' she said. 'She comes and goes, that's all. And she never knocks.'

'I found her a couple of times in my office like that,' he said. 'Where would she go from here?'

'Anywhere. Could be she has a date – some guys like it in the morning. Could be she's going shopping – she likes to do that.'

Rodman asked, 'What happened back in Sioux City?'

'You know about that?' she said.

Boyd said again, 'You talk too much.'

'I'm not telling you a secret, I don't think,' she said to Rodman. 'They blamed Doreen for the thing with Christian, but he started it. I guess they scared him, because he blamed her too. They loved each other – that's what Doreen says – you know, the way fourteen-year-olds do – innocent and dangerous. I guess he dumped her. After him, the other boys went open season on her. She was hurt, so she let them have her. Then one night, a bunch of them got her drunk and did her. When she woke up, they'd cut off all her hair. They humiliated her and made a show of it. When she was seventeen, her stepdad kicked her out or she ran away, and she took a bus to Chicago, and everything happened from there. The old story. It's close enough to what happened to me.'

'Yeah, but you don't kill people.'

'Doreen doesn't either. I wish I had the guts to. You don't screw with a girl's feelings when she's like that.'

'How did Christian come back into her life?'

Raba giggled. 'She walked into the drugstore where he worked. First thing in the morning after she was out all night. Christian stood behind the counter, all nice and neat in his little white drugstore jacket, making eyes at his fiancée.'

'So she killed him.'

She gave that idea an affectionate smile. 'She's bent in just about every way you can bend a girl. But she doesn't hurt people. Ever. For her, it's all about love.'

THIRTY-NINE

As the garage man put the Challenger on a lift at a Midas dealer by I-94, Kelson and Rodman sat in the waiting area and ate chips from a vending machine. Rodman said, 'You think Doreen could've hooked up with Hugo Nuñez?'

'Well, he's got money, if that's all it takes to get to her,' Kelson said. 'But I think it takes more. This man seems to twist her. He set up the killings so they look like she did them, if not me. I don't know if Nuñez is smart enough to do that.'

Rodman thought about it. 'You think she'd spend time with that lowlife anyway?'

'She doesn't seem to mind hanging around lowlifes.'

'Let's visit Nuñez and see what he tells us?'

'Can't go worse than last time.'

So when the car came off the lift with a new tire, Kelson and Rodman drove back to Chicago and parked outside Bomboleo.

The dining room and club were closed until dinnertime, though a *taqueria* connected to the place was crowded. Businessmen in suits stood at a heavy wooden bar and washed down *carnitas* and *al pastor* with beer. The bartender who'd directed Kelson to Nuñez's backroom table was opening beer bottles. He wore a sombrero over his bleach-blond hair.

Kelson caught the man's eye. 'I guess the hat's your idea of fun,' he said.

'Or funny,' Rodman said.

The bartender gave Kelson a long look. 'Your bruises are looking good. You probably should let them keep healing instead of asking for more kicks in the face.'

'What time does Nuñez usually come in?' Kelson asked.

'Who?'

'D'you know where he hangs out before he comes in?'

'I'll tell you what,' the bartender said, 'I'll give you a Corona on the house. Just to be courteous. And then you can leave.' He looked at Rodman. 'I'd give *you* a pitcher, but management would have my ass.'

'I need to see Nuñez,' Kelson said.

'He doesn't talk to guys like you. He grinds them into the bathroom floor.'

'Still need to see him.'

The bartender looked at Rodman, who shrugged and said, 'If he says he needs to see him, I guess he needs to see him.'

The man said to Kelson, 'It's *your* face. He comes in for dinner around eight – unless he eats somewhere else. Either way, we keep a table free.'

'Where is he before then?' Kelson asked.

'Do I look like his secretary?'

'You look like a dick in a sombrero.'

Rodman said, 'If he says it, it must be true.'

The bartender turned red. 'Go to hell, all right? I try to help. I tell you to leave it alone. I offer you a drink. I give you what you ask for.'

Kelson said, 'Last time you gave me what I asked for, I got kicked in the head.'

The bartender looked at Rodman, bewildered. Rodman said, 'Sometimes you can't win.'

So the man said to Kelson, 'You want to get yourself killed? People say Nuñez works from an office in Pilsen. Over a currency exchange. Maybe you'll go there and he'll shoot you. Maybe then you'll stop hassling me.'

Pilsen was a Mexican neighborhood on the Southwest Side. If you drove down the main drag on a Saturday night, you would think you were in Mexico City. 'Where in Pilsen is the currency exchange?' Kelson asked.

The man shook his head. 'Don't know. You'd never catch me looking for Nuñez.'

'We can find it,' Rodman said. 'But we wouldn't want you calling to let him know we're coming.'

Kelson took out a twenty and offered it to the man.

The bartender shook his head. 'I don't want it. I don't want anything to do with you.'

Rodman asked, 'You still offering that beer?'

'Just get the hell out of here, OK?'

FORTY

Most of Pilsen was residential – aluminum-sided single-family houses, old brick two-flats, and, here and there, new three-story condos bought up by professionals edging into the neighborhood. A single strip of businesses lined West Eighteenth Street. Signs advertised a *dentista*, an *Escuela de Futbol*, a *panderia*, a *dulceria*, and a dozen restaurants. Bright murals covered the brick walls with portraits of the Virgin Mary, Che Guevera, scenes of Rio Grande crossings, hardhat construction, and flamenco dancing.

Kelson drove past a narrow redbrick building with a burned-out neon sign that said, *Cash Fast Casa de Cambio*, and Rodman said, 'Whoa.'

Kelson circled back and stopped at the curb.

The Cash Fast windows were dirty and dark, a big MoneyGram decal peeling from the glass, the paint chipping from an advertisement offering *Servicio Rápido*. But lights shined in the windows on the second and third floors.

Kelson and Rodman got out and went to the street door. It was locked. 'We could throw pebbles at the windows,' Kelson said.

'Or we could just walk in.' Rodman yanked the door handle, and the metal bolt tore from its rusted housing.

They went up to the second floor. The door, with a frosted glass top, also was locked. Kelson knocked and a heavy Mexican woman with gray hair opened.

'Hugo Nuñez?' Kelson said.

The woman pointed at the ceiling and closed the door.

So they climbed to the third floor. The wooden door looked thick enough to absorb bullets. There were two locks, one by the handle, one at the top of the jamb. On the other side of the door, a radio played Jimi Hendrix's 'Purple Haze.'

'Ah, well,' Rodman said, and he knocked.

A girl's voice spoke from the other side. '*Quién es?*'

Rodman held a finger to his lips

But Kelson couldn't help himself. 'Sam Kelson, ex-narcotics cop, current—'

'Shh,' Rodman said.

For several seconds, there was silence. Then the lock tumblers clicked, and the door opened.

A child stood in the doorway. She wore a white blouse and blue jeans embroidered with pink and white thread. She had black hair and very dark eyes. She held a little black pistol, which she pointed at Kelson. She said, 'My dad wants to know what you want.'

'Cute,' he said. 'Is your dad Hugo Nuñez?'

'Yes.'

Her answer made him grin. 'That's great.'

She wrinkled her lips. 'What's great about it?'

'He didn't strike me as the type to have a daughter.'

Rodman said, 'We want to talk to him about Doreen.'

She glanced into the room.

Behind the radio noise, Nuñez must have shaken his head.

'He doesn't know her,' the girl said.

'Raba?' Kelson asked.

She looked into the room, said, 'Nope,' and started to close the door.

Rodman jammed a thick hand against it. When she pointed the gun at him, he said, 'Here's the thing. You don't want to shoot me. The cops would come, and who needs that? Even if you managed to do it without the cops, I would bleed out, and with a guy my size your dad would have Niagara Falls down the stairs. And then he'd have to carry my fat ass down to the street.'

The girl smiled, and those dark eyes looked a little crazy.

'We just want to talk,' he said.

She said, over her shoulder, 'They just want to talk.'

Nuñez must have signaled again, because she lowered the pistol and moved from the door.

The room had none of the glitz of Bomboleo, none of the flash a man like Nuñez seemed to need when he went out in public. He and the two men who beat up Kelson at the dance club sat on unmatched leather office chairs. A TV played silently in one corner. An old boombox rested on top of the TV, tuned to WLUP, where Jimi Hendrix put down his guitar and the DJ promised more classic rock after a message. There were a couple of open cans of beer on a table, an open bottle of mescal on a desk. When Kelson stepped in, the men gave him vicious smiles. When Rodman stepped in behind him, the men reached into their belts and snatched pistols into their fingers.

'Good afternoon, gentlemen,' Nuñez said. 'How can I help you?'

Kelson stared at Nuñez's raging bloodshot eye. 'You could start with a pirate patch.'

Nuñez's men pointed their guns at Kelson's forehead.

So Kelson said, 'We just came from the house of a methhead whore who—'

Nuñez held up two fingers with a kind of aristocratic flair. He could have passed as refined except for his eye and his armed companions. 'Who is your Negro friend?' Nuñez gave Rodman his little-toothed grin. 'I grew up in a nice house. We had a Negro maid. She was almost as big as you. I loved that woman.'

Rodman gave him back a big smile that looked as if it could eat Nuñez's little one.

Kelson said, 'This . . . hooker . . . this exotic dancer said the woman who set me up is controlled by a man who sounds a lot like you. Same general look. Access to drugs.'

Nuñez said, 'The last time you came to see me, you accused me of setting you up because of Bicho. I thought my boys persuaded you that you were mistaken. Now I force a girl to set you up?'

'You're behind it. You and Doreen.'

He looked offended. 'I'm a man of honor and faith.'

'Who sells drugs and kills his enemies.'

'I'm a businessman. Violence is unnecessary . . . much of the time.' He signaled to the other men, who set down their pistols. 'You've made me curious. Who is Doreen?'

'As far as we know, she's a girl from Iowa who got into trouble at home, and so she ran away and got into trouble here. I can't help thinking that trouble involves a little Frito like you.'

Again the guns came up.

Again Nuñez signaled them down.

'Once more, you are mistaken,' Nuñez said. 'You are rude. Disrespectful—'

'Disinhibited,' Kelson said.

'But,' Nuñez said, 'I'm content telling you this without violence. Having my boys kick the shit out of you again seems unnecessary. You think I'm a bad man, but I've known cops who are worse. Cops who would shoot a seventeen-year-old boy in an alley. Terrible men.'

So Rodman said, 'Where are Christian Felbanks's parents?'

Nuñez said, 'You are a very big man. Like my old housekeeper. A *rinoceronte*. A rhinoceros, yes?' He looked at his men for confirmation. 'The little eyes so close together.'

Rodman kept his voice low and mild. 'Christian Felbanks's parents?'

Nuñez smiled. 'Doreen? Christian Felbanks's parents? These are people I don't know. But I do know that you are wasting my time.'

Rodman seemed to consider him. 'All right, but if you hear about the parents – or about Doreen, or about anyone out to avenge Bicho's death – we'd appreciate knowing about them. If you want to send your boys out to listen, we'd appreciate that too.'

Nuñez's smile hardened. 'It is a big city,' he said. 'I don't think I will hear about these people.'

'Nah, it's a small town,' Rodman said. 'Seems after a while I know everyone. If nothing else, we try to stay on each other's right side. A man like me and a man like you.'

Nuñez didn't agree to help. But he didn't have his men shoot Kelson and Rodman either. Although Kelson still had all the same questions he walked in with, the conversation went as well as he and Rodman could hope.

But as they turned to go, the WLUP DJ fulfilled her promise by spinning another classic tune – Joan Jett's 'I Love Rock 'n' Roll.'

An image of Nancy stripping off her dress the night she and Kelson first had sex flashed into Kelson's broken brain. 'Dammit,' he said, and spun toward Nuñez. 'Why are you playing this?'

Nuñez gave his daughter a wry smile and glanced at his men, unsure what to make of Kelson's strange turn. 'What do you want me to listen to? *Mariachi*? Shake some maracas like a good little Frito? Maybe play a *corrido* about *los pobres*?'

Kelson fingered his top shirt button, and his hips started to sway.

Rodman saw what was coming, and he reached for him, but Kelson danced across the room toward the little drug lord. He ran his fingers down the man's chest and belly, ran them back up, and pinched his nipples. He would need to talk with Dr P about this. Words rolled off his tongue and over his lips – 'Joan Jett is good for only one thing,' he said. '*Loving*.' He yanked open the top three buttons on Nuñez's shirt.

'Jesus Christ, man,' Rodman said, as Kelson fingered the fourth button.

'Are you fucking with me?' Nuñez said, and his voice rose an octave. 'If you're fucking with me—'

Kelson backed away from the man, still dancing. Most of his brain told him to stop. But the part that mattered told him to *go, go, go*. 'No,' he said, 'if I was fucking with you, I would call you Peewee *Chilito*. I would tell you how when I was a narcotics cop, I would've busted your tiny ass. I would call you a little dog that barks at the big dogs, and the big dogs only want to lift their legs and piss on you.'

'Enough, man, enough,' Rodman said.

But Joan Jett reached the lines where she tells the boy to put a dime in the jukebox, *baby*, and dance with her, and Kelson grabbed Nuñez, pulled him to his feet, and tried to do something between a waltz and a swing-your-partner.

Rodman yelled, 'No.'

Nuñez pulled free and shouted at his men, 'Kill him.'

Maybe if Kelson's behavior hadn't stunned them, they would have done it.

But Rodman got to them before they could raise their pistols. He backhanded one with his huge knuckles and took his gun. He threatened the other with a fist, and the man turned his over to him. He held an open palm for Nuñez's daughter, and she laid her little weapon on it. He emptied the chambers, pocketed the magazines, and set the guns on the floor. He gripped Kelson by the arm and dragged him to the door. 'Until next time,' he said to Nuñez, and they went out.

As they jogged downstairs, Nuñez stood on the landing and shouted insults and threats. *Kelson was dead*, he said. He would chase the *hijo de puta* through the city. He would track him like an animal. Kelson was a *cabrón*, a *maricón*. He would see Nuñez

coming for him, and there would be nothing he could do. He
would die with his *verga* in his mouth.

Kelson and Rodman went out the street door and got into the
Challenger. Kelson said, 'Damn, I hate when that happens.'

Rodman rolled down the window and jutted his elbow out. 'I
like working with you, man.'

FORTY-ONE

Whether or not Nuñez knew other dealers who might
have heard about a plot to avenge Bicho, Rodman did,
though finding the right ones and getting them to talk
was a long shot. It would be even longer if Rodman showed up
with a stranger who blurted out any thought that crossed his mind
and, at the moment, had a hard time keeping clothes on. So Kelson
dropped him off in Bronzeville and drove back through the city to
his office.

As he put his key in the office door, he half expected Doreen
Felbanks to be sitting at his desk in her hot-pink jacket and matching
shoes. But the client chairs were empty. He slid open the top drawer
to see his picture of Sue Ellen. Then he sat and gazed at her. He
was still gazing twenty minutes later when his phone rang.

He had a sense, and, sure enough, Doreen was on the other
end. 'I just came in,' he said.

'I know.'

'Are you watching me?'

'Always.'

He felt a pinprick ache deep in his forehead. He said, 'You're
trying awfully hard to screw with my mind.'

'Maybe you have a little mind and it's easy to screw with it.'

'Maybe.'

'I'm only doing what I'm told.'

'I'm tired of hearing it. And I'm getting the sense it's a lie. I
know about you. Someone hurt you when you were a kid. Maybe
a bunch of people did. So now you're hurting them back. And
maybe you see me as hurting another kid, and so I deserve it too.'

'I think you're confused. And with Mengele, confusion is dangerous.'

'Who's Bicho to you? Of all the kids in this city who've gotten hurt or died, you picked him. Why are you coming after me?' He realized he was still sweating from Nuñez's office.

'You may think you know me, but you don't,' she said.

'But I'm closing in on you, right? Instead of me walking into my office and finding you, you walked into the house Raba Lisle shares with her boyfriend and found me.'

'You shouldn't have gone there. She's innocent.'

'You put her in the middle when you sent her to pick me out of a lineup.'

'That wasn't my idea. Leave her alone.'

'Can't do that.'

'I'm doing this because I have to,' she said. 'But you seem to like it.'

'Ha. I hate it.'

'It doesn't matter. You've got a day and a half,' she said. 'Less than that. You're wasting time.'

'Is that why you called?'

'Mengele said you needed a reminder.'

'Maybe I'm coming after you right now,' he said. 'Maybe you think you're watching me, but I'm really watching you.'

'Don't say stupid things,' she said. 'Even if you're thinking them, don't say them.'

'I see you riding a bus from Sioux Falls to Chicago. I see you getting as big and bad as the city itself. But I also see a little worm turning inside you – a little idea of yourself from before you slept with Christian, this idea of a kid you once were. We've all got those worms. And they hurt, right? They hurt when they turn inside us, and we wish we could pull them out, but we know that they're life itself and we can't kill them without killing ourselves.'

'Yeah, you talk stupid,' she said. 'Maybe Mengele will speed up the clock. Maybe if you check on Dominick Stevens right now, he's already dead, and Mengele has set it up so it looks a hundred percent like you did it.'

'Nope. I'm done with that. From now on, I'm coming after you – you and the man you're with.'

'You're wasting time, and you're going to get hurt,' she said, and she hung up.

So he talked to the dead line – talked because he couldn't help talking and because talking seemed to focus his thoughts after his loss of control with Nuñez. 'What did Dominick Stevens do? Something more than sleeping with Bicho's girlfriend and getting her pregnant? Is this about more than hurt feelings? Does Mengele even exist? Is he Hugo Nuñez? Can anyone explain what's going on?'

Then he dialed Venus Johnson at the Harrison Street Police Station. She answered his question before he could ask it. 'I didn't see it. It's missing.'

'How does a case file go missing?' he said. 'Especially for a big-story death like Bicho Rodriguez?'

'It happens. It could be at the courts. Someone could've pulled it for the DCFS and never put it back. Maybe there's a lawsuit.'

'I'm tired of you and Peters treating me like an idiot,' he said.

'Don't get weird. You were a cop for long enough to know it's as sloppy here as anywhere else.'

'Yeah, but the slop keeps landing on me. I asked for a little favor.'

'It isn't so little – you were a cop long enough to know that too. I could get slapped for just talking about sharing a file with you. If I asked others about it, they would ask about *me*.'

'I'll trade you for the trouble,' he said. 'Christian Felbanks's—'

'I don't trade. That's not how it works.'

Kelson gave her the information anyway. 'Felbanks's parents are gone. There's blood in the sink at his condo.'

She took a sharp breath. 'Jesus, you're like an infected thumb, Kelson. Just talking to you gives me stabbing pains. How do you know they're gone?'

'A friend of mine went there last night.'

'Last night? And you and your friend didn't think you should call it in?'

'I figured you'd blame me for it. Every time I call something in, I end up in lockup.'

'Sounds reasonable from my end. The city's safer that way – and quieter. Do I want to know the name of your friend?'

'Probably not. It's—'

'Don't. Not if it makes my life messier. We'll check the condo, and if we need to talk to your friend, I'll tell you.'

'I need Bicho's file,' he said.

'And *I* need a job where I don't have to deal with infected thumbs like you. But you know what? It ain't happening.'

When they hung up, he called Greg Toselli. Last time they talked, Toselli was having a bad morning and recommended that Kelson either hurt Stevens or take the redhead out of the game by any means. Now, when Toselli picked up the phone, he seemed to be having a better day, and Kelson told him, 'I found out the redhead's name. Doreen Felbanks. She's the cousin of the first victim.'

'Cool,' Toselli said. 'You want me to go with you to talk to her?'

'You mean, take her out of it?'

'I mean, whatever's necessary.'

'I don't know how to find her,' Kelson said. 'Anyway, I thought you wanted to stay away from this.'

'No, I said I wouldn't let you drag both of us down. You know I'll help you off the clock.'

'Yeah, but the clock's spinning. It's as messed-up as my head, and I don't know what's on the clock or off. This Mengele guy is putting me in bed with these people. Everything's collapsing on itself. I—'

Toselli interrupted as if to save Kelson from himself again. 'So, what do you want me to do?'

'Right. I asked Dan Peters's partner to look at the file, but she says it's missing. Peters has cuffed me and thrown me in the back of a cruiser every chance he's gotten, and now his partner's playing sort of nice but the result is the same.'

'He's a tight-ass, but he's clean,' Toselli said. 'I hear the same about his partner. They've got limits and they stay inside them. That comes from too little time on the street. But sometimes you've got to go around the system. You know that and so do I.'

'You still won't hunt down Bicho's file?'

'Give me a call when you locate the redhead. Cut it at the root.'

Kelson promised to call when he had something.

'Cover your ass,' Toselli told him. 'You've only got one.'

Even before the sun dropped below the top of the low-rise building across the street, Kelson locked his office door and went out to the parking garage. As he pulled on to the street and again a half mile from his office, he looked in his rearview mirror and saw a blue Buick Regal a couple of car lengths behind him, but the afternoon sun kept him from seeing who was in the car, and when he slowed for a red light, it peeled into an alleyway by a dry cleaner.

'Don't start,' he said, and drove back to his apartment.

His head ached, and as Payday and Painter's Lane rubbed against his ankles, he popped a double dose of Percocet. 'Time hurts too,' he told Payday, and scooped her up to his chest, where she purred and kneaded his skin through his shirt. He asked her, 'What do you say, do I call Nancy?' If Doreen Felbanks was telling the truth, the man would go after Nancy and Sue Ellen within twenty-four hours – unless he killed Dominick Stevens. Which he wouldn't do. 'Tell her what?' he asked Payday. 'Take Sue Ellen out of school, pack their bags, and run? She'd never do it, never go. She'd laugh at me, say I was crying wolf. Or say she would kick the man's ass. Might do it too.' He scratched Payday's little skull and said, 'Infected thumb? More like a toothache. Nancy knows what to do. Yank it. Tough. Never mess with a dentist.' The double dose of Percocet fishtailed through his arteries, and he felt a pleasant, dizzying warmth. 'The world is what it is, that's all,' he told Payday. He felt like lying down. He went to the kitchen and popped another pill. Then he stretched out on his bed and waited for the room to melt.

He got his best night's sleep since Doreen sent him to Christian Felbanks's condo. Eleven hours straight. He would've gotten even more except for the kittens' mewling. That and the knock on the door.

FORTY-TWO

Kelson rolled out of bed and stumbled to the door.

Peters, his face distorted by the peephole lens, stood in the hallway.

Kelson opened the door and put his hands in the air. 'This routine is getting old,' he said.

Peters said, 'What the hell are you doing?'

'Drag me downtown. I'll call my lawyer and get out in an hour unless you lined this one up better.'

'Nah, I need your help.' Peters looked and sounded exhausted.

'You're screwing with me, right?'

'Can I come in?'

'Is this a trick?'

Peters walked past him into the apartment but stopped when the kittens pranced toward him across the carpet. 'We've got a situation I want you to look at.'

Kelson felt a sudden fear. 'Are Nancy and Sue Ellen all right?'

'Sure – as far as I know. This isn't about them.'

'What's going on?'

'That's the thing – we don't know what to make of it. It's the kind of situation that's better to see.'

'Sounds like you want to take me somewhere I don't want to go.'

'I've been there all night. I don't want to go back either. But it's my job, and you're in the middle even if you don't want to be.'

'What if I say no?'

'Not much I can do. I suppose I could find a reason to throw you in jail again, but I won't waste your time or mine. I'm *asking* for your thoughts.'

'Two days ago, you were sick of me. You wouldn't listen to anything I said. What changed?'

'Come see.'

'Why should I trust you?'

'I'm not telling you to. I guess if I was you, I wouldn't. Take your own car. Turn around if you want to.'

Kelson said, 'I need to shower and eat.'

'Do it fast.'

Five minutes later, Kelson came out of the bathroom, ate a bowl of Cheerios, and rode the elevator down with the detective.

Outside, the sky was clear, though a cold wet wind blew across the damp ground. Kelson followed Peters south in his Challenger. He got a bad feeling when Peters cut on to Halsted. When the detective turned toward North Burling, where Dominick Stevens lived, Kelson said, 'Ah, shit.'

A single police cruiser was parked at the curb two doors down from Stevens's house, and Peters pulled up behind it and Kelson behind him. When they got out, Peters said, 'We're keeping this quiet right now. Mayor's request. But it's a ticking bomb. One of the neighbors will look out the window and do something to tip off the news.'

Kelson's dread felt like a stone in his gut. 'Dead?'

'Take a look.'

Inside the front door, cops had laid plastic sheeting on the floor. One in a uniform talked with another in a lab coat by the stairway. More plastic went up the stairs like a runner. Three cops worked at the top of the stairs.

Peters led Kelson up past them and into Dominick Stevens's bedroom.

Kelson had seen plenty when he worked on the narcotics squad. He'd seen bruised children in vermin-infested houses. He'd seen teenaged girls and boys whose bodies looked chewed up by machines after all the needles they'd stuck in them. What he saw in Stevens's bed was no worse. Christian Felbanks's mom and dad were lying with their eyes closed, a cotton blanket pulled to their chins. They looked almost content, except Christian's mom had no hair – that and they both had neat little bullet holes in their foreheads.

The sight poked at him.

A needle seemed to lodge in the bone above his left eye.

He made a low humming sound in his throat as his words from his last telephone conversation with Toselli came back. *Mengele's putting me in bed with these people. Everything's collapsing . . .*

As if he was scripting his own life.

Peters watched him. 'What?'

'Toselli,' Kelson said.

Peters gave him a look. 'Huh?'

Kelson shook it off. 'Where's the hair?'

'I hoped maybe you could tell me,' Peters said. 'Forensics went over the place and couldn't find a strand.'

Kelson asked, 'Did you pull back the blanket?'

'She's shaved from top to toe. Clean as a baby.'

'And him?'

'Just the hole in his head.'

'I guess that's enough. Where's Stevens?'

'He came in last night and found Goldilocks and her husband in his bed. He's put himself up at the Omni.'

'Why didn't you just tell me about this?'

'I wanted to see your reaction.'

'Which was?'

'You said, "Toselli."'

'Why would I do that?'

'My question.'

'His name was in my mouth. Greg and I talked yesterday. Good man. Principled.'

Peters gave him that look again. 'I've got a question. *You're* into hair, aren't you? I mean, you talk about this redhead.'

'Doreen.'

'Sure. And there's Raima Minhas's braid. And Christian Felbanks's decision to go skinhead.'

Kelson said, 'What are you talking about?'

Peters smiled as if they were getting somewhere. 'When Raima's dad and cousin ID'd her body, they said she was growing a braid. She was supposed to cut it off when she got married. It's a Hindu thing. Did you maybe take it?'

Kelson's mind swam.

Peters said, 'Christian Felbanks liked his hair, the little he had of it. Maybe you have it too?'

Kelson gestured at the couple in Stevens's bed. 'You think I did this?'

'Here's the thing. My partner says you tipped her off to the Felbankses' disappearance yesterday. I don't know why you'd give her that if you did this. But if not you, I don't know what to think.'

'*I* can tell you what,' Kelson said, and he told him Raba Lisle's story about Doreen Felbanks – her teenage relationship with Christian, the boys who pursued and abused her afterward, cutting off *her* hair, the father who kicked her out, the man who, she said, controlled her now. And on and on, until Peters silenced him.

'OK,' Peters said, resigned. 'OK.'

Kelson felt a sudden lightness. 'Do you believe me? About Doreen Felbanks and—'

Peters shook his head. 'I don't know.' His face was sour.

Kelson said, 'This all goes back to Bicho. If you don't look—'

Peters cut him off. 'Just leave him out of it, all right? Let's deal with one fucked-up story at a time. Let's see who this Doreen Felbanks is.'

'Bicho and Doreen Felbanks *are* one story,' Kelson said.

'Just leave it,' Peters said. 'You already gave me enough.'

'Seems like more than you can handle.'

Peters gave him an uncertain look, and then, to end the conversation, 'I hope they didn't tear up your apartment too bad.'

'What do you mean?'

Peters shook his head again. 'Do you really think I just wanted to see your reaction to this? I needed you out so we could look for the hair.' Then he offered to shake Kelson's hand. 'If they'd found anything, they would've let me know by now.'

FORTY-THREE

At Kelson's apartment, the search team had come and gone, getting through the door without breaking the frame, even locking it behind them when they left. They'd closed the kittens in the bathroom, rifled through the clothes in the closet, pulled back the bed covers, and rattled the kitchen drawers. 'Enough to give me an aneurysm,' Kelson said as he gazed at the mess.

The kittens kept away from him, as if they could sense it. 'You guys want a Percocet?' he asked because he badly wanted one himself and wasn't going to take it. 'Too much to do,' he said. 'Too little time. Too many, too few.' He glared at Painter's Lane, who mewled at him. 'I'm babbling like a bald baby.' Painter's Lane moved tentatively toward him. He picked up the kitten, petted her, and set her back on the rug, afraid of what he might do, the razor's edge of a headache seeming to divide his skull bone. 'Poor Mrs Felbanks,' he said.

He went into the bathroom, stared at the vial of Percocet in the medicine cabinet, and told it, 'I'm not your bitch.' He closed the cabinet and laughed at the man in the mirror. 'Ha,' he told him. 'I'm everyone's bitch. And so are you.'

But he managed to get out of the bathroom without sucking the pills from the vial. 'Get on with it,' he said to Payday, and he pulled out his phone and started to dial Toselli's number. Then stopped. He stared at the phone as if it was an oracle. He ended the call. 'Some things, once you say them, you can't unsay,' he told phone. 'Not that that's stopped me before. Maybe nothing I ever said was something to say.' He stared at the phone. It said nothing. So he dialed Rodman instead.

'The Felbankses are dead,' he told him.

'That sucks.'

'Dan Peters woke me with the news this morning. He had a team roll my apartment, looking for evidence that I killed them.'

'That sucks,' he said again.

'Do you have anything else to say?'

'Yeah, Peters looks dirty in all of this. I talked to a Rogers Park dealer last night. He said Bicho sold "recycled." Recycled, as in taken off the street by a cop or stolen from evidence or never cataloged – and then fed back to the street through Bicho. That's what he said.'

'Did the dealer say anything about Peters?'

'No, I don't think he knew who. But Peters has had a hard-on for you since Christian Felbanks died, so why not?'

Kelson said, 'He seemed to take me seriously about Doreen for the first time this morning, but he didn't like me talking about Bicho.'

'Then treat him like he's rotten unless you learn different. What are you going to do now?'

'I need to talk to Nancy and convince her to get Sue Ellen out of the city. I won't touch Dominick Stevens, and so they're next on the list.'

'Maybe you should go with them. No shame in running away if someone's got bigger guns than you.'

'Who would feed the kittens?'

'Take yourself off the table. Change the game. Keep yourself from getting hurt.'

'How about you?' Kelson said. 'What's next?'

'I'm going to take Dominick Stevens out to lunch.'

'What're you talking about?'

'Here's all you need to know – I'm doing this for you. For him too, but mainly for you. You understand that?'

'No, you're confusing me.'

'Good,' Rodman said.

Kelson drove to the Healthy Smiles Dental Clinic.

'Toselli,' he said.

'Do I believe it?' he asked.

'I don't know,' he said.

Dr P had warned that his perceptions might swerve from reality.

'I hope so,' he said.

Nancy's waiting room was painted in a safari theme with big-toothed animals grinning from behind jungle foliage and banana-eating monkeys hanging from the branches.

The receptionist greeted Kelson with a smile as big as the shy hippo's. But when he asked to see his ex-wife, she said. 'That could be a problem. She's doing a cavity.'

Kelson said he had an emergency, and she sent word back. Fifteen minutes later, Nancy came into the waiting room, wearing safety glasses.

The waiting parents looked scandalized when he told her about the methhead prostitute who'd given him details that made him think Doreen Felbanks or the man who was running her meant to harm anyone connected to him – and that meant Nancy and Sue Ellen. Then Nancy jabbed a dental pick at Kelson's chest as she berated him for putting their daughter in danger. As he expected, she refused to flee. She would pick up Sue Ellen from school herself. She would use extra caution. But she wouldn't allow Kelson's selfishness to disrupt their lives.

'Selfishness?' he said. 'I got shot in the head.'

A woman with twin blond-haired boys gathered their toys and scurried from the office.

'I feel bad for you,' Nancy said. 'We all do. But that doesn't change the fact that the rest of us have lives.'

'So blunt,' he said. 'So cold.' He fought the urge but said, 'And still so sexy.'

She poked the dental pick at him. 'Leave.'

FORTY-FOUR

The report of a black man abducting real-estate developer Dominick Stevens outside the Omni Hotel came over the radio shortly after nine. Halfway between Nancy's clinic and his office, Kelson pulled over and listened, then searched for the WGN-TV stream on his phone.

They had video of the abduction from an Omni security camera. A fuzzy-looking Dominick Stevens walked from the Omni carrying a paper cup of coffee. A large black man approached from behind and put a massive hand on Stevens's shoulder. He took the coffee cup, set it on the sidewalk, and then – with his back to the camera, as if he'd scouted security beforehand – dragged Stevens to a white van. He pushed him in through a sliding door, climbed into the driver's seat, and pulled from the curb. Kelson magnified the image. The license plates were obscured.

The anchorwoman said the police were asking Chicagoans to report sightings of white late-model Chevrolet G20 cargo vans. Then she cut to a profile of Stevens and his political and financial friendships.

Doreen Felbanks's call interrupted Kelson's third viewing of the video. 'What are you doing?' Her voice had an edge.

'Don't be mad. You said Mengele wanted me to get rid of Stevens.'

'I said he wanted you to kill him. I said nothing about having someone yank him off the street.'

'Stevens is off the table.'

'No one's off the table,' she said. 'You know what will happen to your—'

'I'm coming after you,' he said. 'You think you've got me, but I'm right behind you.' And he hung up.

Seconds later, his phone rang again but he silenced it. He knew what she would say, knew the threats to Nancy and Sue Ellen, knew the warning about what would happen to him personally if he failed to follow directions. And he knew what *he* would say, what he couldn't unsay. He didn't want to hear or say any of it.

He pulled back into the street and, instead of continuing to his office, drove south toward Rodman's Bronzeville apartment. But then another report came over the car radio. Dominick Stevens had contacted another station, WBEZ. He was safe and with friends, he said. The video and eyewitness accounts were mistakes, misunderstandings.

'Yeah, right,' Kelson said, and kept driving.

Rodman's neighborhood looked as it always did. 'A place that holds on by its knuckles,' Kelson said as he looked out the windshield. 'No pulling itself up. No tumbling in a freefall.' It had people like Rodman to thank for the calm – people who chased drug dealers from the alleys and lived their lives steadily and quietly and with their eyes open for the next threat from above or below. Kelson felt those eyes on him as he got out of his car and scurried to Rodman's building.

He climbed the two flights of stairs to Rodman's apartment and knocked. The door swung halfway open and Rodman beckoned him inside.

Dominick Stevens and Francisca Cabon sat on the living-room couch under the portraits of Malcolm X, Rodman's girlfriend Cindi, and Marty Luther King, Jr. Their baby slept against Stevens's chest. A beaten-up red suitcase stood against the wall.

'Huh,' Kelson said.

'Told you,' Rodman said.

Cindi came in from the kitchen with coffee. She smiled at Kelson. 'DeMarcus said you'd be joining us.'

'I've never been to a party like this,' Kelson said.

'Had to get them out of the way,' Rodman said. 'After dumping the Felbankses in Dominick's bed, someone broke into Francisca's place last night.'

'Bastard tried to kill me,' Francisca said. 'Would've done it too, except I was up with Miguel.' She reached for the baby, and Stevens handed him to her.

'Huh,' Kelson said again.

Rodman downed half of his coffee. 'Like I said, no shame in running away if your enemy's got bigger guns. I invited Francisca and Dominick to spend a little time at our B and B.'

Stevens toasted him with his coffee cup. 'Here's to Nirvana.'

'*Mi casa es su casa*,' Rodman said.

'What the hell?' Kelson said.

'Don't overthink it,' Rodman said.

But a headache dug into Kelson's skull. He asked Francisca, 'You saw the guy who came after you?'

'Wasn't like he was a ghost.'

'Did you recognize him?'

'I recognized the kind. Full of himself. Slick.'

'Good-looking? Highly principled? No man left behind? An angel of death?'

'What do you mean?'

'How'd you scare him off?'

'I'm not stupid. Alone in that building with Miguel? I have a gun. When he shot at me, I shot back. He didn't expect that, I think.'

'Did you hit him?'

'I didn't even aim at him. You think I want to kill somebody?'

'How about your roommate?'

'Elena? She moved out a couple days ago – met a boy at a club.'

Rodman said, 'Francisca called Dominick afterward. She was in his room at the hotel this morning when I picked him up.'

She put a hand on Stevens's thigh. 'Dominick had DeMarcus come back for me.'

Kelson said, 'You went back to the hotel after kidnapping him?'

'Couldn't leave her there,' Rodman said. 'And I didn't kidnap him – I just gave him a ride.'

'And what's the deal with *you*?' Kelson said to Stevens. 'Your girlfriend's like sixteen. You couldn't wait until she graduated from high school?'

'Eighteen, bastard,' Francisca said. 'I finished two years ago. Graduated early.'

'Huh,' Kelson said.

'Racist,' she said.

'Um,' Rodman said, 'we've got important stuff to deal with.'

'I fell in love,' Stevens said. 'Lock me up for it.'

'We do that to men like you,' Kelson said. 'Unless they've got enough money – like you.'

Rodman said, 'What about Nancy and Sue Ellen?'

That shook Kelson out of it. 'I talked to Nancy. She won't budge.'

'Maybe she doesn't get a choice. At least not about your girl.'

'If you try to grab Nancy off the street, she'll break your knees.'

'I don't want to grab anyone,' Rodman said. 'I'm talking about drawing a circle around them. No one gets through.'

'You have friends who can do that?' Kelson asked. 'Because I don't.'

'I can call favors,' he said.

Stevens said, 'And I've got friends.'

That brought a smile to Kelson's face. '*You* I don't get. The man who's doing this will roll over the kind of guy who runs to the Omni when he's scared.'

Stevens gave him back a smile. 'I have the right kind of friends.'

'Accept the offer,' Rodman said to Kelson.

'Fine,' Kelson said. 'Call them.'

'Now say thank you,' Rodman said.

FORTY-FIVE

They spent the morning at Rodman's apartment, planning for eventualities they couldn't really anticipate. 'When you can't see your enemy, you watch every angle,' Rodman said, 'and you also watch from the outside in, because sometimes the first thing that's visible is their backs.'

He made a call, and an hour later a tiny, one-armed man named Marty LeCoeur knocked at the door with his girlfriend, Janet, a big, nasty-complexioned woman. Marty held her hand, caressing her wrist with his little thumb.

Rodman said, 'Marty's the most truly ferocious man I've ever known. I could tell you stories about him.'

The little man seemed to take that as a compliment, but said, 'I keep books at West Side Aluminum. Got no record. I'm fucking clean.'

'Clean because he scrubs up afterward,' Rodman said. 'He doesn't like bullies.'

'Nope, fucking hate them.'

'Once clubbed a guy in the knees with a tire iron for insulting Janet.'

'I'm a fucking knight in fucking shining armor.'

'*I* wouldn't tangle with him.'

'Why would I want to tangle with you, DeMarcus?'

So Kelson told him Nancy's address and explained her schedule. Marty promised to park outside or leave another guard overnight until Nancy and Sue Ellen left for work and school.

'Nancy will feel insulted if she thinks you're protecting her,' Kelson said, 'and when she feels insulted, she gets violent.'

'No problem,' Marty said. 'I'm fucking discreet.'

'You need weapons?' Rodman asked.

Marty looked at him as if he'd made a joke. 'A man like me, they never see it coming.'

When they left, Kelson asked Rodman, 'What favor is he paying back?'

'I set him up with Janet.'

Then Dominick Stevens called Bicho's friend, Esteban Herrera, who worked the downstairs reception desk at the Stevens Group building. He had him write down a list of files and asked him to bring them from his office to Rodman's apartment. 'Tell no one where you're going,' he said.

When he hung up, Kelson said, 'You put a lot of trust in him.'

'I took him in when he had no place to live. Since then, he knows more about me than anyone else I work with.'

Twenty minutes later, Herrera knocked on the door.

He looked up at Rodman as he came in and said, 'Holy shit.' Then he saw Kelson and his expression went from awe to confusion.

Francisca smiled. 'Hey, *guapo*.'

Stevens took a briefcase from him and directed him to Kelson. 'You need to answer this gentleman's questions about Bicho.'

Herrera gave a little shake of his head. 'I don't snitch, you know that.'

'Don't disrespect Bicho's memory,' Stevens said. 'Just tell the man what you can.'

Herrera looked to Francisca for support. She said, 'He's helping Dominick and me.'

'I don't snitch,' Herrera said.

'Who supplied Bicho with his drugs?' Kelson asked.

'Uh-uh.'

'If he didn't get them from Hugo Nuñez, where'd he get them?'

Herrera stared at him hard. 'You're an asshole.'

'A lot of people say so,' Kelson said. 'After Bicho's mom died, who took care of him? Was he on his own?'

Herrera looked at Stevens.

'Talk to the man,' Stevens said.

He looked at Francisca again.

She nodded.

He eyed Kelson as if trying to figure out his game. 'He had an uncle, but that didn't work out.'

'What happened?'

'You ask too many questions. I've got one for *you*. How's it feel to shoot a kid? You get off on that?'

'It feels bad,' Kelson said. 'The worst thing ever. Think of what it would feel like to stick a blade in your own head and twist it. Then think of worse than that.'

'I don't feel for you. You did what you did.'

'And I would do it again. That doesn't mean I like it. Tell me about Bicho's uncle.'

'All I know is he's like you. Says one thing and does another. Like I say, it didn't work out.'

Rodman asked, 'He have a name?'

Herrera stared at Kelson. 'You an ex-cop and all? You can't find out?'

'The records seem to have gone missing,' he said.

'See, that's what I'm talking about. He's a guy like you – trouble sticks to him. If I see a band saw, I don't stick my fingers in it. No, I don't know his name. But he isn't Mexican. I don't think he even *habla Español.*'

Rodman said, 'Dan Peters?'

'Who?'

Rodman moved in close. 'No? You know where we can find this man?'

Francisca said, 'Tell him what you know, Esteban.'

Herrera said, 'It was a couple years ago since Bicho lived with him, and he was there only a month or two before he got kicked out. The rest was rumors.'

'What rumors?' Rodman asked.

'I don't snitch, and I don't tell stories about my friends. But I'll tell you this much – once Bicho moved out, they got on better. He sometimes went over there.'

Kelson said, 'But he never said where that was?'

'Some things with Bicho, you knew better than to ask. But a lot of his trouble started with his uncle. Long as his mom was alive, he played straight. When she was gone, he did a man's work in kid's shoes. Didn't have no choice.'

'Do you know why the uncle kicked him out?' Kelson asked.

'I guess Alejandro didn't live up to his expectations.'

'About what?'

Herrera glanced at Stevens and Francisca. 'Forget it. I don't snitch.'

Herrera left then, and Stevens pulled a pile of contracts from his briefcase and converted Rodman's living room into a temporary business office. Cindi changed into nurse scrubs and headed to a shift at Rush Medical.

Kelson left too and drove to his office. He spent so much time talking to himself in the rearview mirror – debating what Herrera had said and failed to say, commenting on the essential goodness of men like Rodman, wondering about Stevens and whether the love he professed for Francisca was real or corrupt or more likely both, mouthing the name Toselli, mouthing it again – that he almost rear-ended a delivery truck, narrowly missed a woman stepping into the crosswalk three blocks later, and entirely missed seeing the blue Buick Regal with two Mexican men in it, idling at the curb across the street from the parking garage by his office, and the black Chevy Tahoe idling by the garage entrance.

He was still chattering when he cut the engine in the shadows of the garage. Before getting out of his car, he looked once more at the mirror and said, 'I've got to admit Francisca Cabon could do it for a man.'

He answered, 'Not as much as Doreen Felbanks.'

He said, 'It's messed-up that I should even think that way about her.'

And he answered, 'But typical.'

Then he walked down the ramp into the sunlight – and into the hands of Dan Peters and Venus Johnson, who whisked him from the sidewalk into the back of the Chevy Tahoe. Peters got in beside him. Johnson jumped into the driver's seat. The Tahoe shot from the curb. 'What the hell?' Kelson said.

'Shut up,' Peters said, and glanced at the street behind them.

'I didn't do—'

Peters craned his neck. 'I said, shut up.'

Johnson cut hard around a corner and headed for Lake Shore Drive, rolling through stop signs and punching the gas between intersections.

Peters kept his eyes on the streets and buildings.

When they reached Harrison Street Police Station, Johnson got out, scanned the surroundings, and nodded at Peters. Peters said, 'Go,' and he pushed his door open.

Kelson followed them as they ran into the station.

'What the hell?' he said again.

The detectives drew him into a hallway leading to a suite of interior rooms. He'd never been to the rooms even when working on the narcotics squad. He *knew* about them, though. Investigators took especially violent suspects and particularly vulnerable witnesses there. Only the chief and the department heads kept keys to them.

They went into one. Two other men already sat at a table – the narcotics division commander Darrin Malinowski and Kelson's lawyer Edward Davies.

'Hope you don't mind that we called him,' Peters said of Davies.

'What the hell?' Kelson said.

'Take a seat,' Malinowski said. 'You need anything? Water? Coffee?'

'Tell me what's going on.'

Peters and Johnson sat, and when Kelson sat too, next to his lawyer, Peters said, 'One of our own is trying to kill you.'

Kelson tried to process the thought. 'I know.'

'You do?' Peters said.

The wires in Kelson's thinking crossed. 'You?'

'No. Why would you think that?'

'You seem to have a hard-on for me.'

'I—'

Darrin Malinowski said, 'Greg Toselli.'

Kelson knew it was true but said, 'He saved my life.'

'Now he wants to take it.'

FORTY-SIX

'W hen Bicho Rodriguez's junkie mom was dying of hepatitis, Toselli promised he'd take care of him,' Peters said. 'He took care of him a little too good.'
Kelson shook his head.

His lawyer said, 'Toselli turned dirty five or six years ago, when he was on narcotics with you. Internal Affairs has been investigating him since you got shot. A lot of missing drugs.'

Venus Johnson said, 'Toselli grabbed them off the street, but they never made it to the evidence room.'

Kelson kept shaking his head.

'They've got video,' his lawyer said. 'I watched it.'

'Toselli's one of the good ones,' Kelson said.

'He told a CI it's like dumpster diving,' Peters said. 'Reselling drugs headed for the incinerator.'

'Dammit,' Kelson said. 'He brought me a Frisbee.'

Peters looked perplexed. 'I'm sorry?'

'In rehab. He brought me a Frisbee. We threw it outside the center. He smuggled in beer. Nancy and Sue Ellen bought snacks from the machine. Sue Ellen calls him *Uncle Greg*.'

Malinowski said, 'I know this is—'

Kelson was sweating. 'We had a party.'

'I'm afraid it's over,' his lawyer said.

Kelson shook his head. 'Bicho's mom was Toselli's sister?'

'Half-sister,' Peters said. 'Five years older.'

'But she was like a second mom to Toselli,' Venus Johnson said.

'How long have you known about his connection to Bicho?' Kelson asked.

Malinowski said, 'It didn't seem like it would do you any good to know right after you got shot. Toselli looked like the hero in this. We needed one. *You* did. We figured he didn't get to choose his family, and this kind of thing could be poison.'

'How long have you known? Before I got shot, you had me investigate Bicho without telling Toselli. Did you know then?'

'This thing tore Toselli up,' Peters said. 'I did the interviews after the shooting. Toselli's nephew was dead, and you were dying almost. His loyalty was clear. He buried his nephew in a nice little ceremony, but he seemed more worried about you. Seemed like he couldn't do enough for you.'

'He helped when I needed it,' Kelson said.

'We thought he was a good cop,' Malinowski said. 'Tough but clean.'

Kelson's lawyer said, 'After Bicho shot you and Internal Affairs looked into Toselli's relationship to him, they found piles of evidence.'

'They found *traces*,' Malinowski said. 'They're still putting together a case. In the meantime, we transferred him from narcotics to vice.'

'Where he continued his drug dealing,' the lawyer said. 'And now, with his contacts in vice, he's started a sideline of extorting pimps and massage parlors. He's a busy man. Hard to believe he has time to pin on his badge.'

Kelson asked, 'Is that how he met Doreen Felbanks?'

'Seems likely,' his lawyer said.

Malinowski glared at him. 'You're here at our invitation, Mr Davies.'

'No,' Davies said, 'my client's here at my say-so. I can advise him against cooperating at any time. If you try to bury the facts, that time is now.'

Kelson turned to Peters. 'Why are you telling me all of this?'

Peters said, 'You've done undercover work. You know how to handle yourself in the line of fire.'

'So you've got a couple of options,' Malinowski said. 'We can put you up in a hotel room, keep you safe . . .'

'Or,' Peters said, 'you can step back into the line of fire. We'll be watching from a hundred yards away. Like when you worked undercover. We'll be there in a second if things go bad.'

Kelson stared at him. 'You mean like if someone shoots me in the head . . .'

Malinowski said, 'We'd understand if you say no.'

Kelson's lawyer said, 'That's my advice. Walk away.'

'We hope you'll agree to help,' said Venus Johnson.

Kelson said, 'You've had me in and out of the station for the last week and a half. You've pinned me to the wall. What made you change your mind?'

Peters said, 'When I brought you to Dominick Stevens's house this morning, I was making sure about you. We needed to know about you before we moved against another cop.'

'I was a cop too.'

'You left the department under suspicious circumstances,' Peters said.

'Because I got shot?'

'Because,' Peters said, 'you shot first.'

The words slammed Kelson. 'Says who?'

His lawyer looked at Peters with scorn. 'Toselli.'

'It's what he said at the time of the shooting,' Malinowski said. He had the even voice of a man who never admits personal embarrassment. 'We buried it. We didn't want it to hurt you. We didn't want it to hurt the department.'

'*Did* I shoot first?' Kelson asked.

None of the cops answered. His lawyer said, 'They don't know. They only had it from Toselli. He was the only witness.'

Malinowski said, 'We didn't know he was dirty yet. We made our decisions based on who we thought he was. The damage was done.'

'To me.'

'Yes,' Malinowski said.

'Have you gone after him now?'

'We tried,' Malinowski said. 'We raided his house this morning.'

'But missed him?'

'He rigged a shotgun to the front door,' Malinowski said. 'The lead man took a chestful of buckshot. Toselli went out the back in the confusion.'

'So now he knows you're coming?'

'We think he hooked up with another bad cop,' Malinowski said. 'Or an *almost* cop. A guy from your academy class – big guy, smart, strong, but a bad attitude. Name was DeMarcus Rodman. Dropped out. We've got him on security footage with Dominick Stevens outside the Omni.'

Kelson laughed. 'What about Stevens's call to WBEZ?'

Peters said, 'We think Toselli and Rodman forced him to make it. If not, he would've called *us*.'

'Maybe he knows you could trace the call and he wants to stay in hiding,' Kelson said. 'Maybe he knows there's dirt in the department. Maybe he wonders who he can trust.'

'Rodman's dangerous,' Peters said. 'He grabbed Stevens. He's capable of—'

'Rodman's the gentlest man I've ever known,' Kelson said, then said to his lawyer, 'Get me the hell out of here, will you?'

'You're at risk,' Venus Johnson said. 'So are Nancy and your daughter. When we raided Toselli's house, we found a notebook.'

That stung Kelson. 'What kind of notebook?'

'Schedules. Sue Ellen's school. Nancy's work. When they come and go.'

'I've got someone watching them. Don't ask who because I'll tell you and I don't want to.'

'Who?' Johnson asked.

'A little one-armed man named Marty.'

'Don't be an asshole,' she said. 'We've got a bad situation. Do you want us to pick them up and put them in a hotel?'

'Nancy won't go. Too hardheaded.'

'We can try.'

'You can.'

Peters said, 'Work with us and we'll watch you, or let us put you in a hotel too.'

'Why don't you give Toselli's picture to the news?' Kelson asked.

'The higher-ups want him in our hands before the news hits.'

'Control the story?'

'A bad cop in custody is big news,' Malinowski said. 'A bad cop on the run is international.'

Kelson looked to his lawyer. Davies gave him the smallest head shake. 'No,' Kelson said, 'I won't play. You've had this wrong every step, and every time you stumble, I get a bullet in the head or you throw me in jail.'

'Good choice,' Davies said.

'I understand,' said Malinowski. 'We'll arrange for a hotel room and a guard. Keep you safe until we find Toselli.'

'No,' Kelson said again. 'I'm out. You do what you need to do, but leave me alone.'

'Bad choice,' Davies said.

'Stupid,' Johnson said.

'You've got the right to refuse,' Malinowski said, 'but we aren't responsible if you do.'

'I don't like your idea of responsibility,' Kelson said.

So Malinowski and Johnson left, followed by Peters, who said he'd arrange a ride back for Kelson. Davies tried to convince him to take protection and said he could file a civil suit for harassment and intimidation. Kelson told him again he just wanted to be left alone, and Davies left too.

For twenty minutes, Kelson waited alone for his ride. The overhead fluorescent lights buzzed. The windowless walls felt tight and tighter. Kelson looked for an air vent and saw none.

He waited another five minutes. 'Forgotten already?' he asked. He stared at the walls. 'Closing in?'

Another three minutes. No one came. The fluorescent light buzzed. Kelson said, 'Feels like a horsefly eating into my head.'

'Huh?' he asked himself.

'Couldn't they let me sit in the dark?'

'Where I've always been.'

'Percocet?'

'Screw it.' He got up and tried the door. Unlocked. He walked through the halls and out of the station.

FORTY-SEVEN

A wet March wind was blowing. It smelled of the lake and of the old clay soil under the city and of the people who lived on top of it. Kelson flagged a cab and rode back to his office. He ran upstairs, grabbed his KelTec, and checked the magazine. Then he called Rodman and told him about Greg Toselli.

'I never liked that boy,' Rodman said.

'That's it?'

'Nothing surprises me anymore.'

So Kelson went downstairs again and drove home.

As he passed the front door of his building, the blue Buick Regal was idling at the curb. This time he saw the driver and a passenger – the two men from Hugo Nuñez's office.

Kelson stopped a few car lengths beyond the Buick. 'Tracking me like an animal,' he said. He set his KelTec in his lap and shifted into reverse. He stopped again when his passenger window faced the other driver. The man stared at him with cold eyes, made his finger and thumb into a gun, and pointed at Kelson.

Kelson lowered his passenger window and signaled the man to roll his down. When the man did, Kelson said, 'Never pretend to shoot at someone with impulse control issues.'

So the man picked up a pistol from the side of his seat and aimed it at Kelson. He said, 'I'd love to do it, but Hugo wants you for himself.'

Kelson scooped the KelTec from his lap and aimed back.

'Hilarious,' the driver said, and rolled back up his window.

So Kelson parked in the lot and sprinted to the building vestibule. He checked the lobby and mailroom before getting on the elevator. On his floor, he wiggled his door handle before putting his key in the lock.

He opened the door and slipped inside.

And he shrieked.

Doreen Felbanks lay on his bed, petting Painter's Lane. Payday was curled against her belly, purring loudly.

'What the hell,' Kelson said.

'Shh,' Doreen said. She was lying on her side, her head propped on an elbow, like an old painting of a whore, except she wore black Capri pants and a black cashmere sweater. A pair of red high heels lay on the carpet.

Kelson scanned the apartment for other intruders. He forced himself to go to the kitchen doorway. He forced himself to look into the bathroom and behind the shower curtain.

He went back into the main room with his KelTec in his hand. 'Where is he?'

'Oh, put that away. You aren't going to shoot me.' She sounded drunk or high.

'Watch me. Where is he?'

'What if you hit the cat?'

'I'll risk it. Where's Toselli?'

'So you *do* know. A lot of people underestimate you. I did at first. Then the cops broke down his door this morning. He said you must've tipped them to who he was.'

'The cops told *me* about him. Where is he?' He stood away from the window and kept his back to the wall.

'That's the funny thing,' she said. 'After the raid, he came to my apartment and said it was time to clean up. That meant getting rid of me – and you too, though I think he always planned to kill us sooner or later.' Something in her expression seemed pained or sick. 'I ran into my bathroom and went out the window to the fire escape. He shot up the bathroom door.' Her lips quivered, though she could've been faking it.

'Nope. Not this time.' Kelson laughed at her – a forced laugh. 'You've lied and set me up. You've almost gotten me killed. Why would I believe you? Where is he?'

Slowly and with effort, she rolled away from him on to her back. Blood stained the bedspread. Her black sweater looked wet.

Kelson moved toward her involuntarily. 'Oh, shit.'

'Yeah, that's what I said. I almost got out the window.'

He stopped inches from the bed. 'Let me see.'

She peeled her sweater up from her hip and shuddered. Blood spread from her ribcage and belly around her back.

'Why?' Kelson asked.

'Same reason as every man I've ever known. He was done with me.'

'You need help.'

'You know what, he never lied to me. Never pretended I was anyone else. If I did what he told me to, he kept his word. We had an understanding – he never hung Christian's or Raima Minhas's killings on me. I didn't think he'd shoot me, though.'

Kelson pulled out his phone and started dialing 911.

'No,' she said, with strange urgency.

'You're bleeding,' he said.

'Good eyes.'

'You'll die.'

'I don't think so.'

He started dialing again.

She pushed herself up to sitting, though she almost collapsed into herself. 'I'm leaving.'

'Why did you come?'

'To warn you,' she said.

'Liar.'

She tried to stand. Couldn't.

'Dammit,' he said, and shoved his phone in his pocket. He went into the bathroom, soaked a towel, and returned. 'Lie down.'

She did, with a faint smile. 'I knew this about you.'

'Shut up.' He cleaned under her ribcage.

'I knew you were a sucker.'

'I said, shut up.' He went back to the bathroom, wrung the towel over the sink, and wet it again. Then he cleaned her hip and back. The cloth tugged against a flap of skin on her back, and she groaned. The bullet had gone straight through from her belly.

When she caught her breath, she said, 'People keep hurting me if I let them.'

The wound bled freely. He cleaned it with the towel again and made a compress.

She said, 'And you scared Greg. You've got half a brain, and you scared him.' She winced as he pushed the towel into the wound. 'By surviving,' she said. 'By staying . . . clean. By being' – she gasped when he put more pressure on the compress – 'a sucker.'

He bandaged her as well as he could, and then he took out his phone again and started dialing.

'I'll walk out of here before they come,' she said.

'You wouldn't make it to the elevator.'

'I made it here.'

'You had more blood in you then.'

'No hospital,' she said. 'Nowhere Greg or anyone else can get me. I'll give you what you want. You give me what I want.'

'What do you want?'

'Depends. You think I'll live?'

'I've seen people come through worse,' he said.

'You, for instance.'

'Me. But I also knew a dealer with a flesh wound who died of sepsis. He refused to go to a hospital too.'

'Help me get out of Chicago. That's all I want.'

'Back to Sioux City?'

'If you make me laugh, I'll die right here.'

'And what do you think *I* want?'

'Don't you even know?' Again the faint smile. 'You want to make things happen,' she said. 'You want to outsmart people. You want them to love you.'

'And you can make that happen?'

'Maybe a little, if I help you catch Greg.'

'*You* want that too – me to take him down before he takes you down.'

'Sure. And before he takes you down too.'

'Just one problem,' he said. 'You helped him kill Christian and his mom and dad. You helped him kill Raima Minhas.'

'Greg killed them. He set me up the same as you. I had reasons to hurt Christian and the others. And I got Christian to steal drugs from the pharmacy. I did that much. But Greg killed him and the others. If I didn't help him pin the killings on you, he would shine a light on me for the cops. With my background, I'd go down hard.'

'So you tried to send me down instead?'

'I'm a sucker too.'

'No, you aren't. You've never been, or if you were, it's been a long time since you got over it.'

'Do I look like I could kill anyone?'

'Absolutely.'

'Go to hell.' She tried to get up. She almost made it.

'So you're just his tool?' he said. 'Nothing more?'

'I didn't say that. He wanted *all* of me. He wanted the parts no one can buy. The parts no one should give.'

'And now he's trying to kill you.'

'See? I'm a sucker.'

He stared at her. 'All right.'

She looked surprised. 'Yeah?'

'I won't turn you in *yet*. You'll help me go after Toselli. But if you lie again – if you mess with me – I won't bother taking you to the hospital. I'll dump you with the cops.'

'All right,' she said.

'Then take off your clothes.'

She gave him a look.

'I'm not taking you anywhere until I check you for wires. Toselli's run you from every angle. Strip.'

She tried lifting her sweater, but the pain made sweat break from her forehead.

So he did it for her. When she was naked, he ran his fingers up the seams of her pants and sweater. He dropped them on the carpet and checked her shoes. Then he took out his phone again and dialed.

'You bastard,' she said.

But he called Rodman's apartment. When the big man answered, Kelson asked, 'Can you get Cindi to come home from work?'

'What's up?'

'I have Doreen Felbanks. Shot in the ribs.'

'You want to bring her to *my* apartment?'

'She says Toselli forced her to do what she did.'

'And you believe her, why?'

'I'm figuring this out as I go.'

'Best thing you could do is get away.'

'I know that.'

Rodman was silent for a while, then said, 'Why would you want to do this?'

Kelson said, 'Because she's really hot?'

'Not funny. Tell her Cindi and I don't like blood on the rugs.'

Before taking Doreen down the hallway to the elevator, Kelson spread a pack of sliced ham on the kitchen floor for the kittens and filled three bowls with water. Then he tried to get Doreen to take one of his Percocet.

'I don't do that shit,' she said. 'It'll kill you.'

'Like it killed Raima Minhas?' he said.

'Greg did that.'

'No lies,' he said.

'He did it,' she said again. 'I got the pills from Christian – but Greg used them.'

'Fine,' he said, 'go drug-free – let it hurt – die from shock.'

When they rode down and stepped out to the street, Kelson waved at Nuñez's men. They didn't wave back, but the driver started the Buick, and they coasted after Kelson and Doreen as they drove south through the city.

FORTY-EIGHT

When Kelson stopped in front of the Bronzeville apartment building, Rodman came down, lifted Doreen in his arms like a baby, and carried her up the two flights to his door.

Inside, he'd covered the couch with a shower curtain and laid blankets over it. He set her down and gave her a pillow for her head.

'Looks like you've done this before,' Kelson said.

'One mess is like another,' Rodman said.

'Is Cindi here?'

'A couple hours. Short-staffed at the hospital.'

Francisca Cabon and Dominick Stevens stood by the kitchen doorway, keeping away from the wounded woman as if she still could hurt them.

Rodman looked down at her. Her pale forehead was dotted with sweat. 'If you die,' he said, 'I'll throw you off the back porch. Just so you know, that's what we do around here.'

Doreen managed to wink at him. 'Sweet talker.'

'Of course, I could throw you off right now.'

Then he and Kelson spent the afternoon asking her questions.

Toselli trusted just two men, she told them. These men dealt
with the street dealers and, lately, the thugs who strong-armed
pimps and hookers. She had no name for either of the men, though
she'd seen them. One was stocky and black, maybe thirty years
old, with a close-shaved beard. The other was white, with a medium
build, hard features, and black hair streaking gray. Toselli kept
these men at a cold distance, giving them directions over the phone,
exchanging money and drugs in the backseats of cars or through
open car windows.

'Small circle,' Rodman said, 'but a man better have friends in
a time of need.'

Doreen seemed to slip inward to the places in her mind that
haunted her. She mumbled about Christian. She mumbled about
Toselli.

Rodman asked where Toselli might hide, and his soft voice
brought her out of herself. She said Toselli staged his drug sales
from three apartments. She'd gone to one in Edgewater, in a pink
high-rise overlooking the lake.

'How about the others?' Kelson asked.

'Uh-uh,' she said. 'He's para—' A wave of pain seemed to wash
through her, and she looked for a moment like she would vomit.

'Paranoid,' Rodman offered.

She seemed to swallow the pain. 'Uh-huh.'

'Weapons?' Rodman asked.

That smile. 'A lot. He collects them' – then, from inside – 'like
dolls.'

'Yeah, pretty dolls with gunmetal legs,' Kelson said.

They waited until her eyes focused again, then asked about the
people who worked for Toselli. Would they back him in a fight?

She said she didn't know.

Cindi came in as the afternoon darkened into evening. She
brought a bag of antibiotics, bandages, and painkillers. She scowled
at Doreen. Then she filled a syringe with Demerol.

'She doesn't do pain meds,' Kelson said.

Cindi jabbed her with the needle. 'Now she does.'

Cindi flushed the wounds with saline. She pulled dirt from them
with tweezers as if picking for fish bones. She swabbed them with
alcohol. She dressed them with gauze. She said, 'You do know,
baby, you're going to die if you don't get this treated right.'

'Unnh,' Doreen said, as if she'd slipped beyond caring.

That made Cindi smile. 'Demerol cloud,' she said, and she filled a syringe with antibiotics. She injected it into Doreen's flaccid arm, saying to anyone listening, 'Cephalexin bolus. She needs an IV drip, but unless one of you clowns sidelines in hijacking medical supply trucks, she gets what I shoot into her skinny ass. Is that all right with you? I thought so. Now, goodnight to y'all.' She disappeared into the bedroom.

Rodman looked thoughtful. 'I test her patience.'

Doreen's eyes glazed and her breathing slowed. Kelson and Rodman tried to ask more questions, but in the middle of mumbling about a West Side warehouse where she saw Toselli torture a rival drug dealer, she fell asleep.

FORTY-NINE

Kelson and Rodman knew the pink high-rise where Doreen said Toselli based his North Side drug operation. The Edgewater Beach Co-op Apartments used to be a prestige hotel. In its time, Marilyn Monroe and Frank Sinatra stayed there. Then the city dumped a landfill and poured eight lanes of highway where beach umbrellas once shaded cocktail-drinking guests. The hotel went bankrupt, and now the people who lived in the decaying remains dreamed of old elegance but woke to the sounds of rush-hour traffic.

Kelson found an online picture of Toselli that he could show to people who might identify him. Then he and Rodman drove north to the apartment building. When they walked into the sales office, a skinny man in a white turtleneck and thick-framed glasses was turning off his computer for the evening. He gazed up at Rodman from the desk, and his hand floated toward a phone as if he might need help.

In that gentle voice of his, Rodman said, 'We're looking for a friend.'

'Not much of a friend, as it turns out,' Kelson said. 'A real bastard, it turns out.'

'I'm afraid I can't help,' the man said.

Rodman said, 'You don't know that. His name's Toselli. Show him.'

Kelson pulled up Toselli's picture on his cellphone.

The man glanced at the picture. 'I handle sales. I don't deal with tenants.'

'So the guy in the picture *is* a tenant?' Rodman said.

'I'm afraid I've never seen him,' the man said.

'Don't be afraid,' Rodman said. 'Let's turn on your computer and look.'

'I've closed for the day.'

Rodman gave him the gentlest smile. 'Another ten minutes won't hurt, right?'

The man eyed his phone, then the computer. He looked up at Rodman. 'I need to ask you to leave.' But when Rodman reached across the desk and touched the power button on the computer, he jumped back as if Rodman's great arm would uncoil and bare fangs.

'You could say it's a matter of life and death,' Rodman told him.

'Don't hurt me,' the man said.

The computer screen lit up. 'I'm not talking about *yours*,' Rodman said. 'That's the problem – everyone thinks it's all about them. Now sit down.'

The man inched back to the desk.

'See if Toselli has an apartment,' Rodman said.

The man pulled up a database and searched. 'No Toselli,' he said, looking relieved.

Rodman glanced at Kelson. Kelson said, 'Try *Felbanks*.'

'I can't do this,' the man said, but he made the search. Again he looked relieved. 'Nope.'

'Could be a different place,' Kelson said.

'You think?' Rodman said. 'What was Bicho's last name?'

'Rodriguez.'

Without being told, the salesman made a third search. Then he looked like he'd eaten something bad. 'We've got a Rodriguez on the sixth floor.'

'First name?' Rodman asked.

'Gregory.'

'Really?' Kelson said. '*Gregory Rodriguez*? That just sounds wrong.'

Rodman looked at the computer screen for the details. 'You got keys to the units?'

'No,' the man said, too quick.

'Come on . . .'

'I need to close the office,' the man said.

'We only want a peek,' Rodman said.

'I insist.'

'What's another ten minutes?' Rodman asked.

The man said, 'I need to—'

'We prefer to ask nicely.'

They rode to the sixth floor. Then the salesman tried his master key on the door of the apartment he saw on the computer. He looked relieved again when it didn't fit. 'Must've changed the lock,' he said, as if that was that.

But Rodman smashed the doorknob with the meat of his palm. The knob and lock mechanism punched through and fell on the inside carpet.

The salesman said, 'Oh.'

Rodman nudged the door open, and he and Kelson went in.

In the front room, a TV on a wheeled cart played the evening news. There was no other furniture. Kelson turned off the TV and checked the cord. It ran through a timer, set to go on between five o'clock and eight each morning and evening.

'Must comfort the neighbors,' he said, and walked to a bank of windows. Across Lake Shore Drive, the water looked like a slab of slate in the fading light.

The doors to a bathroom and a kitchenette were open. The bedroom door was closed. Kelson checked the kitchen, Rodman the bathroom. Then Rodman went to the closed door.

'No,' Kelson said.

Rodman gave him a look.

Kelson tried the knob and pushed only an inch – until the door resisted. He went back to the TV, unplugged it, and wheeled the cart across the room. He said to the salesman, 'Your tenant's a bastard.' Then he shoved the cart through the door into the bedroom.

A shotgun blasted, and the TV screen burst.

The salesman screamed.

'Not bad,' Kelson said. He reached through the doorway, found a light switch and flipped it. Unsure about other traps, he stared in from the front room. The window shades were down. Metal shelves, stocked with vials of prescription drugs and plastic-wrapped packages, lined the walls. There was no sign of Toselli, no sign that anyone had been in the room recently.

Kelson, Rodman, and the salesman went back into the corridor. A bald man and a graying woman had come out to check on the gunshot. The man scurried into his apartment when he saw Rodman. The woman held her ground. As she complained to the salesman about the disturbance, Kelson called Peters and gave him the apartment address. 'Watch out for trip wires,' he said.

FIFTY

K elson spent the night at Rodman's apartment along with Doreen, Francisca Cabon, and Dominick Stevens. Doreen slept fitfully on the couch, and when Rodman closed the door to the bedroom, the others stretched out on the floor.

At two a.m., Rodman's one-armed friend Marty knocked. He said Nancy and Sue Ellen were safe in their house – lights out, doors locked, no sign of anyone trying to get to them. Police cruisers were passing the house every half hour or so. Two men sent by Stevens were parked up the block. Marty's girlfriend was also keeping watch.

As the sun rose the next morning, Cindi came from the bedroom. Stevens was sleeping on a rug with Francisca nestled in his arms and their baby nestled in hers. Doreen lay awake, staring silently at Kelson, who stared back and said, 'DeMarcus says I'm too trusting. I look too hard for the good in people. I sometimes think I'm just stupid.'

Cindi asked Doreen how she was feeling.

'Like hell,' Doreen said.

Cindi did a quick checkup and said, 'No fever. Maybe you'll live.' She filled a syringe with Demerol.

'I don't do that,' Doreen said.

'Shut up,' Cindi said and stuck her.

'Bitch,' Doreen said.

Cindi filled another syringe with antibiotics and stuck her again.

Kelson stayed on the floor while Cindi went back into the bedroom, put on nurse's scrubs, and left for work. He stayed as Stevens got up to shower and Francisca fed her baby. He watched as Doreen seemed to float away on another Demerol cloud. He said, 'Because, you know, it could be love.' Then he watched as Rodman came from the bedroom and scrambled a dozen eggs.

Before breakfast was ready, Kelson got up and went to the window. The sky hung heavy and gray over the neighboring buildings. In the gauzy morning light, the tenements looked thick and brown. A car and a van passed on the street. A woman walked past, pushing a stroller. A man stepped out from the side of a building – and stared up at Kelson.

'Toselli?' Kelson said.

The man raised a rifle to his shoulder, aimed, and fired.

The window shattered and a bullet passed within an inch of Kelson's head and lodged in the ceiling. Plaster dust rained on him like ash.

Every sane fiber of Kelson's brain told him to drop to the floor. Every properly processing synapse switched from *fight* to *flight*. But the rewiring that enabled him to live alone with two kittens and run an investigation business hadn't been tested in a situation quite like this. His brain all but sparked. He stepped close to the window and yelled at Toselli. 'Two strikes, asshole! A shattered TV and a broken window.'

Toselli pulled the trigger again.

Another bullet flew past Kelson and sank into the ceiling.

Rodman tackled him, mashing him to the floor.

Kelson looked the big man in the eyes so close he could have kissed him and said, 'Three strikes.'

'You stupid son of a bitch,' Rodman said.

'Let me go.'

'You going to yell out the window?'

'No.'

'Truth?'

'Always.'

Rodman got off him. Kelson crawled to the coffee table where he'd left his KelTec overnight. He went back to the window and fired three times down at the street where Toselli had stood.

The bullets pocked the concrete sidewalk. Toselli was gone.

Rodman would've broken Kelson's arm if Kelson hadn't dropped the gun.

'This is what gives my neighborhood a bad name,' Rodman said.

FIFTY-ONE

Ten minutes later, Rodman and Kelson sat at the kitchen table. Dominick Stevens was packing his bag and his briefcase, getting the hell out of a place Rodman falsely promised would keep him safe. The baby cried on Francisca's shoulder, and she yelled at Stevens, calling him a *cobarde* – a pussy, a coward – for running at the first gunshot.

'*Two* gunshots,' he said. 'Five, if you count this idiot's. And I'm not running. I'm walking away. You should come with me.'

'Where to?' she said. 'Your house? That man's been there. My apartment? He's been there too.'

Rodman looked at Kelson. 'He must've followed us back from Edgewater last night. I watched but didn't see him.'

'Someone from his crew could've followed. Could've been anyone.'

'Unless Doreen tipped him,' Rodman said. He went to her. She was floating – somewhere.

'Nah,' said Kelson.

Rodman searched her until he found her phone. He checked call history and shook his head. 'Must've followed us from Edgewater,' he said again.

Stevens said he was going to his office. He would surround himself with people who could protect him. He would stay in touch.

'You're stupid to go,' Rodman said.

'Stupid to go, stupid to stay. Right now, nothing looks smart,' Stevens said.

'*Cobarde*,' Francisca said.

Rodman made a call, and, an hour after Stevens left, Marty came back, dragging a sheet of plywood up the stairs. Rodman nailed it over the shot-out window and then showed the little man to his and Cindi's bedroom.

'Sleep with a finger on it,' Rodman said. 'Francisca will let you know if Toselli comes back. If Doreen's painkillers wear off and she gives you trouble, knock her out however you want.'

The little man slipped off his shoes and lay face up on the bed. He rested a pistol on his belly, looping a finger through the trigger guard. When Kelson and Rodman went out the front door – guns drawn, eyes on every hiding spot below them – Marty was breathing deep and easy, already dreaming of his big girlfriend or whatever a tough little man like him dreamed.

Kelson and Rodman drove north to Nancy's house. The neighborhood was quiet, her driveway empty. They circled the block before pulling to the curb. While Rodman waited in the car, Kelson went to the door and knocked. No one answered, so he let himself in. Every time he'd come to the house since Nancy kicked him out, the contents seemed to have shifted a little, as if spitting him out bite by bite. The weekend after he moved, Nancy rearranged the furniture in the living room – not that she ever complained about where it was when they lived together. Now he put the sofa back where it belonged. 'Haunted,' he said. 'By me.'

He needed to be sure that all was right, as he needed to check his pistol magazine even when he knew it was loaded, and so he climbed the stairs. Sue Ellen had left her bed unmade, the pink sheet and blanket kicked to the foot, the stuffed animal monkey she'd had since she was two years old face down. He went in, tucked the sheets, and propped the monkey on the pillow. Pencil drawings of Payday and Painter's Lane were tacked to the wall above the head of the bed – each of the kittens sketched with a sure, steady hand. 'When did you learn to do that?' Kelson asked.

He went to the bedroom he used to share with Nancy. It looked just as it did when he last slept there. Even with all the danger and confusion, even with the gaze he'd exchanged with Doreen a couple of hours ago – maybe *because* of it – he felt a pang. 'Ouch,' he said. He went to Nancy's side of the bed and sat. He opened the nightstand drawer. Along with a box of Kleenex and a bottle of Motrin, there was a hairbrush. Kelson pulled a tangle of hair from the bristles, smelled it, and stuck it in his pocket.

He went to the other side of the bed. The familiar comfort flooded back. He said, 'What I would do—' then stopped himself again. 'For what?' He opened the nightstand drawer. Like a wave withdrawing and washing in again, nausea rolled over his comfort. There was a man's watch – a stranger's – and a box of Trojan Pleasure Condoms – two of the packets, bright as bubble gum, ripped open and empty.

He grabbed the watch. A Movado, nicer than his own. He crammed it in with the ball of hair.

He went downstairs and out the front door. His Dodge Challenger idled at the curb. He climbed in and stared out the front windshield.

'Anything?' Rodman asked.

'Yeah, a mistake,' Kelson said. 'And a watch.' He fished it out of his pocket and handed it to Rodman. 'I stole it.'

Rodman looked it over, front and back. 'I could get a hundred for it on the street.'

'Yeah, do that. Take Cindi out for dinner.'

'You look sick.'

'I feel it.'

Rodman considered him. 'You're divorced, you know.'

'Yeah.'

'That means she can sleep with anyone she wants.'

'I know.'

'You can too.' Rodman considered him some more. 'When you first saw Doreen Felbanks, you wanted to, right?'

'The first time, yeah.'

'But not now.'

'That would be pretty screwed-up, huh?'

'Really? You still want her? Yeah, that's screwed-up. But there's no accounting for desire.'

'She has the eyes of someone who's seen pain. I've seen it too.'

'So you like her eyes, huh?' Rodman said.

'And have you checked out the rest of her?'

FIFTY-TWO

They decided to talk to Dominick Stevens, and so they drove toward his real-estate office. But Stevens beat them to the check-in. Rodman's phone rang, and Stevens told him, 'I've got a couple more addresses for Toselli.' He gave him one for an apartment on Diversey at the edge of Lincoln Park and another for a townhouse in Dearborn Park, south of the Loop. 'I have property records and databases for co-ops and rental properties,' he said. 'I got to thinking, if he bought the Edgewater place as Gregory Rodriguez, maybe he bought or rented other places that way.'

Kelson and Rodman headed down the lakefront to a wide seven-story building. The redbrick front was scrubbed clean, though AC units stuck out of windows like warts.

Kelson pulled into a loading zone, and he and Rodman got out. The glass front door was locked and secure. Kelson rang the buzzer for the super.

A man's crackling voice answered through the intercom, and Rodman told him they'd come to make an inquiry.

'What kind of inquiry?' the super asked.

'The confidential kind,' Rodman said.

The super said he had no time for confidential inquiries.

'Do you have time to fix the glass in your front door?' Rodman asked.

The super said nothing, so Kelson hit the buzzer again and asked, 'Does Gregory Rodriguez live here?'

The lock clicked, and they stepped into a bright foyer. Then a door at the far end of the lobby opened, and a thick-legged man came out wearing green coveralls. He was about half Rodman's size but didn't look intimidated. 'What do you know about Gregory Rodriguez?' he asked.

'He's a bastard,' Kelson said.

The super glanced from one to the other and decided on Rodman. 'What do you want with him?'

'We need to talk is all,' Rodman said, gentle, 'if you'll let us up to his apartment. He rents here, doesn't he?'

'He *did*. Third floor, rear. When'd you see him last?'

Kelson started to answer, but Rodman talked over him. 'He moved out?'

The super shook his head. 'Apartment fire last night. Burned the walls. Burned the carpet. Holes in the ceiling. No one hurt, but it's a miracle.'

Kelson and Rodman exchanged a look.

'How'd it start?' Kelson asked.

'That's what I want to ask Mr Rodriguez,' the man said. 'The fire inspector does too. Rodriguez has rented here for three years, and you know what? When the fire started, the apartment was empty. Just some metal shelves. Nothing in the kitchen. No toilet paper unless it burned.'

'He's cleaning up after himself,' Kelson said.

Rodman said, 'We need to see.'

The super shook his head. 'Fire marshal closed it. Plywood over the door.'

'You can nail it back up when we're done,' Rodman said.

'You're a funny man,' the super said.

Rodman went to the elevator and pushed the button.

'Should I send the police up?' the super asked. ''Cause they asked me to call if anyone came around about Rodriguez or the fire. They should be here any moment.'

Rodman scratched his chin with a big finger.

Kelson shrugged. 'Could be lying. Probably telling the truth.'

So Rodman said to the super, 'Been nice talking to you.' He and Kelson went out through the foyer.

They drove around the corner, crossed through a parking lot, and pulled into the alley behind the building. Scorch marks licked up the brick side from a broken third-floor window. 'He's scared,' Rodman said. 'He could've burned down the place. Could've killed a lot of people.'

'That doesn't seem to be a problem for him,' Kelson said.

They drove downtown then, expecting more ashes at Toselli's Dearborn Park townhouse. The Dearborn development covered an old train yard south of what once was Dearborn Station. It included high-rise and mid-rise apartments and little streets lined with bleak concrete two-story cubes the developers sold as single-family units.

Kelson and Rodman drove into one of the paved courts leading to a cluster of single units and pulled into a parking spot outside the address Stevens gave them. White lace curtains hung over long rectangular windows in front. A spring wreath hung on the door.

'Huh,' Kelson said.

'Yeah, me too,' said Rodman.

They got out, Kelson with the KelTec in his belt, and walked around the building to the back. More long rectangular windows with lace curtains faced a gated terrace. On one side of a set of French doors, there was a little tiered fountain. On the other side, there was a garden statue of a frog on a lily pad.

'He doesn't strike me as the kind,' Kelson said.

They went back to the front and knocked on the door. Kelson kept his pistol in his waistband but touched the grip under his jacket. Rodman stepped back to the front walk and watched the windows.

The woman who opened the door looked sixty-five, maybe older. She wore blue jeans and a gray sweater embroidered with a daisy. Her short hair was fading from blonde to white. She gave Kelson a pleasant smile and asked what he wanted.

'That's a long list,' he said.

'I'm sorry?'

He said, 'Are you a relation of Greg Toselli?'

'Of course,' she said, eyeing him warily. 'I'm his mom. Are you his friends?'

'That's complicated. Fifteen years ago—'

'Stick to the task,' Rodman said. He scanned the front of the house.

'Greg doesn't live here,' the woman said. 'He has a house in—'

'Schaumburg,' Kelson said. 'Not anymore. The cops raided it yesterday.'

With that smile, she might invite him in for cookies. 'You're mistaken. Greg's a policeman.'

'Not for long,' Kelson said.

The woman seemed amused, and that should have tipped Kelson off. But it didn't matter – at that moment, Rodman charged toward the door, shouting, 'Upstairs window.'

The woman moved to the side, out of the way. But then she

had a revolver in her hand – where she got it Kelson couldn't say.
It was a little .22, but big enough to stop Rodman if she fired it.
Kelson slipped the KelTec from his waistband and stepped inside.
Before the woman could shoot, he held the gun barrel against the
side of her head.

He said, 'Don't.'

As Rodman reached the upstairs landing, glass shattered from
a window. Shards rained on the pavement outside where Kelson
had stood seconds before.

Then a man jumped from the window, hitting the concrete,
rolling, and staggering to his feet.

Kelson shouted at him, 'Toselli.'

Toselli spun. He held a big, black automatic, something
between a pistol and a rifle, with a short barrel and big magazine.
He aimed at Kelson.

But Kelson pulled the woman close, shielding himself.

For a long moment, they stood frozen, Toselli pointing his gun
at his mother and Kelson, Kelson holding his gun against the
woman's head.

Then Rodman started down the stairs.

And Toselli turned and ran.

The woman squeezed the trigger and shot at no one in particular,
the bullet going into the ceiling. So Kelson smashed the woman's
wrist with his pistol grip, and her little revolver clattered to the floor.

Kelson and Rodman ran to the front door.

Toselli was gone.

FIFTY-THREE

K elson made the woman sit at the kitchen table, and Rodman
hovered over her. Her wrist was swollen, but she didn't
seem to mind. She dropped her cookie-baking smile and
looked as hard as a street thug or beat cop. When Kelson started
asking questions, she admitted Toselli let her live in the downstairs
half of the townhouse, while he kept the upstairs bedrooms locked
and off limits.

So Rodman went back upstairs and kicked in a locked door. As in the Edgewater co-op, metal shelves lined the walls, full of prescription opiates and plastic-wrapped packs. A half dozen cartons of drugs lay on the floor.

When Rodman came down, Kelson was sitting across the table from the woman. Rodman turned a kitchen chair backward and straddled it, holding his big, gentle face a foot from the woman's. His eyelids hung half-closed. He asked, 'Where'd he go?'

'Piss off,' she said.

That made Rodman smile. 'My friend here is kindhearted,' he said, 'a real gentleman. But he gets distracted. If it was just me, I would make you eat your gun.' He spoke softly. Nothing could be more terrifying.

She said, 'You don't scare me.'

'That's good,' he said. 'Scared people make bad decisions. They're squirrels on a highway. We want you to think clearly. Add it up. How far can your boy run with us coming after him? Do you want him hurt bad – or worse? The sooner we get him, the better.'

'Piss off,' she said.

Rodman rose from the chair. He balled a fist and cocked his arm back ten inches or so – he would need no more to crush her skull. His chest seemed to swell, and his gentle face became fierce.

She spat at him.

He let his eyelids fall closed, as if to meditate the possibilities the situation offered. Then he opened them and said, 'You're a tough chick.' He grabbed her by the sweater and lifted her from her chair.

Suspending her in the air, he said to Kelson, 'Check the rest of the place.'

Kelson ransacked it. Ever since Bicho shot him, he hated messes, but this wasn't *his* mess. 'Feels . . . weirdly good,' he said. He emptied drawers and cabinets on to the floor, kicking around the contents as he looked for information about Toselli. In a drawer by the phone in the TV room, he found a tattered address book. In a cabinet under the TV, he found three photo albums. He left behind piles of notepads, bills and receipts, spent batteries, ballpoint pens, playing cards, Bic lighters, the souvenirs and garbage of a lifetime. Upstairs, he emptied more cabinets. He upended cardboard boxes from a closet. He pulled down Toselli's metal shelves.

When he returned to the kitchen, he set the address book and photo albums on the table. He paged through the addresses, expecting little and mostly getting it. Under *I*, though, he found an old address and phone number for Inez Rodriguez. He showed the woman the entry. 'Your daughter, right? It's got to hurt,' he said. 'You don't erase a name like this. You don't cross it out. That would be like burying her again.'

She gazed at it but said nothing.

'Greg loved her,' he said. 'Too much or too little or in the wrong ways. He couldn't save her or Alejandro.'

The woman reached as though she would caress Inez's name, but she tried to snatch the book from his hand.

Kelson jerked it away.

Under *R*, he found a listing for Henrico Rodriguez. He showed her again. 'Who's this?'

When she still said nothing, Rodman told her, 'Fight the fights that matter. This isn't one of them. Who's Henrico?'

She gave him a hard look and said, 'My first husband's brother. I haven't talked to him in ten years.'

'Would Greg go to him if he's on the run?' Kelson asked.

Nothing.

He tore out the page and put it in a pocket with the hair from Nancy's brush.

When he finished the address book, he leafed through the photo albums. The first included pictures of the woman's own childhood, teenage years, and early adulthood, ending with shots of her, a brown-skinned man, and a baby girl. He showed her a picture of the baby. 'Inez?'

Nothing.

The second album continued from the first. It included pictures of the woman with another man – a short-haired, stocky white guy with a mischievous smile. In two shots, he wore a police uniform. After the second of those shots, she'd pasted a *Tribune* article about the death of Doug Toselli nineteen years ago when a car crashed into his cruiser at a stoplight. Next to the article she'd pasted the dry remains of a pressed white rose. 'Yeah,' Kelson said, 'it always hurts.'

The pictures of Greg Toselli in the album showed him from the time he was a baby until he was about twelve years old – crawling on a rug, grinning at a birthday party, playing baseball, chopping wood outside a vacation cabin, riding a bike on a suburban street. 'Yep,' Kelson said, and opened the third album. The woman had abandoned it about halfway through. At that point, Toselli looked sixteen or seventeen, old enough to sit in the driver's seat of a green sedan. Most of the other shots of him seemed to come from the cabin where he had chopped wood in the earlier album. Shirtless and wearing cut-off jeans, he pulled the ripcord on an Evinrude outboard on an aluminum fishing boat. He suntanned on a dock. He chopped more wood.

Kelson showed the woman the one with him by the woodpile. 'Where's this?'

Nothing.

'Kind of a getaway, right?' he said. 'A vacation house? A place to escape to when life's crazy?'

She stared at him.

'Maybe somewhere you'd go if the game you were playing turned against you and you needed to hide?'

'Piss off,' she said.

'Now, now,' Rodman said.

'Piss off.'

So Rodman lifted her from her chair once more and said to Kelson, 'Try again?'

Twenty minutes later, Kelson returned with a deed to a property on Keshena Lake two hundred miles north in Wisconsin. Kelson told the woman, 'You can let Greg know when you talk to him that the cabin is out if he's running.'

Rodman said, 'Funny in a country as big as this, there're so few places to hide.'

'Piss off,' she said, the only advice she seemed capable of giving. But as they left the house, she shouted after them, 'I lost his daddy and Inez and Alejandro. I won't lose him too.'

FIFTY-FOUR

As they drove back through the Loop, Kelson said, 'Poor woman.'

Rodman gave him a long, flat look. 'Next time you want to sympathize with someone like that, take away her gun first – before she shoots it.'

'She missed,' Kelson said. 'Should we try Henrico?'

'Nah, she'll warn Toselli we know about him. Same as the lake house.'

'You think it's run and hide for him now?'

'Where's he going to run?'

'He's got to have somewhere.'

'He seems more like the kind who fights if he gets a chance,' Rodman said.

'Does he go to Stevens's office? Back to your apartment? Nancy's house?'

'Or anywhere he thinks he can sneak up behind you,' Rodman said.

'Let's check Stevens.'

But as they drove toward the real-estate office, Rodman's phone rang again.

Francisca was on the other end. 'She's got a fever,' she said. 'And she's talking crazy about that boy Christian again. She thinks he's here with her.'

'What does Marty say?'

'I woke him, but he says she isn't his problem. If she tries to kill me, I should scream and he'll help. If she's just dying, I should let him sleep.'

'Is she dying?'

'I don't know,' she said. 'I think so.'

'I'll be right there,' he said, and hung up. Then he told Kelson to turn around and go to Rush Medical. He dialed another number, and soon he was persuading Cindi to steal more cephalexin and meet them at the emergency entrance. When he hung up again, he said, 'That girlfriend of yours is a problem.'

'Don't call her my girlfriend,' Kelson said.

'Sure as hell isn't mine,' Rodman said.

Forty minutes later, Kelson dropped Rodman and Cindi at their Bronzeville apartment. Then he headed for the Stevens Group building alone. Along the way, he debated Toselli's virtues and failings.

'He put his lips on my bloody mouth to resuscitate me.'

'He framed me and he's trying to kill me.'

'He's a good family man. Of sorts.'

'He's a killer.'

'He loved Inez.'

'He pumps addicts full of stolen drugs.'

'He rushes into a bust in front of everyone else. He jumps from a second-story window and rolls to his feet.'

'He uses his strength to hurt people.'

Kelson recalled the Frisbee and beer Toselli brought him at the rehab center. He recalled the grin on Toselli's face when Sue Ellen first called him Uncle Greg. He recalled Toselli teasing her, saying, *I shoot little girls. Pow! Pow!* He recalled Sue Ellen screaming with laughter. He recalled Raima Minhas's death grimace.

As he pulled to the curb at the Stevens Group building and climbed out of his car, his debate got so heated that he didn't see the man sitting in the silver SUV in front of him. He also didn't see the big, black automatic on the man's lap. But when the man raised the gun and aimed it through an open window, he saw it.

Kelson's brain cross-wired, and before he could shout Toselli's name, Toselli touched the trigger and bullets burst from the muzzle.

Kelson jerked away and dropped to the pavement. He rolled on the concrete and pulled his KelTec from his belt. As Toselli opened his door and climbed out – leading with the automatic – Kelson squeezed two shots.

The rounds sank into the vinyl inside the door.

Toselli dove back into the SUV. He started the engine and the SUV jumped from the curb. It went ten feet and stopped. He shifted into reverse and punched the gas.

The SUV flew back toward Kelson.

Kelson rolled – too slow, it seemed, for the spitting tires. He squeezed the trigger again and again, shooting high into the sky, then into the SUV undercarriage. The skidding tires, the shots from the KelTec, the surrounding traffic – everything went silent in his ears. He was all reflex, his senses as dead as they would be if the SUV had run over his neck.

But he rolled clear. He aimed his pistol at the exterior rearview mirror, with Toselli's face staring at him. He squeezed the trigger, and the mirror exploded.

Then Toselli shifted again and the SUV shot away.

'Huh,' Kelson said.

He scrambled to his feet and ran to his car.

FIFTY-FIVE

Kelson chased Toselli west on Division, slid around a corner and then another and then veered across oncoming traffic to a boulevard, heading north. The street cut through a strip park a half mile long. Toselli charged toward Logan Square, a plot of dead grass and leafless trees dumped in the middle of the boulevard, requiring Kelson to hit the brakes and slide around corner after corner, sideswiping a white Miata, all to stay a block behind an SUV that shouldn't have been able to outrace a Dodge Challenger under any conditions.

They went past tennis courts, an auto-glass store, a Mexican *carniceria*, beaten-down businesses, and beaten-down houses, then under the Kennedy Expressway and north and still north. Kelson shouted at Toselli through the windshield, 'You got a plan? Why not pull over and shoot it out like any normal psychopath?' Toselli drove to the far north of the city, past banks and drugstores, past Maria's Bridal Boutique and A-Z Food Mart & Wireless. Then he cut east toward the Ravenswood neighborhood where Bicho once lived – Francisca Cabon too, until Toselli snuck into her apartment and tried to kill her and her baby.

'Ahhh,' Kelson shouted, as if that meant anything.

But Toselli cut north again before Ravenswood, jumping a curb into Ronan Park, which was another strip of dead grass and leaf-less trees, gray and brown, hugging the banks of the Chicago River. Kelson followed his SUV on to a winding jogging trail. They flew past a bicyclist and an Asian woman with a cane and a German Shepherd. When the trail emerged at a street, Toselli hit the gas and blasted through cross traffic.

'Goddamned squirrel,' Kelson shouted, and hit the brakes – then he took his foot from the brakes and hit the gas too. He clipped the back of a van in the near lane and threaded between two cars in the far lane, then bounced back on to the park trail.

He kept the gas hard to the floor. The ragged branches, the river water, the signs warning against loud music and alcohol consumption blended and blurred. Toselli came up fast on another bicycle, and a moment later Kelson flew past it, screaming. When the trail cut sharp, Toselli's tires skidded from the concrete on to the grass, bounced across a baseball diamond, and found the trail again. Kelson followed. They bumped down the curb on to another street and jumped the curb on the other side.

At Peterson Avenue – four lanes cutting from the Interstate toward Lake Michigan – the park trail forked. One path went through an underpass toward the northern city limit. The other went up to the street. Toselli took the path to the street, which was jammed with cars and trucks. He slammed on his brakes. Kelson hit his brakes too, but his car slid into the back of Toselli's SUV, nudging it into the traffic.

As cars and trucks stopped and horns blew, Toselli nosed across the eastbound lanes, and Kelson inched behind him. Then Toselli floored the gas again, fishtailed on the concrete, and headed west across the river.

A van with ladders strapped to a roof rack was speeding west-bound, and when the driver saw Toselli's SUV lurch in front of him and Kelson's car start to follow, he cut his wheel. The van slid sideways, its tires scraping pavement, then tipped over and spun on its door panels. It came to a rest in front of Kelson.

Kelson shifted into reverse, but traffic filled the road behind him. The van driver climbed up through the passenger's side door, looking ready to kill. Other drivers got out of cars and trucks.

Kelson rolled down his window. A hundred words formed on his lips. A single sound combining all of them came from his window. Everyone paused. Kelson cut his steering wheel and hit the gas.

His car shot into the eastbound lane. The other drivers leaped out of the way, and Kelson went a half block down and rounded a corner. He zigzagged through side streets, cut across parking lots, and came to a rest a mile away in an alley sided by detached garages, chain-link fences, and garbage bins.

He cut the engine and listened to himself breathe – his throat ragged, his blood pumping hard, his skin slick with sweat. Then he swore and laughed at the top of his lungs.

Toselli had escaped, it was true. Maybe he would run now and keep running. Maybe Kelson would never see him again. The thrill Kelson felt was more intense than any he'd ever felt, the adrenaline spike higher. For the first time since Bicho shot him, he felt fully alive. He laughed, and he said, 'The goddamned man wants to kill me and he makes me live.' For a moment, that thought sobered him. 'I suppose I owe him.' Then he laughed again.

He sat still for five minutes.

He heard no sirens.

He saw no cruisers patrolling for a hit-and-run driver.

Toselli didn't come to the alley with an automatic blazing from an open window.

'*Maybe*,' Kelson said, though he didn't know what about.

FIFTY-SIX

K elson drove back to his apartment. He felt an overwhelming desire to see Sue Ellen. But if he rushed into her school and sucked her into his arms, he would scare everyone, especially her. If he called ahead and asked the front office to pull her from class, telling them it was an emergency . . . no, that would do her no good. So he went to see the kittens. To feed them. To pet them.

He knew the danger of easing up after a chase like the one that had just ended, so he circled the block twice before parking. The blue Buick was back, parked up the street, now with just one of

Nuñez's men in it, sleeping behind the steering wheel. The second time Kelson passed, he tapped his horn and watched the man startle awake.

He parked and kept his hand on his KelTec as he crossed from the lot to the building lobby. He checked the stairwell before touching the elevator call button. When the elevator doors opened at his floor, he slipped across the hall to the opposite wall.

'*Maybe*,' he said.

He went down the hall, felt his doorknob, and let himself in. Then another weird sound came from his chest.

Toselli sat at the kitchen table, his hand on his automatic, a finger on the trigger.

When Kelson started to draw back through the door, Toselli brought up the gun and aimed at Kelson's chest. When Kelson reached for his KelTec, Toselli shook his head and tightened his finger over the trigger.

So Kelson stepped into the apartment, leaving the door half open, and said, 'You're really bad about people's private space, aren't you?'

'Close the door,' Toselli said.

'I don't think so.' Kelson went closer.

'You want to drag your neighbors into this? You know what I'll do to anyone who gets in the way. Close the goddamned door.'

Instead, Kelson went to the table and sat across from him. 'Bastard,' he said.

Toselli gave him a vicious smile. 'You can't help yourself, can you?'

'Maggot-headed, shit-sniffing, backstabbing, lying bastard.'

'You done?'

Kelson said, 'You could've been my brother. Even *more* than my brother, you two-faced, snake-in-the-grass bastard.'

Toselli applauded. 'You been studying up for this conversation? Reading a thesaurus?'

'I *died* in that alley with Bicho,' Kelson said.

'No,' Toselli said, 'you should've but didn't.'

'I died. You pumped breath into my lungs.'

'Fine.'

'My blood on your lips. My brains and bone. My . . . dirt. You put your mouth in it. Dirty as licking my ass.'

'Not the metaphor I would use. But you're welcome. You got a couple of years out of the deal.'

'You don't get it. You should've let me die. Then I wouldn't have to look at your backstabbing, ass-licking face.'

'You're a resentful little man, Kelson.'

'You don't get that either. I've got nothing but love. That's what hurts so much. I even love a bastard like you. That's why it's so hard to have to kill you.'

A laugh burst from Toselli's chest. Something like joy. '*You*? Kill *me*?'

'I hate to do it,' Kelson said.

Toselli held his gun as if he would shoot him. 'Anything else?'

'Yeah, you were a bad uncle to Bicho. No better than a child rapist.'

'You don't know when to stop,' Toselli said, and now he showed real anger.

'I don't even know *how* to stop,' Kelson said, and with the passing of his impulsive outburst he felt fatigued. 'You've had plenty of chances to kill me, but you've played this out slow. Tried to make it hurt. You know, I didn't mean to kill Bicho.'

'But he's dead, isn't he?' Toselli said.

'I don't remember doing it. I've tried to put it together. It's like that one memory is in the part of me that got shot away.'

'*I* know what happened. You killed Alejandro.'

'Who shot first?'

Toselli tipped his head to the side. 'If I said Alejandro, that would give you peace, wouldn't it? But if I said *you* shot first – if I swore to it – what would it do to you?'

'It would kill me again,' Kelson said, 'if it was true.'

'That's funny, isn't it? I get to decide what's true. I saw it happen. I saw you shoot each other. I could flip a coin and decide. Heads or tails – you want to choose?'

'I thought you were my friend.'

'You've always been easily led. A good soldier but a bad captain.'

Payday crawled out from under the bed, followed by Painter's Lane. They seemed to sense that something was wrong, but Payday came to Kelson and rubbed against his ankle. When Kelson picked her up, Toselli snapped his gun toward him again as if he was pulling a trick. Kelson put the kitten on the table and petted her.

Toselli looked disgusted. 'What if I gave you a choice? I could let you kill me *or* I would tell you the truth about the shooting – who shot first, whose fault it was. Would you kill me without knowing?'

'In an instant.'

This time, Toselli didn't laugh. 'Put your gun on the table.'

'Why?'

'Because I'll blow a hole in your chest if you don't.'

Kelson pulled the KelTec from his belt and laid it next to Payday.

'How many rounds in it?' Toselli said.

'Six, I think.'

'Take out five,' Toselli said.

'Why?'

'Just fucking do it.'

Kelson did, standing the bullets on the table.

'Chamber the last round.'

Kelson did.

'Now aim at me, but when you do, keep this in mind – if you shoot me, you'll never know what happened between you and Alejandro. If you don't shoot, I'll tell you the truth. I swear.'

'You're insane,' said Kelson.

'Yeah, and you're stupid. Do it.'

So Kelson aimed his pistol at Toselli's head. He held his finger on the trigger and tested its tension.

Toselli stared him in the eyes. He laughed at him. 'You don't even know if I would tell the truth. Maybe I lied after Alejandro died when I told Dan Peters you shot first. Or maybe I described it exactly as it happened. All you know is I'm promising to tell you the truth if you put down the gun. Is a promise enough? The promise of a man who set you up and led you along? But the alternative is nothing. No promise. No chance of knowing. That's what you get if you pull the trigger.'

'Shut up,' Kelson said. His brain cross-wired again, telling him to shoot, telling him never to shoot.

Toselli said, 'I'll whisper it to you. After all this time – all this uncertainty – that seems right, doesn't it? This is just between you and me. Our secret. I'll whisper—'

'I said, *shut up*.' Kelson's finger felt oily on the trigger.

'But once I tell you, you don't get another chance, you understand? That's it. End of the game. You lose. I win.'

The KelTec shook in Kelson's hand. Pulling the trigger seemed impossible. 'You're suicidal,' Kelson said.

'I don't think so.'

Kelson squared the gun barrel on Toselli's chest.

For a moment, Toselli looked uncertain. Then he said, 'All right.' He grinned and stood up. 'Put it down.' When Kelson kept aiming the gun, he waited, as if he had the time.

Kelson slammed the pistol on to the table.

'Right,' Toselli said. He came around to Kelson's side and stood behind him. He touched the muzzle of his automatic to the back of Kelson's head, leaned in so close he could bite him, and whispered, 'My life's over now too, isn't it? Where do I go? What do I do?'

'Tell me who shot first,' Kelson said.

'When I kill you, it'll be like killing myself. In that way, you're right – you'll be killing me too. But it's over for me either way. I've been a cop long enough to know there's no place for me to go.'

'I don't care,' Kelson said. 'Tell me.'

Toselli twisted the gun barrel, as if he would screw it into Kelson's scalp. 'Or I could just shoot you now. Your last thought would be knowing that you didn't know.'

'Tell me.'

'I could—'

A voice came from the hallway outside the apartment. 'Dad?' Little knuckles knocked on the half-open door. Sue Ellen stepped inside.

Toselli reflexively drew the automatic from Kelson's head. He moved around the side of the table and sat, tucking the gun in his lap. Kelson snatched up the KelTec and held it under the table. Kelson's five bullets still stood on end, side by side, an obscene little sculpture.

Sue Ellen ignored it. She saw Toselli and grinned. 'Uncle Greg.' She ran for a hug.

He gave her one, awkwardly. 'Hey, kiddo.'

'Stay away from Uncle Greg,' Kelson said, and when she looked confused, 'He's a bastard and a—'

'*Dad* . . .' she said, but they'd kidded around with Toselli ever since she was a seven-year-old. She scooped the kitten off the tabletop. 'Payday! Did you meet my kittens, Uncle Greg?'

'Uncle Greg doesn't like kittens,' Kelson said. 'He doesn't like nice people. He doesn't like nice things.'

'That's silly,' Sue Ellen said. She brought Payday to Toselli. 'You like *me*, don't you?'

Toselli looked as if he would vomit. He lifted his automatic from his lap and aimed it at Sue Ellen. 'Yeah, honey,' he said, 'I like you.'

Kelson would have shot Toselli under the table to protect Sue Ellen. He would have shot up half the city if he needed to. But a rumbling came from the hallway, and four cops dressed in SWAT gear burst into the apartment. They carried assault rifles and aimed them at Toselli. The lead cop told him to drop his weapon. All four moved close enough to shred him if he disobeyed.

Toselli glanced at them as if unsure. Then he laid his gun on the floor and said, 'Hey, guys, we're all friends, right?' He raised his hands over his head.

FIFTY-SEVEN

Peters wouldn't let Kelson watch Toselli's interview in person, but after Toselli pulled his signature move on a rookie outside the interview room and strutted out of the station with a service pistol shoved into the kid's ribs, Peters let him see the video recording.

'She was dying,' Toselli said to the camera, 'I mean, raking the skin off her face with her fingernails, she needed it so bad. Her husband had just OD'd. Good guy when he wasn't high. Good father to Alejandro. Inez always counted on him to score for her. You know, I couldn't watch her do that to herself. I said I'd take care of her. So I took care of her.'

Peters gave him a blank face and used a nonjudgmental tone, though Toselli knew the routine. 'So you helped yourself to some crack – to help out your big sis?'

'She was into skag by then. But yeah, that's more or less it. Easy to rip off a little after a bust.'

'But you didn't stop at a little,' Peters said.

Toselli had waved away the offer of a lawyer. He knew better than to talk without one, but he also knew better than to think one would do any good. So he acted as if he wanted to cooperate, as if he wanted to come clean.

'My sister had friends,' he said. 'Their friends had friends. A little wouldn't do.'

'Junkies are a friendly group.'

'They've got a shared interest,' Toselli said.

'Shared needles too?'

'Inez already had Hep C when I started stealing for her. She was dying. I eased it for her.'

'I suppose you've got to self-justify or you'd put a bullet in your head.' Even in a seasoned cop like Peters, anger sometimes bled through a blank face.

'Plenty of days when I wanted to do that,' Toselli said.

'So you became a big-time dealer. How about Alejandro?'

'I swore to Inez I would take care of him. I didn't want him in the game. But he was like her – he was already in it when he came to stay with me. He'd nicked from her stash since he was like eleven. Mostly he sold it to the older boys – at first for soda money, later for sneakers and phones – the shit kids like.'

'Why'd you kick him out?'

'I gave him a choice. Cut the dealing or leave. He left.'

'But then you supplied him anyway.'

'He wasn't going to stop. He could get it from me, or he could get it from Chilito Nuñez, who would beat him to death if he came in late or short on cash and would cheat him anyway because Alejandro was just a boy. I told Inez I'd watch over him.'

'Do the excuses help?'

'Call it what you want, he was safer getting it from me.'

'Until Sam Kelson shot him in the chest.'

'Worst day of my life. Worse than when Inez died. When Kelson went into the alley with him, he wasn't supposed to be armed. Department rules. Too much risk to Kelson. I set up the plan so there'd be no gun. Alejandro would rob the drug-buy money from him and escape out my end of the alley. No one would get hurt. I would fuck up the buy-and-bust op and laugh my ass off because I took department money. But Kelson brought a gun.'

'So you decided to square things with him? Set him up. Wreck him. Kill him.'

'I owed it to Inez. I owed it to Alejandro.'

'And you forced Doreen Felbanks to do the dirty work for you?'

'I had to stay out of sight. I figured I might as well put a pretty face on it.'

'How about Dominick Stevens? Why gun for him?'

'He betrayed my nephew with Francisca. Fucking her behind his back. Alejandro never even knew.'

'Why'd you save Kelson in the alley when Alejandro shot him? You could've let him bleed to death.'

'I ask myself that all the time. Alejandro was dead. I saw that. I mean, he had a hole where his heart was. And Kelson was dying. I could've let him go. No one would've known. It could've gone either way. Instinct kicked in. Principles. I saved him. I guess I'm a good cop.'

'Tell yourself that as you sit in jail.'

'I know who I am,' Toselli said. 'I don't expect you to get it. But I'll tell you this, by the time the ambulance pulled out of the alley with Kelson in it, I'd decided to kill him. I would make him hurt. I'd take away any sympathy people felt for him. I'd humiliate him. If I could, I'd drive him crazy. Then I'd shoot him. I'd put a hole where his heart was. You know why?'

'Because you've got a sick mind?'

'Because I defend the people in my life. My sister. My nephew. I defend them the way only a good man does.'

The rookie was supposed to handcuff Toselli before taking him from the interview room. Regulations required it. Common sense did. 'But he's a cop, for Christ's sake,' the rookie said later from his hospital bed. 'You don't cuff another cop, do you?'

As the rookie led him from the interview, Toselli grabbed the kid's throat with one hand and pulled the pistol from his holster with the other. He held the gun to the rookie's temple. Although he made the move silently in the middle of the busy Homicide Room, the whole room seemed to hush.

Then a detective emerged from the closest office with a gun drawn. He stepped close, held the gun about five inches from Toselli's head, and said, 'Nope.'

That made Toselli grin. In a single fluid move, he dropped the rookie's pistol, slapped the detective's gun hand, and, grabbing his wrist, wrenched the gun around so it pointed at the man's belly. He kneed the detective, sending him down against a wall, and swept the rookie's pistol off the floor. He stuck the detective's gun in his belt and crammed the rookie's pistol into the kid's ribs. He announced to everyone in the room, 'Next time, I shoot him and then shoot you.'

No one else drew a weapon.

'Don't come after me,' Toselli added. 'If I see any of you again, I'll kill you. No hard feelings.' Then he marched the rookie out of the back of the station, commandeered a cruiser, and made the kid drive him to the corner of Kimball Avenue and Irving Park Road on the Northwest Side. He used the rookie's phone to tell someone to pick him up there. He scanned the car radio, had the rookie stop a block from the corner, and scanned it again, then ripped the cord from the handheld mic and smashed the radio unit with the pistol butt.

In a little parking lot at Kimball and Irving Park, a man with a medium build, gray-streaked hair, and a mean face stood by a white Plymouth. Toselli told the rookie to pull into the spot next to the car. He said, 'No hard feelings' again, and cracked the rookie's head with the pistol butt.

'And that's that?' Kelson asked when Peters finished telling him.

'Afraid so.'

But Peters misjudged. An hour later, Toselli's escape hit the news – an armed killer-cop taking a hostage and outmaneuvering a whole station of other cops. Now he was running free with a list of targets and a willingness to hurt anyone who got in his way. The TV got hold of a series of pictures – Toselli as a young cop in uniform, Toselli looking heroin chic as an undercover cop in narcotics, Toselli looking like the meanest bastard ever born in his raid gear. The mayor advised citizens to shelter in place and, if they encountered Toselli, under no circumstances to approach him.

Peters streamed the coverage on the computer in his office. He asked Kelson to stay and offer insights. Besides, he said, a lot of cops still pictured Kelson as responsible for Toselli's string of killings. Peters wouldn't want one of those cops to see Kelson and make a tragic mistake. But when a CBS commentator went down that path and speculated on the rumored friendship between him and Toselli, Kelson got up and said, 'That's *so* wrong.'

'Easy now,' Peters said.

The commentator said, 'An anonymous source high in the departmental chain of command says all aspects of Toselli and Kelson's relationship will be investigated. In the meantime, Kelson is in custody—'

Peters yelled at the screen, 'Not *custody* – *protective* custody.'

'Dammit,' Kelson said, and he walked out of the office and then out through the front of the station.

FIFTY-EIGHT

S tanding on the sidewalk, Kelson called Rodman.

Rodman said Cindi had brought Doreen Felbanks's fever down, though she guessed that without a hospital her chances looked about fifty-fifty. But even the mention of a hospital took Doreen out of her Demerol cloud and had her threatening to run.

'How far would she get?'

'She'd crash before she reached the door, but what good would that do?'

'Throw her over your shoulder and take her?'

'Is that what you want me to do?' Rodman asked.

'You think Toselli could get to her in a hospital?'

'He seems to get wherever he wants to go.'

'Yeah, he's doing better than fifty-fifty. Can Cindi stay with her awhile?'

'Sure, but she might leave me afterward. You know, Doreen isn't worth it. Maybe she once was a long time ago to someone. But whatever was good in her is gone.'

'Yeah, I know,' Kelson said. 'But let's keep her until the cops have Toselli again, OK?'

'Your love life, not mine, man.'

'Ha.' When they hung up, he said again, 'Ha.' And to prove he was laughing, he drove to Nancy's house.

But he didn't drive alone.

As he pulled into the street from the station lot, the blue Buick with Nuñez's men in it fell in behind him. Kelson watched the car in his rearview mirror and swore at Peters for broadcasting his presence at the station. But the men stayed back a few car lengths, and when they saw two police cruisers parked in front of Nancy's house, they pulled to the side and cut their engine.

Kelson stopped between the cruisers, one of them empty, the other with uniformed cops in the front seat. When he got out and walked up the front sidewalk, the cops jerked alert, then relaxed as they seemed to decide he was no threat.

He rang the doorbell, and another uniformed cop opened the door.

'Is everything OK?' Kelson asked.

The cop said, 'Who are you?'

But Nancy came from behind and let Kelson in.

Sue Ellen ran from the living room and jumped into his arms. She looked deep into his eyes and said, 'What the hell, Dad?'

'I don't know,' Kelson said. 'I really don't know.'

'Me either,' Sue Ellen said. 'Mom let me bring Payday and Painter's Lane. Just until this is over. I have to keep them in my room.'

'You've got a good mom.'

'The best,' she said.

He set her down, and she ran upstairs to check on the kittens. He went into the kitchen with Nancy. For the first time in his memory, her voice shook. 'Would Greg have shot her?'

He wanted to lie and reassure her. 'Yeah, it looked like it.'

'That asshole. She loves him like family.'

'The department can put the two of you in a hotel room with a guard,' he said again. 'You should take the offer.'

'I know.' She glanced around the room as if the appliances, the walls, and windows were disintegrating even as she stood there. 'Would he have shot you too?'

'I think so,' he said. 'Will you go to a hotel?'

'Yeah,' she said. 'Stupid not to, right? Someone broke in while we were out.'

'*I* came in.'

'And moved . . . things? Took things?'

He dug in his pocket and handed her the ball of hair. 'I also stole his watch.'

'Why?'

He shrugged. 'Jealousy? Confusion? Something.'

'You're scaring the hell out of me,' she said. 'You don't do me any good. You don't do Sue Ellen—'

'Don't say it,' he said.

She stared at him. She gave no sign that she thought they were in this together. He saw only exhaustion. She said, 'I think you should go.'

'You'll do a hotel? You'll keep Sue Ellen safe?'

'I told you I would.'

'Right.' He'd loved her and married her and had a child with her. He'd worn out her love for him. She was hard and beautiful, as tough as anyone he'd ever known. She clutched the ball of hair as if she might punch him. He asked, 'Can I keep that?'

She shook her head, so tough. 'No – no, you can't.'

FIFTY-NINE

Kelson drove back to Rodman's apartment, tailed again by Nuñez's men, and jogged up the front stairs.

Little Marty LeCoeur still slept in the bedroom, while the others watched TV coverage of the police sweeping the city. Doreen sat up on the couch, though her eyes had a Demerol glaze. On ABC, news cameras showed the aftermath of a raid of Toselli's Dearborn Park townhouse. A couple of dozen police cars and tactical vans were crammed into the little court outside the house. Plainclothes cops carried boxes out of the front door. The reporter had to shout over the beat of a hovering helicopter. Standing by one of the tactical vans, Toselli's mother talked with two officers.

'Nice lady,' Doreen mumbled.

'Huh?' Francisca said.

Rodman thumbed the remote, and the channel jumped to NBC. Toselli had just called the news program, and the station was

playing the audio. He ranted about failures of departmental leader-
ship, kids who fall through the cracks, wrongheaded crime-fighting
practices. He sounded more than a little crazy.

Doreen said, 'He's doing . . . it.'

'What?' Cindi asked.

'Shh,' Rodman said.

Toselli said the police wouldn't find him, because he was gone
– gone and never coming back. He was done hurting others,
done getting hurt.

'Ha,' Doreen said.

Toselli said he loved his mom. He loved his dead sister Inez.
He loved his dead nephew Alejandro.

Doreen mumbled, 'He's so . . . damn . . . good.'

'What are you talking about?' Kelson asked.

'It's an act,' she said. 'Dis—' for a moment she lost the second
half of the word – 'Dis*traction*. You lower your guard. He's coming
after you.' She smiled at Francisca. 'And you.' The smile fell. 'And
me.' She wiggled a finger at Rodman – 'I don't know about you'
– then at Cindi – 'You, he doesn't know about . . . but he'd be happy
to have you.'

'No one's guard is down,' Kelson said.

'If you blink,' she said, 'if you look at your . . . shoes – he's so
quick, so damn . . . good. If you take your eyes off for one moment—'

'We get the idea,' Rodman said. 'So how do we beat him at his
own game?'

'You don't. It's' – she did something with her mouth and lips that
looked like an old woman adjusting her false teeth – 'impossible.'

'One of his friends picked him up when he got loose,' Kelson
said. 'Where can we find them?'

She shook her head. The TV ran more video of the raid on the
Dearborn Park townhouse.

Rodman said, 'How many guys can he round up to back him?'

She said, 'When you think you've got him, he's got you. He
likes . . . corners.'

'What are you talking about?' Kelson said.

'Back him into a corner . . . he likes that.'

On the TV screen, the plainclothes cops ran out of the front door
of the townhouse. Other cops backed from the sidewalk to the
opposite side of the court. At the same time, a special operations

truck, carting an object that looked like a bathysphere, drove past the police cars and over the front curb. Two men wearing helmets the size of an astronaut's climbed out.

Rodman asked Kelson, 'Did you see anything that looked like explosives?'

'Nothing,' Kelson said.

'You wouldn't,' Doreen said, as the men in helmets went into the townhouse. 'You should turn that off – if you don't want to see it.'

'I don't mind fighting him in a corner,' Kelson said.

Her face looked sour as she fixed her eyes on the screen. 'I hate watching this.'

Kelson turned off the TV. 'Where—'

Just then, on the other side of Rodman's living room, a spray of bullets smashed the two front windows and tattered the plywood covering the one Toselli shot out earlier.

Francisca screamed. Kelson, Cindi, and Rodman ducked to the floor. Doreen sat on the couch, indifferent. 'See? That's what I mean.'

Little Marty emerged from the bedroom, wide-eyed and furious. With his pistol in his hand, he drifted to the wall by one of the blown-out windows and shot down at Toselli and two other men – the hard-faced one who had picked up Toselli at the Northwest Side parking lot and a stocky black man with a tightly trimmed beard. Nuñez's men were nowhere in sight. Kelson and Rodman crawled to the windows and, after another spray of bullets pocked the plaster ceiling, also fired down at the street.

For ten minutes, Kelson, Rodman, and Marty shot from the windows, and Toselli and his men dodged from parked car to recessed doorway, spraying the building with automatic gunfire. Cindi called 911 and, with the calm voice of a woman who worked in an emergency room, explained what was happening, then explained again when the operator didn't get it – and no, Cindi could do nothing to quiet the noise that made her hard to hear.

When a chunk of ceiling plaster fell on the couch inches from Doreen's head, Francisca got on her knees and shoved her like a queen on a barge across the apartment to a sheltering wall.

Doreen said, 'If he wants to, he can.'

'Can what?' Francisca asked.

'Kill us all,' Doreen said. 'If he wants to.'

In the pauses in the clattering gunfire, approaching sirens wailed.

Still Kelson, Rodman, and Marty shot down at the street. Still Toselli and his men fired into the apartment, filling the air with strange dust.

Until they stopped.

And the dust filtered to the floor.

Then Kelson, Rodman, and Marty stood in the hard silence of the apartment, and a gentle March breeze played through the blown-out windows. They looked at each other, checking for wounds.

As the first squad car turned a corner and headed for the building, Rodman asked, 'Ready for them?'

'All my life,' Kelson said. But when he glanced at Doreen and Francisca, Doreen gave him a look that bored through her narcotic dullness and seemed to plead for help. So he said, 'But get *her* out of here.'

There was no time to argue or ask why. Two more squad cars came around the corner and skidded to a stop behind the first. Kelson's companions could act on his wish without hesitating, or they could give Doreen to the cops.

Rodman said to Marty, 'Take her down the back.' And to Cindi, 'Can you go with them?'

'Where?'

Kelson dug his keys from his pocket and gave her the one for Nancy's house – which would be empty if Nancy had taken Sue Ellen to a hotel. He helped Doreen to her feet between Cindi and Francisca and ushered them out of the back door.

When he returned to the front, seven squad cars were parked on the street, and four cops, pistols in their hands, came up the stairs, stopped at the second-floor landing, and charged up the next flight.

When they reached the landing, Rodman stood in the open doorway with his hands over his head. Kelson stood beside him, hands over his.

SIXTY

All afternoon and into the early evening, a forensic team photographed Rodman's apartment, measured angles of incidence, and pried bullets from the walls and ceiling. Another team collected bullets and casings from the street below. They bagged Kelson's KelTec and Rodman's pistol. News vans lined the curb beyond the police perimeter. Neighbors stood beside reporters or watched from the windows of facing buildings.

Peters arrived and interviewed Kelson and Rodman.

'How many of them were there?' he asked.

'Three,' Rodman said.

Peters looked to Kelson.

He agreed. 'Three.'

'Three of them shot it out with the two of you?' Peters said.

'That's right,' Rodman said.

Again Peters looked to Kelson.

'Plus the little one-armed guy,' Kelson said.

'Goddamn it,' Peters said, 'I'm not fucking around.'

Then Kelson's lawyer, Edward Davies, walked in from outside and said to Peters, 'That's it. No more questions.'

Peters said, 'Who the hell let him in?'

Kelson said, 'I called while we were waiting for you.'

'*I'll* talk to you,' Rodman said to Peters. 'I'll tell you everything I think you need to know.'

When the last cop left – and Edward Davies convinced himself that Kelson needed no more immediate help – Kelson and Rodman swept and secured the apartment. They needed more plywood for the windows, but for now they tacked up blankets. Before hanging the last one, they stared out at the street. Along with bullet-pocked cars and shattered glass gleaming under the streetlights, a police van idled at the curb. According to Peters, the van would stay all night. Another would circle the neighborhood.

'Reassured?' Kelson asked Rodman.

'Toselli's a hyena,' Rodman said. 'I'm with your girlfriend on this one – if he wants to, he can.'

'Don't call her my girlfriend.'

Then the blue Buick driven by Nuñez's men cruised up the street and pulled to the curb about a hundred feet behind the police van. A brown Chevy Impala with tinted windows pulled into the space behind it.

Rodman said, 'What the hell are they up to?'

'Building forces?' Kelson said. 'Getting ready to make a move? Hitting after we've been weakened by another battle?'

Rodman shook his head. 'What are they going to do with the cops here?'

So they hung the blanket and turned on the TV to check the latest on the manhunt.

The police superintendent – a thick-faced black man with a little mustache – said the department had the situation under control. Then he warned everyone to stay inside. He never blinked at the contradiction in his messages. A whole department of good cops was chasing one bad one, he said. He allowed a confident smile. That put the odds against Toselli at around twelve thousand to one.

At the end of the news conference, the reporter recapped the events since Toselli had grabbed the rookie's gun. He described the firefight at Rodman's apartment, narrating over a late-afternoon video of the front of Rodman's Bronzeville building as cops went into and out of the entrance. Then the video cut to Toselli's Dearborn Park townhouse, and the reporter explained that the police bomb squad had pulled out a package of counterfeit explosives.

'Your girlfriend had that one wrong,' Rodman said.

'Or else it's more distraction,' Kelson said, 'and Toselli didn't want his mom sleeping with a bomb.'

Rodman thought for a moment. 'We could use that against him.'

'Blow up his mom?'

'How do you trip up a good man? Exploit whatever's bad in him. How do you trip up a bad man? Exploit whatever's good. Who does he still care about?'

'His mom, apparently. Until this afternoon, I would've said Sue Ellen. Until a couple of days ago, I would've said me.'

'*What* does he care about?'

'His principles. *First in. No man left behind. Relentless force.*

Superior firepower. Expecting the unexpected from others and being unexpected himself.'

'So what do we expect a man to do when twelve thousand cops are chasing him?'

'Run,' Kelson said.

'Sure.'

'Or hide,' Kelson said.

Rodman said, 'A smart man would do anything but take the fight into the open. He would hole up in a safe house or ride a plane to the end of the world. The cops know that Toselli's smart, and so they're shining flashlights into every hiding hole they can think of, reviewing airport security, and checking flight manifests. Toselli knows they know he's smart. And since he's a cop, he knows how they'll spend their energy looking for a smart guy like him. That means he also knows it would be dumb to act smart in the ways they think he will. He'll take it where no one expects him next – no pause for breath – just like when he came here.'

'So he goes back to Stevens's office? Or Nancy's house?'

Rodman shrugged and dialed Cindi's cellphone number.

It rang until voicemail picked up.

He asked her to call as soon as she got the message, then dialed Marty LeCoeur.

The little man's phone rang and rang and rang.

'That's not good,' Rodman said.

Kelson headed for the door. 'Let's go to Nancy's house.'

'Try Stevens first?'

Kelson dialed the Stevens Group building. An after-hours recording gave him a menu of options. Kelson picked the one for the security desk. The line rang twice and Esteban Herrera answered.

Stevens left two hours ago, Herrera told him.

'Did any cops follow him when he left?'

'Guess not,' Herrera said. 'No cops here all day.'

So Kelson tried Stevens's cellphone.

When the call jumped to voicemail, he left the same message Rodman left for Cindi – *Call as soon as you get this.* Then he dialed and left the message again on Stevens's home phone.

When he hung up, he said, 'You want to check on Cindi and the others while I check Stevens?'

Rodman said, 'We should stay together.'

'And ignore which one?'

Rodman frowned. He went into his bedroom, rooted through a dresser drawer, and came out with a nine-millimeter Smith & Wesson – his backup pistol. He gave it to Kelson. 'Go fully loaded.'

Kelson said, 'And how about you?'

'Marty's carrying.'

'Unless Toselli took his gun.' He tried to give Rodman back the pistol.

'You take it,' Rodman said, 'or we stay together.'

'Why?'

'A long time ago I decided I'd rather take a bullet than see someone I care about take one.'

So Kelson stuck the pistol in his belt, but he said, 'Don't take a bullet. It hurts.'

Then Rodman went to check on Cindi, Doreen, Francisca, and Marty, while Kelson drove to Stevens's two-flat on North Burling – the Buick and the Chevy Impala right behind him.

SIXTY-ONE

When Kelson parked in front, the cars that tailed him stopped in the middle of the street. 'One thing at a time,' Kelson said, and stared at the two-flat. The downstairs was dark, but lights shined from the upstairs windows. He thought he saw movement inside one of the rooms, so he dialed Stevens's home number and, when no one picked up, tried his cell.

Nothing.

He removed the magazine from Rodman's pistol, rolled it in his hand, and slid it back in. He climbed the steps to Stevens's front door. No one got out of the other cars.

Kelson rang the doorbell and listened. Although many people were heeding the police warnings to stay off the street, the sound of traffic filtered in from a block away, and then a siren whined over the traffic. The Buick and the Chevy idled nearby. 'Like purring kittens,' Kelson said.

He rang the bell again.

When no one came, he tried the door handle.

It turned – unlocked.

He backed away from the door, stepping down to the front walk. He glanced at the idling cars, then watched the upstairs windows. Nothing moved. So he called Rodman, who was still a half mile from Nancy's house.

'Lights are on,' he said. 'No one's answering. Door's unlocked.'

'Don't do it,' Rodman said. 'Call Dan Peters.'

'Good idea,' Kelson said.

'I mean it,' Rodman said. 'You walk in there, you don't know who's waiting.'

'Only one way to find out.'

'Actually, that's not true,' Rodman said. 'A couple of dozen cops can go in through the front and the back. They can knock down the walls if they want.'

'That would work too.'

'Hang on,' Rodman said. 'I'm calling Peters.'

'Thanks.'

'Don't go in.'

But then, without pulling from the middle of the street, Nuñez's two men climbed out of the Buick, and Nuñez himself climbed from the Chevy Impala. All three carried pistols. As if they'd practiced such things, they chambered bullets at the same moment and drifted toward Kelson.

'Tell Peters to hurry, will you?' Kelson said to Rodman. Then he hung up, climbed the front steps, and went into the house.

The downstairs hall was dark and cool. It smelled like a place where no one had ever lived. Kelson listened, then told the darkness, 'Nothing and—' He yelled Toselli's name. He listened. 'No one.'

As Nuñez and his men came up the front steps outside, Kelson found the bannister in the dark and inched up the stairs. He said, 'If you're up there, Toselli, I'm coming – I wish I was anywhere but – I'm coming. And, Stevens, if you're there and can't speak, there's not much I can do but I'll do it.' He came to the top stair and stopped. He could choose between two brightly lighted rooms toward the front of the house and two dark rooms in back. He moved toward the lighted one where he thought he'd seen movement from outside.

The doorway led into a master bedroom decorated in grays and browns. At one end there was a fireplace, a leather divan, and a thick rug. A black-bladed ceiling fan turned lazily. A king-size bed stood across from the fireplace. In the middle of the mattress, Stevens lay curled on his side.

Kelson heard the front door swing open downstairs, but he spoke to Stevens. 'Hey?'

Stevens didn't respond.

Kelson went to him.

A bullet hole – so tiny and precise it could've been made with an awl – descended through Stevens's ear canal. A shot straight into the brain.

Kelson yelled, 'Toselli, you bastard.'

A voice answered from downstairs.

Then more than one voice.

Then an eruption of shouting – in English, in Spanish, shouting, rage.

Then gunfire – an enormous explosion of ammunition, half a house away from Kelson but as ferocious and extraordinary as when he and Bicho shot each other in a Ravenswood alley.

Footsteps retreated out the front door and down the outside steps. Kelson moved to the front window and watched Nuñez and his men scrambling across the sidewalk into the street. Nuñez dragged a leg as if he'd taken a bullet in the hip. One of his men bled from the neck.

Toselli came out after them and stopped on the sidewalk. As Nuñez and his men leaned for their cars, Toselli raised his gun and squared his shoulders.

He shot.

Once.

Twice.

A third time.

A spot of blood burst from the back of one of Nuñez's men, then the other, then Nuñez. They fell face down on the concrete.

Kelson knew then that Toselli had saved him again. But he knew something else, and Toselli confirmed it by turning from the men he'd killed and staring up at the window where Kelson watched. Toselli pointed up at him and said, loudly enough for him to hear through the glass, 'Not *them. Me.*' Kelson knew Toselli had saved him only to kill him.

Toselli ran toward the house, and Kelson heard footsteps on the stairs.

He'd expected this moment. He would stand by Stevens's bed and exchange gunfire with Toselli. One or both of them would fall. He would never learn whether he or Bicho shot first – but now he didn't care.

He yelled, 'I don't give a fuck.' There was joy in that realization. Bicho shot at him *and* he shot at Bicho. Bicho died . . . and that was as it should be. Kelson lived . . . and that was as it should be too. He yelled again, 'Who the fuck cares?' Then he realized something else. Not only did he remain alive after Bicho shot him, but he really, *really* liked living. Which presented another problem.

So he ran across the room and hid in the closet. He crouched low to the floor – almost, like Stevens, fetal.

He heard Toselli stop at the doorway and look in, then move to the other rooms. From the other side of a wall that the closet shared with the hallway, Toselli called out, 'Kelson?'

If Kelson could have torn out his own tongue, he would have. If he could have bitten into his own flesh and silenced himself – if his damaged brain . . .

'Kelson?' Toselli yelled again. 'Where'd you go, my friend?'

Like a child playing hide-and-seek and unable to contain his excitement, Kelson answered. '*Here.*'

For a moment, there was silence. Then Toselli spoke from the other side of the wall. 'You know how this works now, don't you?' He spoke as if still whispering in Kelson's apartment, as if Sue Ellen had never interrupted.

Kelson answered through the wall, in a voice as quiet as Toselli's. 'You're a real bastard.'

For another moment, there was silence as Kelson waited for an answer. Then bullets blasted the wall, punching holes where Kelson's chest would have been if he'd stood. Dust snowed on him from the wallboard. Toselli squirted another dozen shots, then ran to the doorway and into the bedroom.

As Toselli came to the closet, Kelson stood and threw his shoulder against the cratered wall. He tumbled through into the hallway. As he crawled away, more gunshots blasted from Toselli's automatic.

Kelson scrambled to his feet and ran up the hall. Toselli yelled

after him – his name – something else he meant to send him to
hell – Kelson didn't know what – he couldn't hear – his head was
screaming an insane music. Gun in hand, hand on gun – so tight
the skin could've grafted to the metal – he went to the bedroom
doorway and rounded into the room.

Toselli was groping at the hole Kelson fell through.

Kelson aimed the Smith & Wesson at his old friend's back.

Toselli smashed the wallboard with his gun butt. Then he realized he'd outsmarted himself. He pulled himself from the closet,
stood straight, and turned to face Kelson.

'Ha,' Toselli said.

Kelson shot him in the head.

SIXTY-TWO

They got together at Kelson's apartment, though Kelson
said, 'Having a party after all of this makes no sense.'

'I'll bring beer,' Rodman said.

Kelson said, 'Last time a friend brought beer didn't work out
so well.'

'I won't bring a Frisbee.'

So at eight in the evening on the last day of March, Marty and
his girlfriend Janet arrived with hummus and pita chips. Kelson's
lawyer, Edward Davies, brought guacamole. Francisca was in
Florida, staying with relatives. Nancy didn't come, but Sue Ellen
did. Rodman invited Dan Peters and Venus Johnson. No one
expected them to show, but when they finished their shift, they
did. They also brought beer.

'Bad luck,' Kelson said as he put it in the fridge.

Then Doreen Felbanks came to the door. She wore black leggings
and a big hot-pink angora sweater, which hid her bandages. A
judge had made her wear an ankle monitor, which she'd decorated
with a thin gold chain. She'd gone to a salon, and her hair was
bright, bright red. The other guests stared at her in silence as she
stood inside doorway. But Kelson crossed the room and said,
'Hello, Hot Pants.'

She did look hot too, the others had to admit. Especially considering what she'd gone through.

On the night Kelson killed Toselli, Cindi and Marty hadn't picked up their phones when Rodman called because Doreen started bleeding again as they drove to Nancy's house. Cindi couldn't stop the flow and told her she could go to the hospital or die.

'Let me die,' Doreen said.

They took her to the hospital. In the chaos, they didn't hear their phones ringing. The doctors gave Doreen a transfusion, sewed her up, pumped more antibiotics into her, and put her in a room they used for dangerous patients.

When they released her from the hospital six days later, Peters took her into custody.

Accessory to this.

Accessory to that.

Obstructing the other.

Kelson's lawyer got her out on bail but with provisions and restrictions – the ankle monitor among them. Technically, she shouldn't have been at the party or drinking or chatting with others connected with Toselli's killing spree. Technically, Peters and Johnson should have arrested her for breaking her conditions.

When the building super knocked to say neighbors were complaining about the noise, Kelson invited him in and gave him a Tecate.

Payday sat on the carpet, while Painter's Lane hid under the bed.

Payday looked at the super with green almond eyes. 'You can't have that,' the super said. 'Building rules.'

'It's my daughter's,' Kelson said.

'It's got to go.' The super made a gentle *ntching* sound to get the kitten to come to him. Painter's Lane darted out from under the bed at the sound. 'Hey, how many do you got?' But he grinned as the kittens high-stepped across the carpet as if it was tall grass.

'Just the two,' Kelson said. 'They're service kittens.'

'Never heard of such a thing,' the super said.

'They help with my headaches.'

'I'll need to check with the owners.' The kittens rubbed against the man's ankles.

'Tell them they're for an ex-cop,' Peters said. 'Shot in the line of duty.'

The super tickled Payday's back, and the kitten purred like an engine. 'I'll tell them you'll sue if they don't let you keep them. Americans with Disabilities, right?' He scooped up Payday and made more *ntching* sounds, which made the kitten purr louder. 'It worked for a cripple in another building. Guy with a parrot. Said he needed company.'

Rodman brought the man another beer.

And Doreen helped herself to one. She sat at the dining table, where Sue Ellen was drawing pictures of Payday and Painter's Lane with colored pencils.

The redhead watched Kelson move among the guests.

Sue Ellen said, 'Take your eyes off him or I'll stab you with a pencil.'

Doreen smiled and kept watching. 'He's a good man, isn't he?'

'Depends what you mean by good.'

'A good dad?' Doreen asked.

'He won't get me a horse.'

'Probably for the best. It wouldn't fit in the elevator.'

Sue Ellen put down the green pencil and stared at Doreen. 'Are you going to ask him out?'

'I was thinking of it. He's cute, don't you think?'

'*Eww*. Mom's already got me going to a therapist. I'd need another just to deal with the two of you. Besides, he still loves my mom.'

'Does she love him?'

Sue Ellen screwed up her lips. 'Nope.'

'The world's messed-up, isn't it?' Doreen said. 'Maybe all we can do is ride through it as high as we can.'

Sue Ellen picked up the green pencil again and started shading in Payday's almond eyes. 'Ride on a horse?'

'Whatever gets us from here to there.'

Sue Ellen traded the green pencil for a red one. With a remarkably sure hand for an eleven-year-old, she drew flames by Payday's mouth, as if the kitten could breathe fire or eat it. 'If you ask my dad out, I won't stab you.'

'That's kind of you,' Doreen said. She wiped something from the corner of one of her eyes with a knuckle. Maybe it was a tear.